Stirling Masquerade

Anne-Marie Price

Copyright © 2016 Anne-Marie Price

ISBN: 978-0-9942761-3-1

DEDICATION

To Shirley and Len Daley,
who encouraged me
to believe in my dreams.

The Stirling Breed Trilogy

2016
Stirling Breed
Stirling Masquerade
Stirling Conspiracy

ACKNOWLEDGMENTS

Stella Eversden
A gem of a Proof Reader.

Helen Iles
For convincing me to split
Stirling Breed into three novels.

Rebecca Schulz
For her invaluable information
in regards to beards

Trilogy Review

Stirling Breed

Brought up more a boy than a girl, Lady Antonia (Tony) Stirling had been determinedly resisting the pressure to act like a woman and marry until she met Lord Caleb Delacourt. Now their love threatens the future prospects of at least five people. When an abduction attempt of Tony and her much younger brother, Lord Aidan was thwarted by Caleb, a more daring plan is undertaken. A second abduction is attempted, and when Caleb comes to their rescue again, he is blinded. The trio are transported from England to France. With the very recent defeat of Napoleon at Waterloo, France is a very hostile environment to be trapped within. Even though they manage to escape their abductor, fleeing the country will not be as easy.

FRIDAY
Seeking Sanctuary

There was a church, the Sainte Catherine, at the top of the main street and if Tony understood Captain Sheppard's message, she was to seek help there. It was the early hours of the morning and in a normal village, all its occupants would be curled up in their beds. Hon Fleur, though, was used to smuggling activities and therefore not all its residents were sleeping.

As an Inn door opened and a group of patrons poured out, to aid with the disbursement of cargo, Tony drew Caleb, who still carried Aidan, into the shadows. There was only a short window of opportunity for them to get to the safety of the church before Nigel raised the alarm.

As Tony led them silently from shadow to shadow, she wondered, *have we made the right decision in letting Nigel live? Killing isn't in our nature but it might have been the more prudent option.* There was no uproar from the dock behind them so Tony shelved her doubts as she assisted Caleb up the church steps so that he didn't trip and fall. Taking a deep breath to steady the rising fears that this could be just a trap, Tony reached out trembling fingers to open the door and led her boys inside.

Father Jean Paul

The door of the Sainte Catherine church shut with a tiny click behind them but in the vast emptiness of the holy edifice it sounded like a gunshot. The church was the largest in France made entirely of wood but Tony was not in the right frame of mind to appreciate their surrounding architecture.

1

Caleb released Tony's hand to slide his hand inside his overcoat to draw one of his pistols. Straining his ears, Caleb felt useless without his sight.

'Tony?' His whisper was so soft it could have been the wind moving through the trees.

'The church is empty.' She laid her hand on Caleb's arm and slipping the stiletto blade into her cleavage, she reached up to lift Aidan down. Caleb's boots echoed as they walked cautiously up the centre aisle towards the altar.

When a priest came out of the confessional, his gasp of surprise caused Caleb to raise his pistol as he instinctively moved protectively in front of Tony and Aidan. Tony placed her hand on his shoulder.

'Wait, Caleb.' Stepping around him, Tony spoke to the priest, 'Pere, nous cherchons refuge.'

As Caleb lowered his pistol, the Priest came cautiously closer and he spoke in English. 'Unbelievable! Mark didn't think you would succeed in getting away from your abductor.'

'Mark?' asked Caleb, desperately trying to use his ears the way he had once used his eyes to tell if a man was lying.

'Captain Sheppard,' explained the Priest. 'I'm his half-brother Jean Paul Clavell. Please come and wait in the vestry, you'll be warmer there. Mark won't be too long, he's just gone to visit my mother.' Father Jean Paul gestured for them to follow him through a door that led off from the altar.

The promise of warmth spurred Aidan to eagerly follow the Priest but Caleb was more cautious, still wary of a trap. Although he had lowered his pistol, Caleb did not put it away as he allowed Tony to lead him into the vestry, Jean Paul was amused rather than offended.

'I understand that you're on the run Lord Delacourt but you are in a house of God so could you put your weapon away?' asked the priest. Hesitating, Caleb's muscle along his jaw twitched before he finally re-holstered his pistol. Tony reassuringly caressed her hand against Caleb's arm.

'Sorry Father, but knowing who we can trust is difficult.' She found that hard to admit.

Opening the vestry door, Jean Paul followed them inside. 'Understandable Lady Stirling, especially being in a hostile country.'

Ignoring the adults, Aidan rushed towards the fireplace and sat down on the floor with his fur rug forming a cocoon around him as Tony led Caleb to a chair close to Aidan and helped him to sit down.

Our Family Is Complicated

'You said the Captain is visiting your mother, not our mother,' said Caleb, speaking slowly as if considering his words carefully before he allowed them to pass his lips. 'Yet you have different last names so if you're half-brothers does that mean same mother, different fathers?'

Getting a rug out of a cupboard, Father Jean Paul laid it across Caleb's shoulders. 'Actually the opposite my Lord, like Mark, our father was a sea Captain. Despite his flaws, he was a lovable rogue who remained utterly faithful to the three women in his life.'

'Three women?' Tony looked up startled from where she sat on the floor at Caleb's feet beside Aidan.

Jean Paul chuckled. 'Yes, my Lady, Mark's mother, Edith, he married under his father's name, my mother, Marcella, he married under his mother's name. The third woman was the sea. Each family knew of the existence of the other. I don't remember there being any jealousy between the two human women.'

Tony laced her fingers through one of the hands Caleb had upon his knees. 'So your father was a bigamist? He was actually

3

married to both women at the same time?' She asked in curiosity rather than passing judgement.

Sitting down behind the small wooden desk, the Priest nodded. 'Oh yes, it was a nightmare when Papa died, neither country recognised the legality of the other marriage. Because he died on English soil, Mark was awarded the entire estate as the eldest son.'

'Was that really a lot of money being a Captain of a ship?' Caleb raised his free hand to scrub across the five o'clock shadow already forming along his jaw.

'Mark isn't the first smuggler in the family.' A cheeky grin appeared on Jean Paul's features. 'Don't let him hear me say this but although he looks like a pirate, Mark really is a big softie. He got both our mothers together and asked if they wanted to keep their current home or have a new one. Once that was decided Mark sold everything else and gave half to each mother. Then helped both women to invest the money so they could live comfortably and ensure the future of the younger siblings.'

'He wanted nothing for himself?' Tony's eyebrows rose.

'He was already established in his own home and his ship,' Jean Paul explained.

The Contingency Plans

At the sound of a footfall, Tony looked up defensively but Caleb had already begun to withdraw his pistol, having heard the outer door open.

'Be calm Lord Delacourt, I mean you no harm,' said Captain Sheppard as he stepped further into the room. Relaxing, Caleb removed his hand from inside his overcoat. 'Are you prepared to take us back to England, Captain?' Caleb lay his hand over Tony's and squeezed it reassuringly.

'Of course, my contract with Sutherland is at an end. There is something we need to discuss first.'

Believing she understood what he meant, Tony nodded. 'Naturally you want to know that we have the means to pay for our passage.'

The Pirate chuckled. 'Actually I want to discuss contingency plans. If you let Sutherland live then he may have already alerted the entire village of Hon Fleur to your escape. In that case we won't be able to simply walk back to the ship.'

'What do you suggest we do then?' Caleb drawled, 'Skip?'

This only amused the Captain. 'Option One - we walk down to the dock and board the ship. Option Two - if necessary I walk down openly and you make your way via the shadows down to the ship. If Sutherland causes a manhunt with the villagers then Option Three - you will need to find somewhere to lay low for twenty four hours. Returning to the dock when I bring the ship back into port this time tomorrow.'

'It'll be the last chance for me to get you back to England as the next two days I'm due in Holland and then Finland. If you can't meet up with me tomorrow night then Option Four - will see you head up to Paris to seek help from our British Consulate. It is the riskiest of the options, you'll have to pass yourself off as French, disguise yourselves and travel through a hostile countryside.'

'Don't sugar coat our chances Captain Sheppard, I'm really starting to regret allowing Tony talk me out of killing Sutherland!' Caleb sighed as he held out his hand to assist Tony to her feet.

The Captain laughed. 'Maybe so, my Lord. Do either of you speak French?'

'Well enough,' admitted Caleb.

'Quite well actually,' Tony said, reaching down to lift Aidan up into her arms. 'Let's just hope we only need Option One.'

Good Luck

Assisting Caleb out of his chair, the Captain agreed, 'Yes my Lady, but I like to have back up plans just in case something was to go wrong.'

'Can we go home now Tony?' Aidan lifted his head from his sister's shoulder.

'Yes Little Bear,' Tony turned to the Priest. 'Merci Père Jean Paul.' She accepted the medical bag he had picked up.

The priest smiled. 'Did you think I would refuse to grant you sanctuary when you requested it? If you have to wait for Mark to return tomorrow night, then if you come back here I will willingly hide you.'

Tony was visibly moved by his offer. 'Thank you Father but if the villagers know of your relationship to Captain Sheppard then we'd be putting you in danger from your own countrymen.'

'Well if it comes to needing to flee to Paris, I can at least offer you protection for your reputation.'

Tony shook her head. 'How Father? It'll be maybe two or more nights away from my father's home. My reputation will be non-existent!'

Jean Paul smiled. 'Not if you're already married.' His words were met by momentary silence. Tony cast an anxious glance across at Caleb but he refused to comment.

'That's not possible Father,' Tony finally spoke. 'Firstly I'm not of legal age, secondly we're not catholic, and thirdly we have no marriage licence.'

The Captain laughed. 'Sutherland said he took you away from your engagement party. That means your father approved of Lord Delacourt and the notice will probably appear in the newspapers in London tomorrow or should I say later this morning.'

Caleb reached out his hand towards Tony. 'If we can get back to the Manor before dawn then we can still salvage Tony's reputation. Thank you for the offer Father Jean Paul but we're hoping it shouldn't come to that.'

'Bon chance mes enfants.' Jean Paul blessed them as the Captain opened the outer door and checked the coast was clear before gesturing for Tony to exit ahead of him.

Option One

A shiver ran through Tony as the breeze swept the nippy ocean air up the main street. Aidan dragged his rug tighter around him but Caleb squeezed Tony's arm where his hooked through hers. 'Hand Aidan to me.' Caleb murmured, sliding his hand free to transfer the boy between them.

"I can walk!' protested Aidan but he didn't struggle as Caleb took him in his arms.

Closing the church door behind them, the Captain said quietly, 'If you need to speak, make it in French from now on.'

Slipping his hand back into Tony's, Caleb nodded agreement. He could feel Tony trembling partly from the chilling wind, partly from the same fear that he too felt seeping into his veins.

The Captain chattered in French as they openly followed him down the main street towards the docks. 'It's a pity that you can't see Hon Fleur during the day as it is such a beautiful picturesque port characterised by its houses with slate covered frontages.'

Caleb found it impossible to speak but Tony had a question. 'Why unload in Hon Fleur? Dieppe or Calais are the much bigger ports.'

The Captain chuckled. 'It is because they are larger ports that I don't use them as they are also heavily guarded and regulated; what I transport isn't always legal.' They moved briskly but not so hurried that they would attract the attention of the local people who had finished unloading Sheppard's ship.

The Captain was a well-known figure in the village and he casually acknowledged the villagers as they headed back to the Inn or home to their awaiting bed. The waning moon was still bright enough for face recognition to be possible but it also meant that the shadows were even darker. Tony was wary about the shadows, *they could be useful allies; but they could also be concealing an enemy.*

As they came ever closer to the dock, without any hindrance, Tony's breathing quickened as she felt her heartbeat start to throb against her temples. *It looks like we can make it aboard the ship before Nigel Sutherland has time to stop us but I don't dare believe that we are safe just yet. I don't want to jinx our success.*

Nigel's Recovery

They had just passed the Inn, when they clearly heard a roar emanating from the deck of the ship as Sutherland stormed down the gang plank. Biting back a sob, Tony dragged Caleb and Aidan into the shadows and drew one of Nigel's pistols from her overcoat as Captain Sheppard continued to stroll forward to meet Nigel's rushed descent.

'Problems Mr Sutherland?' The bored note in the Captain's voice was lost to Nigel as he held a handkerchief against his bleeding skull and waved the second letter in his other hand.

'They've escaped! I tried to get y'r men to organise a search party but they're a bunch of morons!'

Captain Sheppard shook his head. 'No, they're doing the job they are paid to do. They work for me and not for you. Losing your prisoners is not our problem.' Thrusting his second letter of instructions into the Captain's hand, Nigel continued to babble even though neither of them could clearly read the text.

'She knows the truth! Me orders are to kill them all!'

'Really? Yet knowing that fact, they left you alive?' That caused Nigel to pause and snatch back the letter.

'That's what she asks me! She wrote on the bottom of the letter. "We spared y'r life more than once, would ya have done us the same courtesy?" I won't get paid if they're not recaptured.'

Sighing, Captain Sheppard turned Nigel and slowly steered him away from the dock. 'You've an opportunity to make a new start for yourself. If you kill them, you'll never be able to return to England again. If you raise the alarm of the escape with the local people, even though they are English aristocracy, you're also English and you may end up just as dead.'

'Kill me and they don't get paid.' Pulling his arm out of the Captain's grasp, Nigel turned back towards the dock.

The Pirate chuckled. 'You don't appreciate the raw, seething emotions still prevalent after Napoleon's recent defeat by Wellington. These people will have your head on a spike and will be more satisfied with that result than any money you can offer them.'

Ya Work For Me

There was a moment of hesitation as Nigel considered the Captain's words. 'They got to ya didn't they? Y'r hiding them! They're here aren't they?' Nigel's eyes darted around the moonlit street, peering desperately into the shadows. 'Whatever they offered ya, I'll double it!'

'It doesn't work like that.' The Captain tried to get Nigel to focus on him and not the shadows where Tony and her boys were hiding.

'Y'r a pirate aren't ya?'

'I don't work that way otherwise I would've helped them escape before we even left England but you were my client first.'

'Then ya still work for me?' Nigel peered at him closely.

Drawing out his pipe, the Captain took a moment to light it. 'You ceased to be my client the moment we docked in France. Take my advice Sutherland, walk away before you do something you're going to regret.'

Option Three Then?

As Nigel seemed to be contemplating his options, Tony felt Caleb press against her back and his breath warm next to her ear.

'Can you make the shot?' He breathed in French.

'I'm not confident that I wouldn't hit the Captain.' Tony managed to whisper back. 'He's going to incite the locals to hunt us down isn't he?' Caleb paused as Nigel continued to scan the surrounding area for his hostages.

'Yes, he's not going to give up. Option Three?'

Pocketing her pistol, Tony dragged in a deep breath as she took Caleb's hand. 'Yes.' Sighing she cast one look back at the ship in regret. 'So close.'

'We'll make it home, elfling,' Caleb squeezed her hand, 'but I won't risk your lives to do it tonight.'

Dashing away the tears that threatened to fall, Tony nodded. 'I know, I had just hoped… let's go.' Turning away from their thwarted escape path, Tony squared her shoulders and with a determined resolve led Caleb and Aidan down towards the rear of the Inn. Without looking back, they headed away from the port of Hon Fleur, away from the ship that could take them back home, back to safety.

Their feet had just stepped onto the main road that would lead them north east when they heard the result of Nigel's rabble- rousing as excited, blood thirsty Frenchmen streamed out of the Inn to hunt for English aristocracy. Caleb lifted his head and appeared to be scenting the air.

'We're not heading for the church?'

Tony cast a surprised look up into Caleb's face. 'No, we're not, but how can you tell?' She asked.

'The sea breeze is no longer hitting the back of neck but my left cheek,' explained Caleb.

'Oh I see. Well the church is the first place they'll search so we're heading for a house where I hope we can hide until

Captain Sheppard returns. It'll probably take us about an hour on foot to get there.'

Caleb pulled up for a moment. 'In that case, I need Aidan to hop onto my back so I can carry him a little easier.' He lowered the boy to the ground but Aidan didn't immediately comply.

'I can walk for a while Caleb. I don't want to be a burden to anyone.' The boy was trying to be so brave but he was cold, tired and very frightened. Caleb drew Aidan into a hug as he knelt before the boy.

"You're not a burden Aidan. It's just that we could possibly cover more ground if you're carried and on my back, my hands can be free to protect you and Tony if the need arises.'

For a moment, Aidan returned Caleb's embrace before allowing Tony to lift him onto Caleb's back and wrap his arms around Caleb's neck. Once Tony had adjusted the fur rug so that it was secure around Aidan, Caleb straightened to his feet and reached out his hand for Tony. With only the moonlight to guide their way, they left their hunters behind them.

The Du Bois Country House

It was nearly over an hour later that they approached their destination. Although she didn't say one word of complaint Tony was relieved that they didn't have any further to walk. Shoes suitable for dancing or drawing room, were definitely not suitable for walking in the dark, over uneven ground or even long distances.

I long for my practical male attire but I will say not a word of my discomfort. Nor will I reveal the fear that Phillippe Du Bois may be away from his home. I have my hopes pinned on the fact that my Fencing Master could possibly be our only friend in such a hostile domain.

It was still dark as Tony led her boys around to the rear of the house and scooping up a handful of pebbles, threw them one at a time up to an upstairs window. Caleb moved closer to the wall to surround himself and Aidan with shadows.

The sound of the angry mob could still be heard in Caleb's head although the only sounds he could actually hear were the pebbles clinking against the glass of the window and subtle noises of night life. When the window was thrown open in anger, Caleb instinctively tried to draw Tony into the protection of the darkness.

'Arrête ça! Stop that you vandals. I have a shot gun and I'm prepared to use it!' yelled a woman in French as she thrust her head out of the window.

'Louise?' Tony drew her arm out of Caleb's grasp. 'It's Antonia Stirling.'

There was a momentary pause. 'Lady Tony? Is it really you? Come to the kitchen door belle fille.' The woman's head disappeared and the window was closed again. Tony led the boys around to the side of the house.

Checking to ensure that Aidan wasn't freezing, Tony rubbed her hands along his back to keep his circulation flowing. In a very short period of time she saw a light inside the house coming towards them. When Louise opened the door for them, Tony breathed a sigh of relief that she could get her boys safely indoors.

'Lady Tony, I can't believe it's really you.' Louise set down her candle before pulling Tony into her buxom embrace and kissed both her cheeks.

'Is Phillippe here? We could really use his help.' Tony asked as Louise turned to lift Aidan down and hugged him as well.

'I'm sorry ma cherie, Phillippe's father died two days ago so he had to go up to Paris. What has happened my Lady? We had heard that you and Master Aidan had been abducted and rescued nearly a week ago. Have you eloped with your handsome young Lord? Does Papa not approve of your rescuer?' Louise closed and locked the door again before taking Tony's hands between her own.

'We were abducted again and brought across to France. We're on the run but...' Tony hesitated about voicing her doubts.

'If you're here alone,' Caleb said, 'then we're placing you in danger if our hunters come looking for us.'

Chuckling Louise patted Caleb's cheek. 'I think not belle fil. François! It's Lady Tony!' She called up the back stairs.

'François?' Tony face relaxed into a tired smile. 'Your little brother?'

'Not so little now, ma cherie.' A naughty laugh escaped from the comely, plump Frenchwoman.

François

Down the stairs bounded a God. His hair tousled from the bed, his bronzed, muscular, toned body poured into underwear that was too small for him as he loosely tied a dressing gown around him. Laying eyes on an astounding Tony, the God broke into a devastating smile and enfolded her into his embrace as he broke into a warm welcome. As François kissed Tony on both cheeks, Louise took pity on Caleb's lack of sight and explained.

'Lady Tony won't have seen François since he was a gangly youth. He's grown into a fine specimen of manhood.'

Caleb wasn't certain he liked the idea of a God embracing his fiancée but was startled to be taken firmly by François and also kissed upon both his cheeks.

'So the story that you were rescued by a handsome young Lord was actually true.' François bent down to pick up Aidan. 'But what have you done to your young man, Lady Tony?'

She reached out to brush her hand through Aidan's hair. 'I'll explain everything but I must get Aidan somewhere warm.'

Louise reached out to take Aidan. 'François, we'll need hot chocolate. I'll get a fire started in a guest bedroom and then make up the bed for you.' Leading them up the backstairs, Louise was surprised when Caleb slightly altered her plans.

'Make it a servant's room. It needs to be easier to cover up our presence that way.'

Looking at him sharply, Louise finally nodded. 'Come to my room then, my Lord, but unless your hunters know Lady Tony intimately, they won't know to come to this house.'

Tell Nanny Everything

There was a speaking silence as neither Tony nor Caleb answered her and Louise's eyes widened in surprise.

'Mon Dieu! Have we come to that?'

Tony was spared the need to answer as Aidan tugged on Louise's sleeve as she lowered him to the ground.

'I need the lavatory Nanny,' the boy's words made Louise's relationship to the Stirlings a little clearer for Caleb.

'I'll come with him,' Caleb offered, reaching out his hand towards Aidan.

Louise handed Tony matches to light the fire as she led the men out of the bedroom again and down the hall. She returned alone and quietly closed the bedroom door as Tony knelt before the fireplace and fed pieces of crumpled paper into the fire.

'Tell me everything belle fille.' The gentle encouragement in her ex-Nanny's voice was nearly Tony's undoing and she needed a moment to compose herself before telling her story. As she started to warm up, Tony began to discard her outer garments, being careful to withdraw Nigel's pistols out of her overcoat before throwing it over the nearby chair. Slipping off her shoes, Tony wasn't surprised by the blisters already formed on her feet and briefly wondered, *how will I be able to walk back to the docks again?*

Louise knelt down behind Tony and as she listened to their story began to remove the pins, ribbons and crushed flowers that had adorned Tony's hair for her engagement party. When Caleb and Aidan came back into the room, Louise had moved

Tony to the stool in front of her dressing table and was brushing out Tony's hair. Aidan led Caleb to the arm chair beside the fireplace before curling up on the floor as close to the flames as he dared.

Naughty Boy!

Undoing his overcoat, Caleb drew out one of his pistols and laid it across his lap. As Louise plaited Tony's hair, both women watched as Caleb's leg twitched with nervous energy. When Louise had finished her hair, Tony slipped onto the floor at Caleb's feet and laid her hands over his.

'I know this is scary Caleb and you don't know these people but you need to get some sleep.'

Louise went across to a dresser and pulled out a nightgown. 'We'll stand guard over you, Lord Delacourt. François and I would rather die than let anything happen to Lady Tony.' Laying her hand on Tony's shoulder, Louise assisted her to her feet. 'Time to change for bed, my Lady.'

A depressed little sigh escaped from Caleb and Tony glanced back at him in concern. 'What is it Caleb? Are you in pain?' She reached out to caress her hand along his shoulder. Caleb captured her hand and pressed her palm against his lips.

'I wish now more than ever that I could see!'

Louise gasped at his audacity. 'Oh non, non, if you could see, my Lord, I would at this point be throwing you out of the room!'

Releasing Tony's hand, Caleb caressed his fingers slowly up her arm. 'You wouldn't consider describing everything as you undress?' When his hand slid down her shoulder to cup one of Tony's breasts; Louise smacked his hand and lowered it back into his lap.

'Naughty boy! There'll be plenty of time when the bandages come off and you're married for you to see each other naked.'

Louise drew Tony beyond Caleb's reach as she assisted her out of the silk dress and into a very sensible nightgown.

Unsuccessful Valet Duties

Aidan didn't pay attention to any of the adults until François entered with a tray of hot chocolate and some additional nightwear thrown across his arm. Putting down the tray on the dressing table, François handed Aidan his mug before he gently laid his hand on Caleb's shoulder.

'Let me help you, my Lord.' Kneeling down in front of Caleb, François slid his hand down Caleb's arm until it rested upon his knee.

'I can manage, thank you.' Caleb squirmed uncomfortably.

Chuckling, Tony ran her hand through François' hair. 'Behave François, this one is mine.' She headed for the door. 'I won't be long,' she added.

François took his hand from Caleb's knee and started to remove Caleb's boots. 'Pity... I could make you both very happy.' François smiled angelically up at Tony as one of her eyebrows rose in answer. Wagging her finger at the French God, Tony left the room and headed down the corridor to the bathroom.

Although Caleb had misgivings about the younger man's actions, he didn't have the strength to protest as he realised that he was extremely tired. Boots and stockings removed, Caleb rose to his feet as François assisted him to undress while Louise changed Aidan into a nightgown.

Made uncomfortable by François trying to remove his underwear, Caleb resisted at first until Louise spoke, 'I'll wash all you clothes, my Lord, and have them dry in time to get you to the ship later tonight.'

With incredible reluctance, Caleb allowed the remainder of his clothes be removed. His cheeks flushed in embarrassment,

Caleb held out his arms to slip into a borrowed nightgown but when it didn't eventuate, he reached out a frantic hand for something to make him decent.

'Vous êtes magnifique!' François made Caleb jump startled as he caressed his hand along his Lordship's stomach.

'Not appropriate François!' Louise reprimanded her brother, taking the nightgown away from him and assisted Caleb into it. She eased his Lordship back into the arm chair before placing a mug of hot chocolate into his hands. 'My apologies my Lord. François can't resist a beautiful body.'

Caleb wished that his face wasn't so hot and flushed. 'I'm honoured, I think, but I'm a one woman man.'

'Good to hear, my Lord. I'll just go and light the fire in my brother's room for you.' Louise didn't make it to the door before Caleb stopped her.

'Wait! No need, I'm not letting Tony or Aidan out of my sight... my protection.'

The Frenchwoman tutt-tutted. 'Now my Lord that's hardly acceptable. Lady Tony's reputation...'

Currency Exchange

A hard laugh came from the doorway. 'My reputation is probably now non-existent Louise. Would it ease your mind to know that Caleb and I are actually engaged?'

Louise clasped her hands in delight to her ample bosom. 'Oh my Lady really? It's not because of what happened during the first abduction is it?'

As Tony closed the door behind her, she went as scarlet as Caleb. 'No it's not but I'd like to know how much of the truth has become common knowledge even here.'

'Phillippe Du Bois keeps up with all the London news. Once it is light, I'll go to the markets to get supplies for you. The only thing is... I've only got a small amount of housekeeping money until Phillippe returns.'

17

Tony went across to the dressing table where she had left the Doctor's medical bag and retrieved one of the silk bags of money. Handing it to Louise, she apologised, 'I'm afraid all we have in English currency.'

'That's all right, my Lady. I can get some of it changed for you. Just in case you're stuck here for longer than you expect.'

'Thank you,' said Caleb, 'but we don't want to put you in danger Mademoiselle Louise.'

Sitting on the edge of Louise's bed, François had been silently urging Tony to sit beside him and drink her hot chocolate. He looked up mildly interested as his sister counted out the money in the purse.

'There's always the safe. If you're carrying a large amount of English money it could cause problems if you have to pretend to be French to get to Paris.'

Louise hesitated to agree. 'Yes, but I'm supposed to only open the safe in an emergency.'

Her brother chuckled. 'I think this can be considered an emergency Lou.'

Pointing at the medical kit, Tony said, 'Actually François makes an excellent point. We couldn't explain having English money of any quantity on us. There's another purse of money in the bag.' As Louise drew out the second purse, Tony added, 'Be careful with that one, it has my jewellery in it as well as the money.'

None of Those Stray Kisses!

Sorting out the contents, Louise found Tony's engagement ring. 'Ooh! So you really are engaged! My heart sings for you!' Louise kissed Tony on both cheeks and then startled Caleb by also kissing him.

'Hey! Stop that! I know you French are supposed to be passionate people, but I don't like stray kisses!'

Slipping off the bed, Tony knelt down beside Caleb's chair and tousled his hair. 'Does that include me?' She asked.

He captured her hand and pulled her closer as his other hand cupped her face so that he could kiss her. 'You are the exception to that rule!'

Entwining her fingers through his, Tony drew Caleb to his feet. 'I'm glad to hear it. We need to try and get some sleep.' She led him across to the bed and sat him down on the edge of it.

'Is there room for Aidan in the bed or is he staying in front of the fire?' Caleb asked, sitting up as François drew the covers of the bedding over him. Louise removed the cushions off the seating under the window and laid them on the floor beside Aidan. François rose to his feet and lifted Aidan onto the cushions and placed a small cushion under the boy's head.

'It's best he stays in front of the fire.' Louise collected up all their discarded clothing as Tony slipped into the bed beside Caleb. 'We'll make certain the fire keeps burning while you sleep.' Pausing at the door Louise smiled. 'Do you want François to stand guard in the room with you or outside the door?'

'Hum! Would we be safe?' Caleb asked.

Chuckling, Louise suggested. 'Are you worried for yourself or Lady Tony? François is very good at what you're afraid of. I'll leave you to discuss your concerns while I organise some supplies for you.'

Do You Like Men Or Women?

As Louise quietly closed the door behind her, François sat down on the edge of the bed beside Caleb. He had taken their empty mugs and placed them back onto the tray. Tony put a hand over her mouth as she yawned.

'I know I'm supposed to understand what's going on but I'm being a little slow on the uptake,' said Tony. 'Are you attracted to men or women?' She addressed François.

An enchanting smile appeared. 'Actually both,' admitted François. 'Phillippe encouraged me to cultivate my ability to appeal to and to satisfy either sex.'

With the hot drink warming them from the inside, and the adrenalin rush from being chased subsiding, Tony yawned again as she laid down, snuggled against Caleb. 'What does Louise mean that Caleb is afraid of that?'

Slipping his arm around Tony, Caleb's laugh was a little forced. 'In one way François is free to indulge in his sexual fantasies whereas I am constantly fighting to keep control over my desires. In society's expectations of my protection of your reputation, I should be keeping you at arm's length. Forcing a distance between us could make you feel that I don't care and drive you into the arms of one who is free to satisfy your need for intimacy.'

Frowning, Tony laid her hand lightly on Caleb's chest, 'But I don't want François, I want you and I understand that we're supposed to wait until after we are married.'

Caleb laughed again. 'I find it absolutely frustrating! Being so close to you and not being able to give into our desires!'

Pinching his arm Tony said, 'I said I understand it not that I like it! Does... does François' attraction to men worry you?'

When Caleb did not immediately answer, Tony raised herself up onto one elbow so that she could see clearly the conflicting emotions that he was attempting to conceal.

'Are... are you afraid that you are attracted to men?' She added, her voice soft and gentle.

Swallowing on the lump in his throat it was a moment before Caleb could answer, 'You shook my understanding of myself that first evening at the Stirling Arms. To be fair it had been six years since I had seen Lady Antonia, you were still only a child then, and you had always been in female attire for those formal affairs. So the night I met Lord Tony, I no longer knew who I was. I've never before had any curiosity or sexual desires for other men and yet the moment I saw you, I was attracted in a way that had never happened before.'

'But… it wasn't long before you realised the truth.'

'True,' Caleb agreed. 'But I was worried that I might be attracted to you only in male attire.'

Tony dragged in a sharp breath. 'And are you?' Her voice was little more than a whisper.

His smile should have been enough of an answer for her. 'Do you really have any doubts after your experiments the other night?' Caleb reached out to caress his hand along Tony's arm. She wondered if her face was as flushed as it felt.

'So, when we're married how do you want me to dress?'

'However you want to dress my beautiful elfling. Although…' Caleb paused as he slid his hand down to caress against her stomach.

'Although what?' Tony was almost afraid to ask.

Smiling, Caleb placed a kiss against her forehead before locating her lips. 'Although when you swell with our first child, you might find a dress more comfortable than breeches.'

'Oh!' François' exclamation startled the embracing couple. 'Sorry but you've given me a brilliant idea for a clever disguise. Now go to sleep and don't do anything I would do!' The Frenchman jumped off their bed and headed out the door.

Overcome by a fit of giggles Tony could only cling to Caleb as she tried to keep from waking Aidan. Tracing his finger along Tony's jaw, Caleb raised her face so that he could locate her lips.

'One kiss and then we should try to sleep,' he suggested, caressing his finger across Tony's rosebud lips. Managing to control her giggles, Tony permitted her betrothed just one kiss before snuggling into his embrace.

'Do you think it's safe to be in the same bed, my Lord, or should I join Aidan on the floor?'

Caleb's arms tightened around her. 'You're not going anywhere. To be honest, elfling I'm so tired right now, I wouldn't be able to even undress you, let alone satisfy you.'

Caressing her hand along his chest, Tony said, 'Rain check then, my Lord?'

'Definitely my elfling!' Caleb sighed and tried to relax. *We need to give sleep the opportunity to heal and rejuvenate our spirits for the long journey ahead.*

Three In The Bed

It is nice to feel so warm, to be so comfortable, and to feel safe. Even though the darkness is still very real, it is no longer frightening and overwhelming. Uttering a deep sigh, Caleb wrapped his arms tighter around Tony and he pressed his lips against the back of her neck.

They both lay on their sides, Tony's back curved into his chest. Running his hands down to encircle Tony's waist, he was startled when his fingers ran into a head of curly hair.

'What on earth?' Releasing Tony, Caleb struggled to sit up.

'Sorry big brother,' said Aidan, 'I had a nightmare.'

Scrubbing a hand across his own face, Caleb replied, 'That's all right. You can help me down the corridor.' He threw back the bedding and rose to his feet to stretch all his muscles.

'All right.' Aidan jumped out of bed.

Tony slipped out of the sheets, already missing the warmth of Caleb's body and picked up a dressing gown that Louise had borrowed from Phillippe Du Bois. 'Put on this dressing gown,' Tony said, 'Louise will bring up breakfast, or in this case luncheon as soon as we're ready.'

Putting his arms out to assist Tony in getting the dressing gown on, Caleb asked, 'Why can't we eat downstairs?'

'Louise doesn't want us to be visible from a downstairs window.'

Caleb tied his dressing gown closed. 'I see. All right little brother, lead the way.' As Aidan took his hand Caleb tried to not think about all the problems they would have to face that day.

Clothes Make The Man... Woman

The meal Louise presented them was simple but excellent and Caleb complimented her skill in the kitchen. While a blushing Louise cleared away, François assisted Caleb and Aidan to dress. Tony had unwrapped Caleb's shoulder and decided that it didn't require fresh dressing before he changed into clothes supplied from Phillippe's closet.

Louise found some children's clothes from the last time Phillippe's nephew had stayed there and Louise threw one of her own dresses over Tony's head. Looking at herself in the full length mirror, Tony was a little dubious about this new look. Louise was a big busted, plump woman and her dress hung a little tragically over Tony's graceful curves.

'Eh... Louise I don't want to complain but don't you think I'll attract attention in an ill-fitting dress?'

Louise only laughed. 'We haven't finished yet. Something Lord Delacourt said to you gave François an idea. As part of your new look. I'm going to dye your hair black, and Lord Aidan's as well.'

Unconsciously, Tony ran her plait through her fingers. 'It won't be permanent will it?'

'A couple of washes and it will be gone completely.' Louise patted her arm reassuringly. 'My Lord, François is prepared to shave you if you want but the developing beard does slightly alter your appearance.'

Caleb rubbed his hand against the stubble on his face. 'I suppose it's impossible to hide the bandages over my eyes. That must be a dead give-away.'

François had been having a silent tussle of wills with Aidan as he tried to brush the boy's curly hair. 'I've an idea but it will depend upon the Doctor's instructions.'

Tony had begun to unplait her hair. 'I need to re-dress and put ointment on his burns daily.'

'Do the burns have to be covered or just the eyes?' asked François.

'I... I don't know. We have to keep the burns clean and anointed but I don't know about covered,' Tony admitted.

François rose to his feet. 'Give me a minute, I have to get something.' He left the room as the two women looked at each other puzzled.

Sitting Caleb down on the edge of the bed, Tony carefully unwrapped his burns bandages before peeling off the gauze pads. 'Keep your eyes closed Caleb,' she ordered as she wiped a water soaked swab across his burns.

'How... how does it look?' He tried to keep his tone unconcerned.

Tony answered immediately, 'Actually a lot better than yesterday.' She picked up the medical bag and drew out the jar of ointment. As Tony was applying the ointment to Caleb's face, François came back into the room.

'Place the small pads back over his Lordship's eyes and then put these on over the top.' François handed Tony a pair of spectacles with black lens. 'During the day it will be less obvious. At night or when you get back to Stirling Manor you can re-bandage his wounds.'

Looking at the spectacles, Tony was a little dubious but following François' instructions, she put clean pads over Caleb's closed eyes and slipped the black lens spectacles over the top.

'Well?' Caleb queried as Tony placed her hand under his chin to raise his face so that she could examine him.

'I think it'll work but… I am worried about being able to keep the burns clean and sterile.' Tony lowered her head so that she could kiss Caleb's stubble rough cheek.

'That had better be you Tony!' Caleb reached out to grasp hold of Tony's hand and drew her down on to his lap.

'Can't you tell the difference?' She wrapped her arms around his neck and caressed her lips against his. He tightened his hold around her waist.

'I think you'll need to do it a couple of times just so that I can be sure!' Laughing, Tony permitted Caleb one more kiss before Louise drew her to her feet.

'Now my Lady, I need you and Lord Aidan to come with me and I'll dye your hair black.' Louise headed for the door.

'It is only temporary isn't it Louise?' Caleb asked, reluctantly allowing Tony out of his embrace.

'Yes my Lord. Will you be all right until we return?' Louise urged Aidan to his feet.

Caleb didn't even hesitate, 'I'll be fine.'

'I'll stay with Lord Delacourt,' offered François, 'I think there's something I can help him with.'

Tony cast a speaking glance over her shoulder. 'No touching, François!' She warned.

An angelic smile answered her. 'Not unless he touches first Angel!'

You're Not A Liability

François crossed the room to close the door behind them. 'Now then my Lord… I know what is worrying you.'

Caleb sighed, 'I doubt it!' He drawled, just a tiny bit nervous as François moved back across the room to sit beside Caleb on the bed. 'Are you as good looking as I think you are?' Caleb added.

'That's really not for me to say, my Lord.' There was no disguising the amusement in the Frenchman's voice. 'But that isn't what troubles you. Her Ladyship's love for you is absolute. It's the loss of your sight, even if it may be only temporary, you feel as useless as Lord Aidan to protect all of you.'

I would dearly love to damn François' impertinence but I have to honestly admit the younger man has hit the nail squarely on the head. 'Yes,' Caleb sighed, finally accepting his fears. 'I suppose you have the answer my French God?'

François chuckled. 'Actually I do. A way that you can see through Lord Aidan's eyes. Imagine that in front of you is the face of a clock.'

'You are joking, aren't you?' There was no hiding the scorn in Caleb's voice.

'Hear me out my Lord, it'll all make sense in a moment.' François laid his hand on Caleb's shoulder as he rose to his feet. There was a minor tussle of wills when François tried to take Caleb's hand into his own. The Frenchman uttered a deep sigh.

'Please work with me.' He waited patiently while a muscle twitched in Caleb's cheek as he debated his next move. Finally, reluctantly, Caleb stretched his hand out towards François. The Frenchman contained a smile as he knew that the moment he spoke it would be obvious in his voice.

'Straight ahead is 12 o'clock.' François moved Caleb's hand to point straight in front. 'Three o'clock is directly right and nine o'clock is directly left.' François moved Caleb's arm as he explained.

'And six o'clock is directly behind me?' concluded Caleb.

'Yes my Lord, but if you and Lady Tony are back to back to protect each other, you won't have to be worried about the directions between three o'clock and nine o'clock. Lord Aidan knows how to tell the time. He can be your eyes and together you are more than an asset to her Ladyship.'

Giving Caleb time to digest this information, François dropped his Lordship's hand back into his own lap. Very quietly

François moved around the bed until he stood behind Caleb and the bed.

'Do you know where I am, Lord Delacourt?' He spoke clearly and waited.

'Well since you're behind me, I'd hope that Tony would be protecting my back. Otherwise I'd guess you were at five o'clock.' Caleb turned around to point almost directly at François' heart.

'Bravo, my Lord! If you had a gun, I could now be dead.'

What A Change!

A surprised voice came from the doorway. 'Why should Lord Delacourt want to shoot you François? What did you do?' Louise led the Stirling siblings back into the room. Aidan slipped around Louise's skirts to plonk himself on the cushions in front of the fire.

'Nothing Lou, I was just suggesting a way for Lord Delacourt to overcome his temporary disability.' François paused as he took in the changes to the siblings as Aidan dried his hair, now black, in front of the fire and Tony sat down at Louise's dressing table as the older woman brushed Tony's hair. Now black waist length hair. 'Mon Dieu! What a remarkable difference that has already made!' François moved around the bed to study Tony more closely.

'Tell me please,' Caleb quietly asked.

'They both now have hair as dark as midnight,' explained François. 'Lord Aidan will easily pass as your son.'

Caleb held up his hand to stop François from saying anything else. 'If you make the comment that Tony could easily pass as my daughter, I will find you and punch you in the mouth.' Caleb warned.

Louise chuckled. 'That won't be necessary, my Lord, something you said earlier to her Ladyship gave François an idea.

Lady Tony won't be disguised as your daughter, but as your wife… your very pregnant wife.'

Both his eyebrows rose in surprise as Caleb asked, 'Not just pregnant but very pregnant? Won't that hamper Tony's movements?'

Laying her hair brush down in the dressing table, Louise tapped Tony on her shoulder. 'Join Lord Aidan in front of the fire and get your hair completely dry, my Lady, while I explain.' When Tony had settled on the floor beside her brother, Louise sat down to the chair her Ladyship had just vacated.

'When its dark, François will drive you back to Captain Sheppard's ship but we can't ensure that you'll get on board so you'll then have to head north east to Paris. Colouring your hair may not be enough of a disguise. Also if they do look for you here, you can't leave your silk dress behind. So I'll secure a bag around her waist, under her dress as well as most of your money and jewellery.'

Deep in thought, Caleb stroked his chin. 'So this is just about concealing Tony's expensive attire?'

'Only in part. Men are generally more hesitant about rough handling a pregnant woman. Your story too will prevent people asking too many questions,' added François.

'If you seriously doubt we're going to get aboard Captain Sheppard's ship, why not head straight to Paris from here?' Caleb asked.

Tony knew the answer to this one. 'If there is the slightest chance, even if it is remote, that we've the opportunity to get home before dawn then we have to take it.'

The Cover Story

Caleb sighed, 'All right then, so what's our story going to be?'

'It is very simple, my Lord,' stated Louise. 'You are Captain Rene Du Bois, his wife Bella and their son Henri. Your injuries are from the recent campaign at Waterloo and you're all travelling up to Paris for your Uncle Luke Du Bois' funeral. You must never lapse into English, even when you believe that you're alone.'

'You have really thought this through,' Caleb stated.

Louise nodded. 'Yes my Lord. It is essential that you have your story straight now, making up lies on the spot is very hard to do especially in another language.'

Thinking this over, Caleb absently scrubbed his hand across his face. 'I have only a civilian's understanding of what happened between Bonaparte and Wellington. What do I do if someone asks me about the campaign?'

François smiled. 'But no one will ask you, my Lord, our defeat at the hands of the English at Waterloo is very raw and very painful. Believing you're a veteran of our army, only a drunk or an imbecile will ask you any questions. If that happens, then do that thing you do with your jaw by clenching your teeth. Say in a hollow voice that you don't want to talk about it. Anyone with the questioner will shut them down immediately.'

Louise agreed, 'So long as you don't let anything fluster or betray you, it will be possible to bluff your way through anything.'

Shifting her position to continue drying another section of her wet hair, Tony ran her hand over Aidan's hair to see how his was drying. 'I won't risk exposing Aidan to the night air if the odds are low that we can possibly succeed getting on that ship.'

The French brother and sister exchanged a glance. 'There are no guarantees in life belle fille,' said Louise, 'it might all go off without a hitch or you might run into a hundred and one different obstacles and never make it to the dock. But you can't pass up any chance that you could be home before dawn breaks.'

'You could be having breakfast with your father,' added François.

Aidan reached up to take Tony's hand into his own. 'I want to go home Tony.'

Sighing, his sister relented. 'All right Little Bear, we'll try to board the ship tonight.' With her free hand, Tony tussled Aidan's hair. 'I'd like to go home too.'

Waiting For Nightfall

Rising to her feet, Louise said, 'I'll find a couple of books from the library but you'll have to stay out of sight up here.'

François chuckled. 'It'll be a couple of hours before we can safely head out when it is dark. I'm sure you can find something to fill in the time.' His wicked laugh brought a rush of colour to Tony's cheeks.

'You really are unbelievable aren't you? Is sex all you think about?' asked Tony.

'Oh Angel, once you try it, you won't have to ask that question.'

Louise urged François towards the door. 'Try to get some additional sleep, belle enfants. You may be awake in the wee hours of the morning.' The older woman paused on the threshold. 'Oh and Lord Delacourt…'

'Yes Nanny, I'll be a good boy and keep my hands to myself.' Caleb's lips twitched into a smile.

Shaking her head, Louise laughed. 'The virtuous will be rewarded.'

Out in the hall they could hear François' wicked laughter, 'But being virtuous isn't half as much fun!'

'Oh François!' Louise pushed her brother away from the door. 'You're not helping Lord Delacourt's resolve to be a gentleman! Something you know nothing about!'

Tony winced at that low blow. 'Louise! That's a little harsh.'

François laughed and retorted, 'I am what she made me!' He disappeared before his sister could clip him around the ears.

Our Future Children

When Louise had quietly closed the door behind her, Caleb rose to his feet and carefully made his way around the bed to join the siblings in front of the fire. Accepting the hand that Tony held out to him, Caleb sat down on the floor.

He was rather surprised when a small cold hand slipped confidently into one of his. Caleb released Tony's hand so that he could find Aidan's other hand.

'Sitting in front of a fire, you shouldn't be this cold.' Caleb briskly rubbed the boy's hands between his own. Rising to her feet, Tony went across to the dresser and checked one of the top drawers until she found a pair of ladies mittens. *They'll be way too big but at least they'll keep his hands warm.*

'Now you know why I fear him getting cold.' Tony took her brother's hands out of Caleb's and slipped the woollen mittens onto Aidan's cold fingers As Tony sat down again, Caleb reached out until he touched her shoulder and caressed his fingers through her hair.

'Your hair isn't dry enough yet Tony.' Reluctantly Caleb released her so that she could move closer to the fire again.

'If you're going to be so heavily pregnant, one question we'll have to be ready to answer is what names have we considered for the unborn child.'

'Alexander.'

Caleb's eyebrows rose. 'You didn't even have to think about it.'

'Or Paul, Angelica if it is a girl. It'll have to be something French.' She gave a gurgle of laughter at his look of surprise. 'When Papa was considering possible names for Aidan I started to think about what I would like to call my own children.' Tony fanned her hair in front of the flames to speed up the drying

31

process as Aidan wrapped his fur rug tightly around him and lay down on his cushions.

'I like the name Margarette like Grandmama,' Aidan yawned, scrubbing his hand over his eyes. 'I could call her Maggie until she's a young Lady like Tony is now.' As Aidan yawned again, Tony knew that her young brother was already half asleep again.

'That's a nice name Little Bear. Go to sleep and we'll try to not disturb you.' Tony brushed her hand against Aidan's hair to ensure that it was completely dry before moving his cushions closer to the fireplace.

Sweet Distraction

Assisting Caleb to his feet, Tony led him over to the window seat away from Aidan. 'Do you want to get some more sleep?' She sat down in the window beside Caleb and took his hand between her own.

'Let's see what Louise finds for us to read.' He intertwined his fingers through Tony's and raised her hand to his lips. 'Unless there's something else you'd rather be doing.' Caleb raised her hand a little higher to press his lips against Tony's wrist. Uttering a nervous laugh, she was glad that Caleb could not see how she blushed.

'Caleb! François got to you didn't he? I thought you were trying to be a true gentleman!'

Chuckling, Caleb permitted himself a second lingering kiss against Tony's inner wrist. 'I didn't say what we could be doing, that suggestion was completely out of your pretty little brain. I think that maybe François has put ideas into your head.' *Even without the use of my eyes I know that she will be blushing furiously.*

'Well what else am I supposed to think when you kiss me like that and your voice lowers to a seductive tone?' Tony traced her free hand along Caleb's roughened jaw line and turned his cheek to claim his mouth with her own. Giving into the sweet delicious temptation of Tony's willing, gentle lips; Caleb took control of the kiss.

Releasing her hand, Caleb drew her closer into his embrace and her gentle kiss turned into a more demanding, more passionate one. As she ran her hands up his chest to entwine behind his neck, there was no saying where that kiss may have led them as Louise returned to the bedroom at that moment.

Reluctantly, Caleb released Tony's lips as she pushed gently against his chest in embarrassment. He refused, though, to remove his arm from around Tony's waist.

'My apologies, my Lord, but perhaps its best that I did interrupt you before you got swept away on a flood of emotion.' Louise laid a couple of novels as well as a morning newspaper into Tony's lap.

Glancing over them, she was surprised that the novels were in English and the newspaper was that morning's London Times. Tony looked up as Louise straightened the bedcovers.

'This morning's paper all ready? Is there anything in it?'

Nodding Louise sat down on the edge of the bed. 'Your engagement is in there, nothing about the second abduction, though, there is another mention of the first abduction a week ago.'

A Truth Universally Acknowledged

Laying the newspaper down on the floor at her feet, Tony turned the novels over to look at the covers. 'There's no Author listed on the books,' Louise stated, 'but I believe that they're by the same Lady.'

'Sense and Sensibility was published in 1811, Pride and Prejudice in 1813 and Mansfield Park in 1814. I think I read the first one when it came out.' Tony opened one novel and flicked through the pages to the beginning. '"It is a truth universally acknowledged, that a single man in possession of a good fortune, must be in want of a wife." ' She read aloud before glancing up a little provocatively. 'Well my Lord, are you in want of a wife?'

Caleb tightened his embrace around Tony. 'Not in the least.' A gasp of shock was torn from Louise but he hadn't finished. 'I'm not in want of a wife as I have already secured the one I want.'

'Oh! I thought you meant...' Louise wasn't sure how to end that sentence.

A rueful smile appeared on Caleb's face. 'This might not be how I thought I'd be celebrating my engagement but I'm not regretting any of the choices I've made.'

Louise cooed as Caleb's hand travelled down Tony's arm until he located her hand and raised it to his lips.

'Now then ma belle enfants, are you going to behave yourselves or do I need to chaperone you?'

Caleb's smile could have dimmed the sun. 'Tony can read the newspaper to me.'

'Ah Hum! Behave yourselves and there could be chocolate mousse for supper.'

'Yes Nanny.' Chuckling, Caleb sat back against the window sill. Picking up the newspaper, Tony settled between Caleb's legs and leant back against his chest. Louise took the books from Tony and placed them on the floor close enough for her Ladyship to reach.

Heading for the door, Louise paused and looked back at the engaged couple as Tony located the article about their first abduction and folded the paper so that she could read it aloud. It was an image that would stay with Louise forever. *An idyllic portrait of a young couple, deeply in love and at peace with the world. Although the first part is true, I pray that the latter will not be too far away.* Louise quietly closed the door behind her.

A Quiet Afternoon

That afternoon was spent rather idyllically, hidden away from prying or murderous eyes. Once Tony had read all the articles that Caleb was interested in, Aidan was finally awake and wanted something a little more to his taste than the novels written by Jane Austen. Louise had found a couple of children's books for Tony to read, but had hesitated to bring them up as they were in French. *It is a good opportunity for Aidan to practice his translations,* Tony thought.

The trio had a very pleasant meal of roast chicken, several vegetables and of course the promised chocolate mousse. Tony had tried to convince Louise and François to join them but Louise insisted that she and her brother would eat their dinner downstairs.

As the daylight started to fade Tony began to grow increasingly nervous although she attempted to keep that hidden from Caleb and Aidan. Her brother was happily employed with cleaning up his chocolate dessert but her fiancé was not unaware of Tony's conflict of emotion. Caleb's hand travelled across their makeshift dinner table to lay comfortably over the top of her hand.

That simple wordless gesture caused Tony to sigh and smile as some of the tension left her. *We're going to undertake a huge risk returning to the seaside village of Hon Fleur. Nigel Sutherland will have turned the local people against us with promises of money or the opportunity to string up three English aristocrats.*

It is soothing to watch Louise fold and pack into a carpet bag Aidan's and Caleb's clothing which are now dry. It's as if we're going for a picnic down along the river. Nothing seems to faze Louise's composure. My silk dress is carefully folded and placed into the pouch that will be secured around my waist.

Most of the money that Louise had exchanged for our English currency will also go into the pouch as well as all our jewellery. A small amount of French money will go back into a silk purse then into the Doctor's bag to either pay Captain Sheppard to sail us home again or to pay for our passage up to Paris.

Tony's New Figure

François was sent out to harness up a pair of horses to the cart while Louise stripped Tony out of her borrowed dress and petticoat to attach the pouch securely around her waist before redressing her again. As Louise tightened the dress sash around Tony's waist and tied it into a bow behind her back; Tony glanced into the free standing full length mirror in the corner of the room. A gasp of surprise escaped from Tony, bringing Caleb sharply to his feet and around the table to join her.

'What is it? What's wrong?' Caleb reached out for Tony's hand and she placed his over her suddenly swollen abdomen thanks to the pouch underneath her dress.

'I wish… that you could see me at this moment.' Tony whispered, awestruck at becoming instantly about eight months pregnant. 'But after we're married, it probably wouldn't be long before you'll be able to see this become reality.'

Allowing Caleb the opportunity to caress his hands over her new swelling, Tony could almost imagine this was real. 'This is what it will look like when your child is inside of me. Our child! Oh Caleb, I had been nervous about this next step in my life. Getting married, having children as it all seemed a life time away from the facade I was living, pretending to be something I'm not.' *I feel radiant as if I really am pregnant. This is what I had been searching for all my life even though I hadn't been aware of it.* Caleb's hands left her new abdomen to travel up her arms to cup her face.

'I can hardly wait for that day! My love! My life! My salvation!' He kissed her passionately, drawing Tony into his arms which was a little difficult with her new figure. Louise

36

turned to her dressing table and briefly hunted through a jewellery box before turning back to the embracing couple.

'You'll need this,' Louise slid a gold ring onto the second last finger on Tony's left hand.

Reluctantly Tony drew herself out of her fiancé's arms and hugged Louise. 'Thank you Nanny, for everything you and François have done for us.' She kissed the older woman on both her cheeks before picking up the Doctor's bag and the carpet bag packed by Louise.

'We'll never forget the respite you offered us in this dangerous adventure.' Caleb reached out for Louise's hand and bowed low over it as she blushed and curtsied.

'I'm sorry we can't take you in the carriage but Phillippe used it to drive his mother up to Paris. Let me carry those down for you,' Louise took the bags away from Tony, who then took Caleb's hand to lead him down the back stairs. She paused long enough to be certain that firstly they had left nothing behind to betray Louise after they had gone and secondly, perhaps most importantly, that Aidan was securely wrapped up in his fur rug as he followed his sister.

François had the horses and cart waiting outside the stables. If possible they didn't want to be seen from the front of the house. Louise loaded the bags before assisting Tony to first lift Aidan into the back of the cart, and then help Caleb up before he in turn assisted Tony up beside him. *My new body shape is more difficult to manoeuver than I had first thought and is going to take some getting used to.* With the three of them huddled in a corner of the cart, Louise threw a large blanket over the top of their laps as Aidan curled up in his sister's arms.

'Bon chance ma belle enfants! Remember from now on, speak only in French.' Wrapping her shawl tightly around her shoulders, Louise waited until the cart had disappeared out of sight before she headed back into the house. Until François returned, she would make absolutely certain that there were no clues left behind to suggest that the Stirling siblings and their blind hero had ever been there.

Back to Hon Fleur

The journey was made in total silence as the tension increased the closer they approached Hon Fleur. François hid the horses and cart a little distance from the village and led the masqueraders in on foot. Louise had packed away Tony's flimsy shoes into the carpet bag and lent her a sturdy pair of half boots as well as a pair of thick socks to protect Tony's blistered feet.

Aware that they were in danger, Aidan was uncharacteristically quiet as he clung tightly to his sister's hand. Through the fading light, François led them to the Inn beside the dock to scope out access to Captain Sheppard's ship, which had already berthed.

Outside a window of the Inn, hidden in the shadows, Tony and François peered cautiously inside the public bar room. At the sight of Nigel Sutherland having collared Captain Sheppard and refusing to let the pirate out of his sight, Tony gasped in surprise and Caleb instinctively reached out to support her as she seemed about to collapse.

'It's Patrick!' She whispered. *Although he had been an obvious suspect behind our abduction, I had never truly believed that my cousin could hate me so much that he would wish us all dead.*

Overhearing A Conversation

Through some clever piece of devilry that Tony didn't want to know how he did or how he knew how to do it, François jemmied open the window and easing it by a fraction, they were able to hear what was being said.

'You're barking up the wrong tree gentlemen,' drawled the Captain, 'your escapees won't be anywhere near here. They'll be safe in Paris by now, or on their way back to the Lady's father.' Bored with the discussion, Captain Sheppard stoked his pipe and took his time to light it.

'Then why did ya come back here if not to pick them up?' demanded Nigel.

Patrick was pacing up and down the room, barely able to contain his nervous energy. 'They have to be somewhere! My God, she's on her own in a foreign land with a child and a blind man! Why did you do that to him? Why bring them here at all?'

Nigel threw a look of scorn at the fine gentleman who was so easily falling apart. 'I was following the orders I was given. I can't help it if y've had a change of heart.'

'For God's sake! I don't care what your orders were, I want Tony back alive!'

Nigel uttered an ugly laugh. 'Even if the boy and the hero are taken out of the picture, she'll never have ya! So can ya be happy enough with just the title of Earl without the hand of the Lady?'

Tearing his fingers frantically through his hair, Patrick was almost beside himself. 'If it makes Tony happy, return all three of them alive and well. I don't know what you were offered but my uncle will ensure that you're still paid if they are returned unharmed.'

Nigel snorted in disgust. 'What sort of man are ya? If I'd been in y'r shoes I'd have broken her in years ago. Letting her run around the county in male attire! She was more of a man than ya are! Ya had a penis man! Why didn't ya ever use it?'

Roaring in anger, Patrick slugged Nigel in the face and although the big man was rocked on his feet, it didn't knock him over.

'Don't talk about my cousin like that!'

'I'm glad to see y've got some balls little man but don't do that again or I'll knock ya into next week!' Briefly Nigel massaged his aching jaw.

Withdrawing his fob watch out of his waistcoat pocket, the Captain sighed. 'Are you going to hold me here all night? If I'm to make it to the Sussex coast before sunrise to avoid the coastguard, I need to set sail now.'

Patrick waved a dismissive hand but Nigel was less complacent. 'I'll escort you aboard, Sheppard, that way ya can't smuggle the escapees on without anyone noticing.'

Captain Sheppard shrugged his shoulders in boredom. 'As you wish Sutherland but you're wasting your time remaining here in Hon Fleur.'

Option Four?

As Nigel followed the Captain out of the Inn, François touched Tony on the arm and gestured with his head back in the direction of his cart. Taking Caleb and Aidan by the hand, Tony followed François away from the port. Their disguises weren't going to fool Nigel and he wasn't going to let anyone get on that ship that night.

Once they were loaded once more into the cart, Tony ensured that Aidan was well wrapped up as François drove them back to his own village. A tremor of fear ran through Tony and in agitation she dashed away the tears that threatened to overwhelm her.

Yet another night spent away from my father's house. Is this why Patrick wants me alive and not dead? So that he can enjoy the ruin of my reputation? Now isn't the time to dwell upon this question as I am faced with the dangerous task of getting my blind fiancé and young brother safely through a hostile country where the state of my reputation will be the least of our problems.

Drawing up outside the Inn, the White Goose, François assisted them out of the cart and embraced them each in turn.

'From here you can purchase tickets for the stage coach to Paris. I must return to Louise in case your cousin thinks to look for you there. Remember, speak only in French.' François kissed Tony again. 'God grant you wings beautiful angel.'

Picking up their bags, Caleb followed Tony and Aidan into the Inn. Dragging in a deep breath they stepped into their assumed roles and a world filled with so much danger that Tony felt her knees tremble beneath her. From now on they must be Captain Rene Du Bois, his wife Bella and their son Henri.

The French Masquerade

Trying to look tired and not scared, Bella led her boys into the public bar.

'Good evening, I understand we can book a passage to Paris from here?' Bella addressed the publican in French as she took the medical bag out of Rene's hand.

Laying down the glass he had been polishing, Guy, the publican, smiled. 'You're in luck madam, one is due in about half an hour. The next after that isn't until six o'clock tomorrow morning.

Removing her purse from her bag to pay for the tickets, Bella turned slightly to speak to her son, 'Henri lead your papa to the fireplace. We won't have long to wait.'

By now the other patrons in the Inn had taken in their appearance and their deductions about Rene's dark glasses are justified as he accidently brushed against a chair in his path and stumbled slightly.

'It must be pretty important to drag your young child and blind husband out at this time of night?' Guy handed the tickets to Bella.

She sighed. 'Rene feels that he has to attend Uncle Claud's funeral.' Laying her hand over her abdomen Bella smiled. 'I thought Phillippe would understand our difficulty to travel up to Paris but Rene insists on going anyway.'

The publican's eyebrows rose. 'You're Phillippe Du Bois' cousin?'

Bella gestured with her head towards Rene as she slipped her purse back into the Doctor's bag before turning to join her family.

'Look Madame Du Bois, the stage isn't always on time, can I get you a pot of coffee?' offered Guy as Bella caressed her hand against her husband's hair where he sat in an arm chair and Henri sat at his feet as close to the fireplace as possible. Henri looked up with his huge eyes.

'Hot chocolate please.'

Bella hid her smile as Guy melted under the pleading look, not surprised really that the puppy dog eyes worked just as easily on the French as it does on the English.

'Right away Master Henri,' the publican's indulgent expression changed suddenly. 'Oi! Marius! Where's your manners? Give the lady your chair!'

Rene chuckled. 'Disturb the drunk not, Keeper,' his hands reached out instinctively to surround Bella's waist and drew her down onto his lap. 'I may have lost the use of my eyes but my lap is still good enough to support my wife.'

The First Inquisition

Settling herself more comfortably so that she was not sitting directly upon one of his guns, Bella placed her medical bag down beside the carpet bag. The drunk Marius stirred enough to stare unfocussed at the young couple.

'You a Du Bois?' Marius drawled.

One of Rene's eyebrows rose hauntingly. 'Yes, Captain Rene Du Bois.'

'Captain? Is that how you injured yourself?'

Guy slammed his hand down on the bar. 'Marius! It's none of your business!'

Rene took Bella's trembling hands between his own as he replied calmly, 'It's all right Monsieur, yes I was injured at

Waterloo. A shot blast too close to my face destroyed my sight. Anything else you'd like to know?' There was a touch of steel to Rene's voice that even the drunk managed to recognise.

'Was it as bad as everyone makes out?' Marius wasn't about to be completely suppressed. The colour drained from Rene's face as his lips thinned in pain. Guy came out from behind the bar and smacked Marius across the back of his head.

'Shut your gob Marius!' The Innkeeper pressed a small tumbler into Rene's hand. 'Here Captain, not all of us are insensitive to what you brave men went through for our country.' He patted Rene on the shoulder before going back to collect the hot chocolate from the kitchen for Henri.

Rene took a sip from the tumbler and both his eyebrows rose. Guy had given him a very excellent quality cognac. Knowing Bella's aversion to alcohol, Rene didn't mention what he was drinking but took small sips of the liqueur to enjoy it while it lasted.

The Stage Coach

When the coach drew up outside the White Goose Inn, its keeper carried their bags out for them, passing them up to the driver to secure on the roof of the carriage. As Guy assisted Bella to ascend into the coach, she pressed some money into his hand.

'For the refreshments,' she explained.

Flushing, he tried to hand the money back. 'No Madame, it was my pleasure.'

Rene reached out to lay his hand over Guy's. 'You have a business to run and your own family to feed, but thank you for the gesture.'

Sniffing, the Innkeeper bobbed his head and accepted the money. He saw them safely into the coach before closing the door. He whisked out a big handkerchief as he saw a small hand waving to him while the vehicle pulled away. Blowing his nose defiantly Guy stepped back into his establishment.

The rest of his night was fairly routine – throwing out the drunks, locking up, finally able to head upstairs to his bed and his own wife. Something, though, about that young family had affected him. So when his wife stirred in her sleep and turned over to look up at him as he slipped into their bed, Guy placed a tender kiss upon her lips and drew her into his arms. *I have so much to be grateful for and aren't going to take it all for granted again.*

SATURDAY

The Accident

The stage coach was cold and despite the late hour quite crowded. Due to her extended stomach bulge it wasn't comfortable for Henri to sit on his mother's lap, so he willingly wrapped his arms and his fur rug around Rene. Despite the roughness of the road and the cracking pace the driver set; Henri now full of hot chocolate, proceeded to drop off to sleep.

Bella closed her eyes and tried to relax her mind and body but it was necessary to grab hold of the strap beside the door to stop herself being pitched onto the floor with every bump or jolt of the carriage. Half an hour into their journey Bella was just wondering if she was going to survive several hours of a rough ride when they began to slow down for the village of Beuzeville.

Even so Bella kept a tight grasp on the door strap. Which was just as well for when a dog ran out in front of the coach they veered off the road. They struck a large pot hole and the jolt fractured the wheel shaft forcing the coach violently onto its side.

The woman seated beside her screamed, falling into hysterics. Bella saw no point in creating needless noise and held onto her strap to stop from falling too hard upon the other passengers. Glancing across at Rene, Bella was relieved that Henri was secure in his father's arms.

The carriage door was ripped open from outside and the anxious faces of a couple of Ostlers from the Inn appeared. As hands reached in to help the trapped passengers, Rene handed Henri up before reaching out to locate Bella and assist her out of the coach.

Being a true gentleman Rene helped his other fellow passengers before allowing the two strong lads to haul him out of the overturned coach.

Too Much Noise

For a moment Rene was lost, there was too much noise surrounding him to distinguish between the different sounds. The horses were screaming in agony, the back two were managing to get to their feet but the front pair had broken their front legs in the fall. The woman who had been sitting beside Bella was having hysterics.

Having been pulled out of the carriage, the woman had tripped over the dead body of the driver who had fallen off his box when the coach went over and had broken his neck.

Having been rudely awoken, Henri was naturally upset and Bella had her hands full comforting him as she knelt on the ground, Henri sobbing in her arms. There was no point calling out as Rene wouldn't be able to hear over the noise.

Taking deep breathes Rene tried to suppress the rising feelings of panic. Looking up Bella put her fingers to her lips and whistled to catch the attention of an Ostler.

'Direct my husband over here and those horses need to be put out of their misery.' Bella ordered, lifting Henri into her arms as she rose to her feet to wipe his eyes and blow his nose.

As the Ostler took Rene's arm, Bella turned to face the hysterical woman and slapped her face. 'Pull yourself together Madame! Sir, if you're not injured, throw a blanket over the driver. Is there a local Doctor nearby? Her natural Authority had people running to do her bidding.

Taking Command

Beuzeville was a little market town, in the Normandy region and a long way from their goal to reach Paris. Leon, the Keeper, of the Inn, the Renegades, made his way through the injured bodies and the over-turned carriage to Bella's side.

'I've already sent one of my boys for the Doctor. Shepherd the injured into my establishment and I'll take care of the horses. Madame, you shouldn't be carrying your son in your condition.'

By this time Rene had joined them and Bella laid her hand on his arm. 'Are you injured?' She asked.

'My shoulder's a little sore but I'll be all right. Give Henri to me.' Rene reached out his hands for their son as Bella took the rifle the Ostler, a Groom at the Inn, brought out to the Innkeeper. Passing Henri to Rene, Bella strode over to the horses and calmly put a bullet into the brain of each suffering animal.

The loud crack of each shot polarised everyone around them and Bella threw the rifle back to the Groom. The hysterical woman stared open mouth at Bella who sardonically raise one eyebrow.

'Are we going to have any more histrionics from you?' The woman mutely shook her head and scurried into the Inn with the other passengers.

The Renegade Inn

Chuckling as Bella took his hand, Rene followed her into the Inn, 'Not everyone has your nerves of steel Bella.'

'Maybe not but that noise was beginning to annoy me.' Bella glanced around and found the Innkeeper directing the passengers into chairs as his wife, Claire, assessed their injuries. 'What can we do to help?' Bella asked.

Claire cast a quick scrutinizing glance over Bella's family and made a rapid decision. 'You've enough to contend with Madame.

Take your family up to room six and one of the boys will bring up your luggage. You won't be able to go on any further tonight.'

Looking up from a broken arm he was examining, Leon, the Keeper, added, 'I'll send the Doctor up to check you over once he has dealt with these people.'

The very thought of being examined and their secret being revealed sent a chilling wave of fear through Bella but linking her hand through Rene's arm, she somehow managed to smile.

'Thank you but it's more important that I get my son warm.'

Leon bowed his head. 'I'll have my girl come up and light the fire.' He gestured to his teenage daughter Michelle, who had been assisting her mother, to follow them up the stairs. Glancing at the Innkeeper's pretty daughter, Bella was surprised into thinking, *She is only just younger than me.*

Carrying a candle, Michelle lit those already in the room before kneeling in front of the fireplace to light the kindling already set up. Easing Rene down onto the edge of the bed, Bella glanced around the room and was pleasantly surprised. It was clean, well aired, the sheets seemed to be fairly fresh and as the fire took hold, it didn't emit too much smoke into the room. Henri immediately slipped out of Rene's arms and dropped to the floor in front of the fire, wrapping his fur rug firmly around him.

Heading back to the door, Michelle paused to hold it open as one of the Ostlers brought in their carpet and medical bags. *I am surprised but relieved that our luggage has survived the crash,* thought Bella. *I had been wondering how I was going to tend to Rene's burns if we had lost our supplies.* Bella thanked both the servants and tipped them as they left, quietly closing the door behind them.

Assessing Their New Injuries

Sitting down on the bed beside Rene, Bella slipped her hand into his and was a little annoyed that her hand was shaking. 'If the Doctor wants to examine the baby, we'll be immediately exposed as imposters.' Bella spoke softly so her voice didn't carry to her son.

Rene squeezed her hand. 'We could make a run for it or insist that you don't need to be examined.'

'Won't that look suspicious? Who wouldn't naturally be worried about the effects of a crash upon their unborn child? Do you… do you think we could bribe the Doctor to let us escape?' Annoying tears prickled in Bella's eyes as doubt could not be kept out of her voice.

'Help me undress. If we must, we'll tell the Doctor the truth. I need you to massage my shoulder just in case we have to fight our way out of here.' Rene undid the buttons of his coat and waistcoat, turning slightly as Bella released his hand and assisted to strip him down to his waist.

Placing a tender kiss against his bare shoulder, Bella gently ran her hands over both his shoulders. He winced a little as she touched the shoulder blade where not that long ago he had suffered a bullet wound but there was no evidence of any serious break, fracture or injury.

'Muscle damage,' Bella said, moving so that she sat behind him on the bed. 'You probably tensed up trying to protect Henri.' She placed both her hands upon Rene's shoulders and began to massage his muscles.

'Ow!' Bella immediately withdrew her left hand and massaged it absently with her right.

'What is it? Are you hurt?' Rene turned so that he could reach out his hand to lay it over hers.

'I've only just noticed the pain. I must have sprained my wrist hanging onto the strap. I'll be all right.' She patted Rene's hand and urged him back around before beginning to massage his shoulders using just one hand.

Doctor Maurice Lambert

Every so often Bella caressed her lips against his bare flesh. Leaning back into her embrace, Rene uttered a deep sigh. 'Now elfling, don't start something that will be interrupted by the Doctor,' he drawled softly.

Bella placed another kiss against his skin as she chuckled. 'Am I putting wicked little ideas into your head, darling Rene?' Her arms slid sensuously around his neck from behind and her next kiss was against Rene's neck. Bella's hands travelled admiringly down the hard muscles of his chest as her breath whispered softly against his cheek.

Before he could do more than capture Bella's hands beneath his, there was a knock at the door and a hastily dressed middle aged man immediately entered the room. He carried a medical bag similar to Bella's but it didn't stop Rene automatically reaching for one of the pistols on his hips. Casting a quick glance over her shoulder, Bella tapped Rene's arm reassuringly.

'It's all right Rene, it's just the Doctor.' Bella gently slid his hand off his weapon as the tired Doctor set his bag down on the table.

'Good morning, I'm Doctor Maurice Lambert. Nice of you to strip down ready for my examination.' There was a twinkle in the Doctor's eyes as he approached the bed.

'I'm Captain Rene Du Bois, this is my wife Bella and our son Henri,' explained Rene, steeling himself for the discovering of the truth.

'Well then Captain, let's have a look at you. My, my, you have been mistreating that fine specimen of a body.' The Doctor ran his expert eye over Rene's healing bullet wound as well as his pulled muscle before turning his attention to Rene's burns.

Carefully removing the dark glasses and then the gauze pads over Rene's eyes, Doctor Lambert tilted Rene's face up to get a better look in the candle light.

Sliding off the bed, Bella searched through her medical bag and presented the ointment Doctor Stevenson had given her to Doctor Lambert.

'Hum, I'm sure the Doctor who treated you would have preferred you kept the burns covered but I suppose it would make you more conspicuous, my Lord.' Doctor Lambert soaked a swab in the basin of cold water situated on the table beside the window.

Their Mask Slips

His statement was met by stone cold silence as he cleansed Rene's forehead.

'What did you call me?' Rene knew that he hadn't spoken soon enough but to say nothing at all would be suspicious.

A chuckle answered him. 'That bullet wound is less than a week old, your burns only a day or two old. Mind you, the erection is the result of her Ladyship's caresses. Oh, don't look so hunted my dear child, I'm not a snitch.'

Having cleaned the burns, the Doctor reapplied the ointment before replacing the pads and re-bandaging the whole burn site, he said to Bella, 'Take off your trench coat and jacket, my dear and I'll look you over. I'm very impressed with your disguise. The dyed hair is a nice touch but I have to admit the baby bump is a stroke of genius.' As Bella was having trouble using her left hand to remove her clothes, the Doctor assisted her to disrobe.

'I think it's just my wrist.' Bella spoke quietly, being careful of what she said, 'so what happens now Doctor Lambert?' She asked the question that they had all been thinking. Laying her clothes over the end of the bed, the Doctor picked up her hand and began his examination.

'Just a sprain, my Lady, but you could also have some shoulder or neck pain.' Doctor Lambert's fingers travelled up her arm and along her shoulders and neck. The additional wince confirmed the Doctor's assessment.

He wrapped a short length of bandage around Bella's wrist. 'I'm sure you can keep each other amused massaging each other's aches. Now what about this young man?' With a little difficulty he dropped to his knees on the floor as Henri reluctantly sat up right.

'I'm cold.' Henri tolerated being examined, slipping off the mittens as the Doctor took both his hands.

'So you are. You've had bronchitis or pneumonia haven't you little man?'

Henri cast a frightened look up at Bella. 'I... I don't know. I remember coughing and coughing. Always cold. Maman?'

'Yes Doctor, we nearly lost him twice to the cold. He's a little terror for falling into the stream at home.' Dragging in a deep breath Bella wished she wasn't shaking so violently. 'Will you please answer my question Doctor Lambert?' Her voice came out as little more than a whisper. She automatically reached out to assist the Doctor to his feet.

Drawing a small notebook and pencil out of his coat pocket, he briefly wrote down an amount of money. 'My fee for my services,' he explained, handing the piece of paper to Bella. Bemused, she silently took out the silk purse from her medical bag and paid the amount written down. The Doctor didn't even count the money but slipped it into his coat pocket and taking back the piece of paper, signed it before placing it once more into her hand.

Will You Betray Us?

To still her trembling, Bella slid her hand into Rene's. Doctor Lambert smiled fatherly at them. 'Now, my dear, you and your family can be considered my patients and I take Doctor/patient confidentiality very seriously. Anything you admit to me, I will reveal to no one.'

Bella choked back a sob. 'Aren't you interested in the reward? Sacrificing English aristocracy on a pyre of democracy?' There was a considerable tremble in her voice even though she was trying to be flippant.

'I stand by my Hippocratic oath. I won't betray you. Is there anything I can do to help you?' The Doctor took Bella's other hand and squeezed it reassuringly.

'If you don't alert anyone to our true identity, we'll be eternally grateful,' said Rene.

'Of course my Lord.'

Exhaling slowly, Bella managed to slow her shaking. 'How did we betray ourselves? Was it just Rene's wounds or have we done something?'

'According to Claire, the Innkeeper's wife, you went deathly pale when Leon said he'd send me up to your room. I told her that it was probably just the realisation that the accident may have put your baby in jeopardy.'

'I'll try to control that in future Doctor.' Bella felt faint at the thought of how easily she had betrayed them.

Doctor's Orders

There was a knock at the door as Doctor Lambert packed up his medical bag. Leon, the Innkeeper, entered upon Bella's 'Come,' and brought a bucket of fire wood and some chair cushions.

'My apologies Captain Du Bois, all the spare cots are taken up with injured passengers. I hope your little fellow will be comfortable enough on some cushions in front of the fire. I heard you tell my wife that it's important the boy is kept warm so I also brought up some more kindling.' Shutting the door behind him as he entered, Leon took his loads across to set up the cushions for Henri.

'Thank you, that's very kind of you,' said Rene, 'we'll have a cat nap before the next stage is due. If you could wake us half an hour before it's due to depart.'

The Doctor, picking up his bag, made a tut-tutting noise. 'The next stage coach is due about 6.30 o'clock and it'll be fairly crowded. I recommend that you get a decent rest and have a late breakfast before boarding the midday coach. There'll be fewer passengers and you won't have to rush.' Placing the bucket down by the fire, Leon assisted Henri onto the cushions.

'Doctor Lambert's right Captain. There's plenty of time for you to get to Paris for your uncle's funeral.'

Rene stiffened, his hand tightened around Bella's. 'You know who we are? How?' He tried to keep his tone light.

'Someone else boarded the stage from the White Goose and they overheard Guy questioning you about your identity. Someone downstairs mentioned your dark glasses and disorientation once you were out of the coach. Also there was a considerable surprise when Madame Du Bois took the weapon to put the injured horses down rather than the Captain but once Noel had explained your past it all made sense.' Leon hoped that they hadn't offended the young hero.

As Rene relaxed, his charming smile emerged. 'Perhaps we will accept your offer and take a later coach. I should've listened to Bella who was hesitant to take Henri out during the night. I just didn't want Phillippe to think we couldn't make an effort to attend Uncle Luke's funeral. Thank you.'

Respectfully, Leon bowed his head. 'Can I offer you something to help you sleep?'

Puppy dog eyes were raised from the cushions on the floor. 'Can I have hot chocolate please?'

Bella touched her husband's arm in a silent question and he sighed. 'Oh yes, let's all indulge and have hot chocolate. Thank you gentlemen.'

The Frenchmen took this dismissal in good grace and the Doctor patted Rene on his good shoulder as he headed to the door. He couldn't, though, resist a parting jibe. 'Remember after such a jolting, you'll need to be very delicate handling your wife. Some gentle massages to ease your aches, nothing more… amorous.'

I don't need to be able to see to know that my own cheeks are flushed and it is easy to assume that Bella's would be as well. It was a low blow but an accurate one, mused Rene. They heard the Doctor chuckling to himself as he headed down the passage as Leon quietly closed the door behind him.

How Amorous Is Too Amorous?

While they waited for the hot beverages, Bella made them more comfortable. Removing Henri's and then Rene's boots. Hanging up any of their discarded clothes. Placing the cushions from the arm chair onto the floor beside Henri for a pillow before adding a couple more pieces of kindling to the fire.

'Bella…' Rene's voice was soft and inviting.

'Hum?' Bella wasn't giving him her complete attention. Yet. She removed her own boots and placed all their shoes neatly under the table.

'How amorous do you think is too amorous?' There was no hiding the amusement in his voice and Bella turned to stare at him as a gasp escaped her. Glancing back briefly to see if Henri was paying any notice to them before she sat down on the bed beside Rene.

She traced her hand lightly over his bare chest and slowly down the front of his breeches. Rene tried to stifle the moan that rose to his throat as Bella caressed him lovingly.

'Are you certain I shouldn't be massaging your shoulder Rene?' She slid her hand inside his breeches and wrapped her fingers around his erection.

He sighed in pleasure. 'This is more therapeutic!' He was about to give into the wonderful sensation when a tiny thought of propriety hit him. 'Henri isn't watching us is he?' *I don't want Bella to stop but I don't want to damage that innocent boy's fragile psyche.*

'He's only interested in the flames. Shall I... shall I stop then?' Bella caressed her lips against Rene's cheek and then his lips. As she felt his sigh brush gently against her lips, Bella used her free hand to pick up one of his hands and slid it inside the bodice of her dress.

Automatically his fingers moulded and curved around Bella's breast and he teased across her flesh as she firmly stroked his erection. Their kiss deepened, intensified, smoothing Rene's moan of pleasure as she brought him to climax.

Hot Chocolate For All

While Rene struggled to catch his breath, Bella cleaned him up and slid a rug around his bare shoulders. *I'm not insulted that his hand had fallen away from my breasts. This had been about his need and it might mean that Rene will sleep a little better.* When a knock fell on their door, Bella briefly kissed Rene's cheek before going to hold the door open.

Michelle carried a tray over to the table before pouring out three mugs of hot chocolate. That caused Henri to become interested in the adults again. He leapt up to accept a mug out of the hands of the Innkeeper's pretty daughter.

What surprised Bella was that Henri didn't return to his cushions and his contemplation of the flames but carried the mug of hot chocolate to the bed and placed it into his father's hands before coming back to Michelle to collect his own mug.

He raised worried eyes to meet Bella's. 'Have I done something wrong Maman?'

Bella pulled herself together. 'No, not at all.' She accepted her own mug from Michelle as Henri went back to his cushions.

'I thought I should help you a bit more... with Papa,' explained Henri, sipping his chocolate with considerable enjoyment, 'until he gets his sight back anyway.'

Michelle headed back to the door, 'Leave the tray outside your door and I'll pick it up later. Any problems just tug on the bell and we'll come straight up.'

Picking up her own mug of chocolate, Bella took a sip and sighed in pleasure. *It is easy to see why Henri loves it so much.* 'Thank you Michelle.' Bella locked the door after the girl had left before joining Rene on the bed. In companionable silence they enjoyed their night cap.

When he had finished his drink, Henri put his cup back onto the tray on the table before he lay down on the cushions and drew his fur rug over the top of him. Bella slipped off the bed, threw extra wood onto the fire before placing a spare blanket over Henri. Once Rene had finished his drink, Bella placed both their cups on the tray beside Henri's and threw back the bedding.

'Are you going to wear your guns to bed?' Bella unbuckled the belt of his scabbard and laid it and the sword on the table before starting on the gun holsters.

'Place one under my pillow and the other on the bedside table for me.' Rene allowed the pistols to be removed from his hips before he stripped off his breeches and made his way around the bed so that he would be lying closest to the door. Slipping between the sheets, he checked that Bella had put the pistols where he had asked her to place them.

Resisting Temptation

Taking the empty holsters to the table, Bella slipped her dress off over her head. She stood in a full length petticoat and hesitated in undoing and removing her body bump. Bella put out all the candles but the one on the bedside table. 'Should I leave on the baby bump? Do you think the Doctor will keep our secret?'

Rene held out his hand towards her. 'If he hadn't, they would've knocked down our door by now. Come to bed wife.'

Slipping the padding onto the floor beside the bed, Bella took his hand and joined him under the sheets. Before allowing him to draw her into his arms, Bella blew out the remaining candle beside their bed. She felt a twinge of apprehension but also excitement as Rene's lips sought hers and she could feel the warmth radiating from his naked flesh through her thin petticoat.

'Rene...' Bella managed when he allowed her the opportunity to speak at all. 'We shouldn't start something we can't finish.'

Chuckling, Rene traced his forefinger across her shoulder. 'Don't you think I can keep control over my actions or are you worried about Henri hearing us?'

Bella captured his hand and briefly raised it to her lips. 'We don't have Mary to throw cold water over us this time, or to smother our cries of... enjoyment and I don't want to give Henri nightmares. Besides which...' Bella hesitated over how to explain her concerns.

'If you tell me you don't love me anymore, I think I'll cry,' he teased.

Bella couldn't help but smile. 'I love you more and more each and every hour that I am with you!' *I wonder if Rene can hear me blushing with every word.* 'Mary... Mary warned me that...'

He tenderly brushed his thumb against her cheek. 'That men are brutes? That it isn't always enjoyable the first time?'

'No! Yes!' Bella silently cursed herself for making a mess of everything. *Why can't I just say what I have to say? Why does his closeness, his warm almost completely naked body pressed against mine cause me to become am addled brained twit?*

'Which is it Bella, yes or no? Or do you want me to drop this line of question?'

Sighing, Bella tried to pull herself together. 'No to the first, yes to the second but… it's not what I was trying to say. Mary said that breaking the… maidenhead does hurt briefly, it's the… blood loss the concerns me. It's not much but it can mark the sheets and would give away our disguise.'

'I see. It raises another delicate question, when do you expect… your monthly visitor?'

'We have three weeks before that would betray us. So you understand that it isn't that I'm afraid to be intimate with you but that the blood and noise evidence would give us away.' She caressed her hand against the silky mat of hair on Rene's chest.

'So what am I allowed to do then? Can I at least snuggle with my wife?' He tried to keep his tone light but her caressing hand was very distracting.

'Snuggling is definitely allowed Captain,' Bella wrapped her arms around his neck and willingly met his lips in a kiss. When Rene wrapped his arms around her to draw her closer, she willingly permitted it.

As their kiss deepened in intensity and his hand slid into the neck of her petticoat to cup her breast, again Bella permitted it. In fact she enjoyed, thrilled in it, longed for it to continue forever. For that caress to lead into more glorious emotions but they had to restrain their desires. For now.

Rene felt Bella shiver, not from the cold but from desire and realising that she was struggling to retain her control, he slowly removed his hand from inside her petticoat to wrap both hands around her waist. Releasing her lips, Rene pressed a tender kiss against her shoulder.

'Good night my elfling.'

She relaxed into his embrace 'Sweet dreams my love.' Laying her head on his uninjured shoulder, she could feel him shaking in silent laughter.

Three In A Bed... Again

It really is a surreal feeling. So euphoric. To wake up in the arms of my loving husband. To feel our son snuggled in the bed between us. Our unborn child safely growing inside of me. The future has unending potential for a very happy, fulfilled life. Bella's eyes flew open as something tweaked her awake. *Son snuggled between us? That was it.* Bella slid back the bedding to see if the imagery was in fact a reality. Yawning as he rubbed his eyes, Henri reached out to thread his hand into the material of Bella's petticoat.

'Sorry Maman.'

Bella tenderly caressed her hand against Henri's hair. 'That's all right baby. Another nightmare?'

He shook his head. 'No, I got cold. The fire died down. You and Papa are so warm.'

A chuckle came from the other side of the bed. 'Body heat is probably more beneficial than a dying fire,' Rene stated, his own hand searching to cover Bella's and she sighed deeply.

'I should have realised! I should have put more kindling on the fire before we went to sleep.'

Henri yawned again. 'It's not your fault Maman. This is nicer though. More... more like it should be.'

A lump in her throat made it impossible for her to speak as she blinked away the sudden tears that appeared. Smiling, in understanding, Rene's hand left hers to locate Bella's currently flat stomach.

'And baby makes four?' He teased, knowing full well that just the touch of his hand would bring a shy blush to her cheeks.

'I'd… I'd better put my bump back on.' Throwing back the bedding, Bella slipped out from under Rene's hand. As she bent down to pick up her padding, she kissed Henri and then Rene on the cheek.

'I need to pee,' Henri stated as he sat up and stretched.

'Find me some clothes, Henri and I'll come with you.' Rene tested his shoulder for stiffness and damage as he threw his legs over the edge of the bed. While Bella slipped the baby bag under her petticoat, Henri jumped to his feet and brought his father his clothes. Making certain that the baby bump was securely attached, Bella smoothed down her petticoat and unwrapped the bandage around her left wrist before having a quick wash in the hand basin.

Dressing Bella

While the boys were out of the room, Bella took care of her own toiletry needs before slipping her dress on over the top of her head. Her damaged wrist made it difficult to tie the sash behind her and the baby bump made it impossible to put on her half boots.

Giving up even trying, Bella re-wrapped her wrist before brushing out her hair and attempted to fashion a simple style but her injured wrist refused to co-operate. Throwing the brush down onto the dressing table, a colourful expletive escaped from Bella as she gripped the painful limb with her other hand.

A giggle behind her, caused her to spin around in surprise. She hadn't heard the knock at the door or Michelle quietly enter.

'Sorry, I didn't think there was anyone around to hear me,' apologised Bella. 'I hadn't counted on having to deal with any more injuries. Henri will start to think that body parts begin to fail you once you reach one and twenty!' For the briefest moment she wondered, *did I swear in English or in French?*

Michelle smiled as she turned Bella around to do up the sash behind her back. 'You over-estimate what men really think about; the only thought that boy of yours will be able to wrap his head around will be the state of his stomach!' Sitting Bella down on the edge of the bed, Michelle assisted with her boots before putting up Bella's hair.

To support the Bar-maid's theory Henri led Rene back into the room and declared, 'Maman, I'm hungry.'

A speaking glance was exchanged between the two women before they broke into giggles.

'We can't have that Master Henri,' stated Michelle, 'How about you put on your shoes while I help the Captain and we'll see what we can do about some luncheon.'

Henri immediately picked up his boots and sat down on his cushions to put on his footwear. Bella unwrapped the bandages around Rene's eyes to bathe and anoint his burns while Michelle assisted him with his own boots. With the dark glasses once more holding fresh eye pads in place, Bella packed away her medical kit as Michelle ensured their clothes had been repacked into the carpet bag.

Rene attached his pistol holsters once more to his hips before attaching Bella's sword over the top. Their overcoats were thrown over the edge of the bed for Bella to pick up as they left the room.

Leading the family downstairs, Michelle refused to let Rene carry the bags so that he could have one hand on the staircase balustrade as the other held his son's hand. Bella had their overcoats flung over her arm as well as Henri's fur rug.

'All the other crash passengers have already left,' explained Michelle as she settled them at a table closest to the fireplace. 'Some by the 6.30 stage, the rest by the noon coach. Doctor Lambert said to not disturb you. That it would be better for the baby if you weren't immediately stuffed into an overcrowded, noisy and bumpy carriage too soon.' The Innkeeper's daughter placed their bags on the chair beside Henri as Rene and Bella sat down opposite the boy.

'Would you prefer a breakfast meal, otherwise I whole-heartily recommend Mama's luncheon. Unless you're still suffering from morning sickness - then I can arrange tea and toast.

Elevating his head slightly, Rene breathed in deeply. 'Something smells divine. Whatever it is, that is what I want.'

Michelle smiled. 'Mama has just taken quiche and chicken pies out of the oven.'

'That does sound wonderful,' agreed Bella. 'A little bit of everything and I'll see what I can get Henri to eat.'

Ruffling the boy's hair Michelle said, 'As an inducement there is crème caramel for dessert.' Henri's eyes lit up; he did like his sweets.

Not Defenceless

When Michelle headed out to the kitchen to assist her mother in dishing up their luncheon, Bella stood up and opening the medical bag, drew out her purse. For a moment she laid her hand over Rene's.

'I'm just going to settle our bill with the Innkeeper,' she explained but didn't move until he nodded. As Bella made her way to where Leon stood behind the bar. Rene's hand lowered to rest upon the hilt of his sword.

Although the other passengers had departed, the Inn was not empty. With the loss of his sight, Rene had been aware of an increasing heightening of his other senses. His hearing in particular. *There is the clatter of cutlery, the clinking of glassware, the soft hum of conversation and the occasional flick of the pages of Henri's picture book. There is something else, something more subtle, underlying all other noises.*

It caused Rene to tighten his grasp around the hilt of his sword. *The sound is of heavy breathing, not completely a wheeze but more of an occasional whistle and struggle to get any air into clogged lungs. It isn't just a general sound but one that appears to be slowly approaching our table.*

When the hairs on the back of his neck began to stand on end, Rene rose swiftly to his feet and drew out his sword. He brought it down hard in the direction of the chair beside Henri. A satisfying yelp told Rene that he had struck an outstretched hand.

'I don't care if your intention was to steal our meagre belongings or my son, but I promise you try for either again and I will draw your blood!' Rene's softly and coldly spoken words sent a chill throughout the bar room.

Jerome, The Thief

Grabbing his shotgun, Leon came out from behind the bar and strode forward to confront the thief.

'I warned you about your light-fingering ways in my establishment Jerome!' Leon pushed the thief away from the tip of Rene's sword. 'You stupid fool, haven't you heard a word about who this man is?'

The weasel little man sneered at the Innkeeper. 'A war hero? Should I get down on my knees and lick his boots?'

Looking up from his book, Henri raised angry eyes. 'I will not be kidnapped again!' He clenched his hand into a tight little fist and hit the thief at the highest point he could reach. Small his hand may have been but it brought tears to Jerome's eyes and a curse to his lips as the boy punched him in the groin.

As colourful words streamed from the thief's mouth, a diabolical smile appeared on Rene's face and he felt a surge of pride in his son. A strange noise had been heard when Henri's blow had made contact and laughing he turned to Rene.

"Papa, his pee pee jingles like the cat's bell!'

As realisation of what the boy meant struck the other patrons, Jerome tried to make a run for the door. Leon reached out to grab the thief by the scruff of his neck.

'Check your pockets gentlemen, our Jerome has been dipping his fingers again.' Leon restrained the thief's attempt to break away. 'Turn out your pockets Jerome or I'll let the Captain skewer you with his sword!'

'All right! All right!' Reluctantly Jerome emptied his ill-gotten haul out onto the table. Bella returned to kneel down beside an upset Henri as he looked at her with troubled eyes.

'Mama, did that man want to steal my book? Nanny gave me this book! He can't have it! It's special!' The little boy was close to tears and Bella wrapped her arms around him to cradle him against her breast. *I just pray that no one else had realised the significance of Henri's words that "he didn't want to be kidnapped again"* worried Bella.

'It's all right baby, he's too stupid to know that your book is special. Papa won't let him take you or your book Henri.'

Jerome's eyes lit up. 'Is the book worth something then?'

Sighing, Leon clipped Jerome around the ears. 'You really are thick aren't you? They're not talking about monetary value. For a five year old it is sentimental value!' Leon collected up the stolen goods and put them into his own pocket before marching the thief towards the door. 'Don't show your face in here again Jerome,' the Innkeeper said, throwing the thief physically out of his pub.

With that accomplished he turned his attention to returning the stolen property to its rightful owners. Bella sat down beside Rene as he re-sheathed his sword and resumes his seat. Michelle and her mother, Claire, brought out their luncheon and as no one else appeared to have heard or understood Henri's slip-up, Bella breathed a sigh of relief.

A Peaceful Luncheon

A very healthy distance was observed around the Du Bois family as they enjoyed their luncheon. After the display that the Captain was not an easy target no one was prepared to chance the possibility of suffering the same fate as Jerome.

When Rene asked for Leon's wife, Claire, to appear, she was worried there had been something wrong with their meal. She almost passed out as he smiled and spoke in a highly complementary way about her cooking.

'Oh thank you Captain Du Bois! I'm so glad you enjoyed it.' There was no hiding the relief in her voice and Bella laughed.

'Don't be so pleased, Claire, or Rene may decide to stay here for a couple of days on our way home so you can improve my cooking skills.'

Smiling Claire said, 'I'd be more than happy to teach you, Madame Du Bois but I think you've enough on your hands at the moment.'

A maidenly blush tinged Bella's cheeks as she laid her hands tenderly over her baby bump. 'Perhaps better now than in a month's time when I'll feel like a beached whale and Rene will have to roll me out of bed again.'

Laughing, Rene reached out to place his hand over Bella's. 'I look forward to it. This time, though, I'll have Henri to help me.'

A Boy Or A Girl?

With six children of her own, Claire had a very strong maternal instinct and knowing that Rene wasn't angry, she was interested in the young family. In fact she was encouraging her daughter, Michelle to marry her sweetheart Eric, Doctor Lambert's son.

'Do you have any preferences with what you're expecting?' asked Claire.

'Girl,' said Rene.

'Boy,' said Bella.

Not to be left out Henri added, 'I want one of each!' Margarette will be as beautiful as Mama and Alexander will be brave and handsome like Papa.'

Claire smiled at the boy's enthusiasm. 'I hope you get to use both names.'

A groan came from Rene. 'Don't encourage him, twins have been known to run in both our families.'

'I just want a healthy, normal child,' Bella added, 'but any more road accidents and Doctor Lambert said I could spend the next month in bed or I could lose the baby.'

Sighing, Claire had to agree with the Doctor. 'I'd stay away from the stage coach then. They drive and set a wicked pace to get to Paris on schedule. I'll talk to Leon about where you can hire a horse and carriage to complete your journey without breaking your neck or your budget.' Reassuringly she patted Bella's shoulder before approaching her husband behind the bar to help out the young family.

Andre Guillaume

A middle aged gentleman, impeccably dressed, cautiously approached the masqueraders. Even though he didn't have Jerome's breathing problems, he was aware that Rene was following his movements.

'My apologies for eavesdropping Captain Du Bois but I was wondering if I could be of service to you? May I approach? I mean your family no harm.'

'Of course Monsieur...' Rene gestured to the chair beside Henri, rising to lift the bags down to place them onto the floor at his feet.

'Andre Guillaume.'

Bella's eyes lit up as she looked across at him in interest. 'The novelist?' There was a considerable note of awe in her voice as it dropped in volume. Andre bowed as he sat down beside Henri.

'Yes Madame.'

One of Bella's eyebrows rose as a cheeky smile twisted her lips. 'The renowned reclusive novelist?' She was answered by a smile as Andre shrugged expressively with his whole body.

'Most of the time that is true but there are times I need physical contact with real people and not just the characters who inhabit my head.'

Rene's whole body stiffened and his lips thinned. 'If you're suggesting that my wife perform certain acts as a way of paying for our passage...'

Andre reached across the table to lay his hand over Rene's. 'I have no designs upon your wife's virtue. All I want are some stimulating discussions.'

'Discussions?' There was no hiding Rene's scepticism as he drew his hand away.

'There are rare times when I like to talk, others where I just want to listen. It aids me creatively.'

Bella nodded. 'Is that how you get your plots?'

'No Madame Du Bois but it does help me to develop well rounded characters. Mannerisms, quirks, flaws. It's about making the character more realistic to the reader.' Andre drew out his fob watch to check the time. 'If you're interested in accompanying me, I'll be leaving in about ten minutes.'

'Thank you Monsieur Guillaume,' said Bella, 'we'll just freshen up and meet you outside.'

Andre rose to his feet and bowed before Bella led Henri towards the stairs. Michelle called out to them before they mounted the first step.

'We have amenities downstairs to save you trying to climb all those stairs. 'Michelle led Bella and Henri towards the back of the Inn.

Andre placed his hand upon Rene's shoulder. 'If you want to pick up your bags, I'll guide you through the tables and out the front door.'

Rene Voices His Doubts

Picking up their luggage Rene waited until they were outside before he addressed Andre, 'You're being very nice to perfect strangers Sir.'

A chuckle answered him. 'Suspicious is not a good colour on you Captain Du Bois. Not everyone has an ulterior motive to everything they do.'

Rene felt rather than heard Bella and Henri join them out in the afternoon sunshine. 'You can understand, though, my need to protect them?' Some of the tension left his body as Bella laid her hand on his arm.

Andre smiled. 'Oh yes that I most definitely understand.'

'Bella, did you pick up Henri's book?' Rene laid his hand over the top of hers. 'I wouldn't want to get into Paris to find out we have to come back for something our son has left behind.' The amused tone of his voice suggested that this had happened on more than one occasion.

'It's here Papa, can I...' Henri chuckled as he tapped his book against his father's arm.

Rene cut him off. 'Oh no, I'm not going to have you or your mother read all the way to Paris!'

An Interesting Little Story

As he assisted the family into his carriage and handed their bags to his driver to secure them on the back, Andre chuckled. 'Actually I want to discuss a plot idea that I've become interested in and I think you can help me iron out some of the details.'

Settling down on the front seat with Henri, Bella was surprised that a famous Author would want their assistance.

'What on earth could we possibly do for an intellectual such as yourself?'

Taking his place beside Andre, Rene sighed. 'No Bella, Monsieur Guillaume is going to tell us a story. We just have to listen.' Rene checked his weapons. *If this is going as I think it will then I don't know how we are going to escape. The carriage has already started to move so jumping isn't going to be a likely option.*

Leaning back in his seat, Andre steepled his fingers. 'A little real life story has come to my attention and I'm thinking of either tackling it as a piece of fiction or as a straight forward non-fiction story.'

Realising what he meant, Bella sighed. 'Oh I see, so what are you planning to do with this information?'

His eyebrows rose in surprise. 'Surely I just explained my plans.'

'So you're not interested in the reward?' asked Rene. He could feel his heart pounding against his chest.

'No I'd rather have the story.'

Bella was puzzled. 'Why? I'd thought that most people would jump at the chance to make easy money?'

Andre smiled. 'I'm not most people. Why don't I start at the beginning and you can interrupt if I get anything wrong or miss something?'

'Wouldn't it just be easier if we just told you the story?' asked Rene, trying to keep his voice friendly and unconcerned.

Andre chuckled and patted his hand. 'Humour me Lord Delacourt, I'd like to see how much of the story I have correct.'

Wrapping the fur blanket around her son, Bella drew him closer to her. 'Don't you think that putting the story down on paper will place those who assisted your hero and heroine in danger? Even if you changed their names, someone could still recognise them.'

'Yes, that could be a problem. Maybe we can publish only in England until the French people are ready to accept the masquerade you have pulled off to perfection.'

'And yet you saw through the disguise,' drawled Rene, his hand unconsciously lingering on the hilt of his sword.

Andre smiled. 'I've very sharp ears. Even if Leon had heard or understand your brother's exclamation, I'm not certain that he would've betrayed you. Neither of you flinched when Lord Aidan declared, "I will not be kidnaped again." and yet if Jerome had even half a brain and realised what that meant it would've meant a messy end to your masquerade.'

Henri had been having trouble following the conversation but as he realised that he betrayed them, his eyes filled with tears as he raised them to Bella's face. 'Oh Mama, I'm sorry! He's not going to make you do nasty things now like that pig man? Everything is my fault!' As he burst into tears Bella cradled him comfortingly in her arms.

'No it's not your fault, Little Bear.' Bella accepted the handkerchief that Rene held out to her as Andre hurried to reassure of his intentions.

'I have no interest in disgracing your sister, Lord Aidan, I am in admiration at the depth of your disguise and how well you have travelled in such a hostile environment.'

With his hand still on the hilt of his sword, Rene frowned. 'Yet it hasn't been as hostile as I feared it could be. Our disguise is fairly basic and has been penetrated more than once but neither of those men have immediately handed us over to the enemy for the reward or the thrill of killing three English aristocrats. Why is that? Dumb luck? Have we been blessed in being discovered by decent men? Or once you have your story, Mr Guillaume will you drive us back to Nigel Sutherland in Hon Fleur and collect the bounty on our heads?'

Reassuringly Andre patted Rene's hand. 'I'll deliver you to Paris as agreed. Why you haven't been betrayed may be because

71

they are honourable men, they have no need for the reward or their hatred for anything English is not as strong as their fellow countrymen.'

Laughing lightly, he moved his hand across to lay upon the one Rene had still poised over his sword. 'Don't cut me down until I've tried to explain myself. In the masquerade you're a beautiful young family. Touched by the harshness of war, the defender of your loved ones. The story you've chosen is a good one. There is respect for our soldiers trying to return to a normal life after such a disastrous campaign. When the veil slips, there might be anger at the misrepresentation, but there is also admiration at the sheer bravery that you're all showing to pull off a ruse in a desperate attempt to just get home. It's so hard to put it precisely in words why I can't find it in me to betray you. I bet it was the same for Doctor Lambert.'

Drying his eyes and blowing his nose, Henri looked curiously across at Andre. 'Does that mean we can go home Maman?' Until Bella told him otherwise, Henri would not drop the facade.

'I believe it does Henri.'

Sighing, Andre removed his hand from Rene's. 'Now then let's start at the beginning…' Slowly the Author pieced together the truth and discarded false rumours as they swiftly covered miles of French countryside on their journey to Paris.

Fine Tuning The Details

To be brutally honest with myself, mused Rene, *I have to admit that Andre is incredibly well informed. In actual fact, far too well informed. Although Bella has to correct his story a little bit where details are probably known only by us, there is some knowledge that surprises me. The Author's knowledge of what happened at the French seaside village of Hon Fleur and at the Du Bois country house is obviously a surprise to Bella too.* Andre smiled and let them in on a little secret.

"Florence, my wife... my late wife was a Du Bois. So it was natural for me to drop in on Louise on my way up to Paris. Louise didn't want to tell me but François thought I might be of use to you if you ran into trouble along the way.'

Bella laughed in delight. 'Did Louise describe us for you then?'

Shaking his head, Andre smiled. 'No François said it would test my observational skills. Now if I was in the middle of a novel I probably wouldn't know what day of the week it is.'

Abruptly, Rene reached out and firmly grasped Andre's arm. 'The carriage is turning around!'

Bella glanced out the window. 'It's all right Rene, there are some road works which we have to go around.'

Rene released the Author's arm with an apology. 'Sorry but recent events have made me paranoid.'

'Quite understandable my dear boy.' Andre slipped a calling card into Rene's breast pocket. 'Promise me that you'll contact me after you're home and safely wed.' Chuckling, he leant forward and laid his hand over Bella's fake baby bump. 'By the time we go to press you'll probably have made this a real pregnancy.'

Raising her hand to press against her flushed cheeks, Bella shook her head. 'Do you really think anyone would want to read our story?'

Andre stroked his chin as he released her. 'Yes I do. It has romance, adventure, danger, cross-dressing and family betrayal. I just hope that it has a happy ending.'

'So do we,' sighed Rene, 'but unlike writing a novel, we can't guarantee that can we?'

Have You Been Naughty Children?

Andre raised a mocking eyebrow. 'I can see you keep this charming fellow around for his overwhelming optimism!'

A wicked smile twisted Rene's lips as he drawled. 'Believe me that is not why Bella keeps me around!'

Bella gasped. 'Rene!'

A chuckle came from Andre. 'There is one thing I've always wondered… what considerations do you have to take when making love to your very pregnant wife?'

Bella stuttered in embarrassment. 'I… I took off the padding before getting into bed. In any case we… we didn't… Rene has been a complete gentleman throughout it all.'

Rene continued to grin wickedly. 'It's all about satisfying any little wish my dear wife may have.'

Gasping at his audacity, Bella retorted, 'Oh really? That's not how I remember it Rene! How amorous is too amorous? My hand inside your trousers?' She had placed her hands over her son's ears.

Rene had the grace to blush as he defended himself. 'I seem to remember offering to satisfy your needs but you had doubts that I could control myself if we started anything.'

Uttering a crow of laughter Andre clapped his hands. 'You two have been playing with fire. There's more to your alone time than you've let on. Have you naughty children been experimenting how close you can get to the flames before you get burnt?'

The use of the word "experimenting" swept Rene and Bella back to their time in his bedroom at Stirling Manor. They became rather flushed at the memory of their pleasuring each other. Their naked bodies covered in beads of perspiration as they discovered release. More than once. A twinkle entered the Frenchman's eyes as he realised some of this from the guilty expressions on their faces.

'Oh naughty, naughty! Perhaps I should stick around and play chaperone?' Andre laid his hand over Rene's. 'Having announced yourselves as a Du Bois, you at least will have to attend the funeral Rene, I'll pick you up. We can rely on Phillippe to keep your secret.'

Bella groaned at the stupidity of using the Du Bois name. 'I had hoped that we could be on a ship back to England before night fall! When is the funeral planned?'

'Tomorrow morning,' answered Andre, removing his hand from Rene's as the carriage drew up outside the exclusive hotel, the Grand Duchess.

The Grand Duchess Hotel

Descending from the carriage, Andre assisted the family down before he embraced each of them. Rene put on a brave face as the Frenchman hugged and kissed his cheeks. *If I'm going to pretend to be French, I am going to have to tolerate their fondness for stray kisses.*

'Thank you Andre, I'll send Phillippe a note as soon as we have booked into a room.' Bella was a little more enthusiastic in returning his embrace than Rene had been.

'Behave yourselves, adorable children,' Andre smirked, 'and try to stay out of trouble.'

Accepting their bags from the driver, Rene could not help but laugh. 'Is that sound advice from an expert?'

Wrapping his fur rug around Henri, Bella looked up startled as she exclaimed, 'Rene! Don't be rude! Andre has been nothing but kindness to us.' She linked her hand through the crook of Rene's arm to lead him into the hotel.

'We humbly thank you for your condescension Master Wordsmith!' With considerable elegance but still dripping in irony Rene bowed to Andre.

As Henri bounced up the front steps of the hotel, Andre chuckled as he patted Rene's cheek. 'Keep that up my boy and you could be mistaken for aristocracy!' Andre laughed as Rene flushed up in embarrassment over his lapse.

'We wouldn't want that now would we?'

Bella tugged on Rene's arm to lead him up the steps before Andre and Rene did something they might later regret.

The sight of the severe black livery of the hotel staff slightly daunted Henri's enthusiasm but he managed to say, 'Bonjour, I'm Henri. Do you have any room for us?'

The hotel Clerk, Victor, was a father with a tribe of children and smiled kindly down at the boy. 'Bonjour Henri, let me have a look in our book.' Victor raised his eyes to smile at Bella and Rene as they approached the reception desk. 'Perhaps a room on the first floor to save you having to climb too many stairs.'

Rene stiffened in indignation. 'I'm blind, Sir, not decrepit!'

'I'm sorry sir,' the Clerk stuttered, casting a beseeching glance at Bella. 'I meant no disrespect to yourself.' Sighing, she laid a calming hand upon Rene's arm.

'Rene, I think the kind man was offering for my sake rather than yours. Being eight months pregnant remember? With a five year old toddler, remember?'

'Oh!' Rene's anger immediately deflated. 'I'm so sorry, I thought… I'm a little prickly about my disability.'

Victor's professional smile returned. 'Not at all Sir. Madame if you would like to sign in?'

'Of course.' Bella released Rene's arm to enter their name into the registry book.

Glancing down at the entry as he flicked his fingers to the Porter, Victor said, 'Hugo, take up the bags for Captain Du Bois and his family to room 124 please.' Victor handed a key across to Hugo. 'You'll be here for Senator Du Bois' funeral tomorrow then. Will you be staying long with us?'

'At least a couple of days.' Bella removed her purse from her jacket pocket and counted out enough francs to cover at least two days room and meals. She smiled at Victor. 'Save you having to ask for a deposit,' she explained as she handed the money across to the Clerk.

He smiled in relief. 'Thank you Madame Du Bois.'

76

Taking Henri's hand, Bella followed Rene and the Porter up the stairs. She refused to offer assistance but was relieved that her husband used the hand rail to steady himself.

Contacting Phillippe

'Mama, I'm cold,' Henri stated as they entered their room. Bella pressed her other hand against her son's forehead.

'I'll have a fire started immediately.' Bella rushed into the room, pressing a coin into Hugo's hand before she bent down with a little difficulty due to her baby bump in front of the fireplace.

'Allow me Madame.' Hugo pocketed his tip and took her place in front of the fire so that she could pull a rug off the bed to wrap it around Henri. Guiding Rene to an arm chair, Bella placed a tender kiss against his cheek before sitting down at a neat but elegant little desk under the window.

While Henri curled up on the floor as Hugo made up the fire, Bella wrote smoothly and elegantly across a sheet of the hotel stationery. She didn't look up until she had patted the letter dry and folded it. Picking up the stick of wax to seal the letter, Bella was surprised to find Hugo standing beside her.

'Allow me Madame Du Bois.' He melted a small amount of wax to seal the paper and turned it over so that she could address it to Phillippe Du Bois. 'Is there anything else I can do for you Madame?'

Shaking her head, Bella rose to her feet and followed Hugo to the door. 'Not at the moment, thank you Hugo.' She handed him another coin. 'That is for the boy you send with the letter.' She closed the door behind the Porter and locked it with a sigh.

Analysing Our Options

Pausing to check on Henri and adding a little more kindling to the fire before she planted herself on Rene's lap, Bella slipped her hand inside his jacket and drew him into a passionate kiss. He willingly wrapped his arms around Bella's waist but had to rearrange her as she was sitting on one of the pistols.

'Well wife, what do you have planned for us now?' Rene traced his hand up her arm to reach her cheek and drew her mouth back to his.

'We have a couple of options.' She had obviously been thinking this through. 'One - I leave you and Henri here and I go to the Embassy alone. Two - I could write a note to the Ambassador and hope he'll visit us. Three - We wait for Phillippe to be available so that he could escort me. Four - We all go to the Embassy.'

Lovingly caressing his hand across Bella's baby bump, Rene mused, 'You'd rather we left Henri here even though the sun is shining outside.'

'But the wind is quite chilly and he is already complaining that he's cold.'

'I'll be all right Mama.' Came Henri's voice from the fireplace. 'We need to let Grandpapa know that we're safe.'

Bella sighed. 'How are you feeling Little Bear?'

'Tired.'

'Are you hungry?'

'Not really?'

She stiffened. 'Oh dear!'

Assisting her to sit upright, Rene was concerned. 'That's not a positive sign is it? I thought he was always hungry.'

Bella removed herself from Rene's lap. 'Not when he's sick.'

'I'm all right!' protested Henri. 'I'm just tired.'

Raising her dress and petticoat Bella undid her baby bump and removed it, Rene's head tilted slightly as he listened to her actions. 'What are you doing?'

Opening the baby bump, she removed the purse with her jewellery as well as Rene's card case and his signet ring. 'We're going to need a few of the items we hid to prove our identity.'

'Oh,' he sounded extremely disappointed. 'I was hoping that you were stripping off for your poor husband's benefit.'

Caressing her hand through Rene's hair, Bella chuckled. 'If all is well then perhaps this evening, my love.' She bent down to permit him one passionate kiss before reattaching the padding around her waist.

'We'll all go together to the Consulate as I'm not letting either of you out of my protection.' Rene rose out of his chair and checked his weapons. Bella slipped their valuable possessions into her jacket pocket before bending down to untangle Henri from one blanket and hoisted him and his fur rug up into her arms.

Involuntarily she winced and swapped Henri to her other hip to take the boy's weight off her injured wrist. Opening the door, Rene held his arms out towards her.

'Give me Henri; you shouldn't be carrying him in your condition.' Bella didn't disagree and handed him over before locking the door behind them.

'I can walk Papa.'

Rene paused but finally he eased Henri to stand on his own feet. 'All right but you're not to let go of my hand.'

'Yes Papa.'

Out And About In Paris

On their way out of the hotel, Bella paused beside the reception desk to speak to Victor. 'If Cousin Phillippe arrives before we're back, tell him we should only be about half an hour.'

Victor smiled. 'Of course Madame Du Bois. Be careful out there, we've had reports of pick pockets in the area. Even in broad daylight.'

'Thank you, but they'll have to be seriously desperate to take on my husband!'

Victor blinked twice before glancing bemused across to Hugo, the Porter, who expressively shrugged his shoulders.

A mischievous smile appeared on Bella's face. 'Don't let his blindness fool you into thinking Rene isn't a dangerous man to cross. Good afternoon gentlemen.'

Rene waited until they were outside the hotel and strolling down the avenue before he spoke, 'Was that wise Bella?' He tucked her hand through the crook of one of his.

'Most definitely my love. We're not safe just yet and a little healthy fear may come in handy if we're cornered later.'

Instinctively Rene's hold on Henri's hand tightened and his pace quickened. Even though the late afternoon sun was beaming brightly down upon them, Rene felt an icy cold chill race down his spine. They were far from safe and he just did not have Bella's confidence that he could protect them.

Ambassador Sir Malcolm White

Stepping through the front door of the British Consulate, Rene contained any relief as they were met by a self-important young man.

'The Ambassador sees no one without an appointment!' declared Arthur Hopkins.

Sliding her hand from Rene's arm, Bella withdrew her husband's card case out of her jacket pocket and handed the supercilious public servant a card.

'I think Sir Malcolm will grant us a minute of his valuable time.' Bella's eyebrow rose in a challenge as the young man read the name on the card and jumped in surprise.

'Wait here please!' He showed them to a couple of chairs in the foyer before disappearing up a flight of stairs to the offices above them. The explosion of words that followed could be heard in every corner of the Embassy.

'You fool Hopkins! Why didn't you bring them straight up?'

The self-important young man grovelled and followed the Ambassador as he rushed down the stairs. Sir Malcolm White came to a halt at the sight of three virtual strangers. Smiling Bella rose from her seat and held out her hands. 'Have I fooled even you Uncle Inky? Do we look completely unrecognisable?'

Laughing, Sir Malcolm closed the distance but instead of taking Bella's hands, he wrapped her in a big bear hug. 'My dear girl! I would never have guessed. Come, there's a fire in my office and Hopkins can make us some tea.'

'I've really missed a good cup of tea.' Bella sighed as she was released and drew Rene and Henri to their feet. 'Sir Malcolm, I don't know if you're acquainted with Lord Delacourt?'

Rene bowed gracefully but kept a tight grasp on Henri's hand. 'Uncle Inky?'

Bella laughed as Sir Malcolm led them upstairs to his office.

'Sir Malcolm was at school with my Papa. I think the origin of the nick name had something to do with Sir Malcolm being rather a successful writer of love notes to the Dean's daughter.'

Embarrassed, the Ambassador closed the door behind them and sat Henri down on a chair beside the fireplace. 'Unsubstantiated rumour my dear child! Please have a seat my Lord.' Placing her hand under Rene's elbow, Bella led him to a chair opposite Henri's.

As he poured a glass of brandy, the Ambassador looked them over a little closer. 'So the rumours that your abductor blinded you were true. I'd thought it was impossible for you to get this far. You must tell me everything,' Sir Malcolm placed the brandy glass into Rene's hand before drawing up two more chairs so that Bella could narrate the whole adventure so far.

Once More Telling Their Story

Arthur Hopkins was dismissed the moment he brought in the tea tray and the Ambassador served the tea himself, not wanting to interrupt Bella's tale. With his tea cup in both hands and his rug tucked firmly around him, Henri had slipped off the chair and sat on the floor to soak in the warmth of the flames. Sir Malcolm White shook his head in disbelief a couple of times but didn't speak until Tony had finished.

'Unbelievable! I would've laid good odds on nearly all Frenchmen being only too glad to get revenge upon English aristocracy. I'll have word of your safe arrival sent to your father but getting you home…'

Rene spoke for the first time since Bella had started to narrate their story. 'Having taken on the name of Du Bois, we'll have to stay in Paris until after the funeral. Then it'll be assumed that we simply headed south for home again.'

In considering their options, Sir Malcolm stroked his chin. 'Do you think you're safe enough with Phillippe's family? I know that he'd never betray you but the reward for your capture is very tempting.'

Amused Bella laid her hand over the Ambassador's. 'Thinking of turning us in, Uncle? Have your gambling debts got the better of you?'

Uttering an embarrassed laugh, Sir Malcolm said, 'No my dear, I'd never do that to you.'

Henry Becomes Ill

'Mama?' The empty tea cup slipped out of Henri's fingers and landed on the carpet in front of him.

'Yes baby?' Bella bent down to pick up the cup and placed it carefully on the tray.

'I'm cold.'

A little surprised, Sir Malcolm chuckled, 'That close to the fire you should be well done by now Lord Aidan.'

Taking Henri's comment a little more seriously Rene leant down to place his hand upon the boy's forehead. 'Bella, he's sweating and shivering.'

She knelt down and forced Henri's head up to look more closely at him. Glancing up again, she directed her next statement to the Ambassador. 'Your waste paper basket Uncle Inky, immediately.' Sir Malcolm handed Bella the bin just in time as Henri lurched forward and vomited.

Rene sighed. 'That doesn't sound good.'

Starting to cry, Henri was a little incoherent. 'I don't wanna be sick! I wanna go home!'

'I know baby, it won't be safe to leave Paris for a couple of days.' The five year old's tears made it hard for him to breath. From experience Bella knew that it wouldn't be long before Henri started coughing. 'I need to get Henri back to the hotel… now.'

Sir Malcolm pulled a bell to summon his Secretary. 'Have my carriage brought round immediately and send a message to Doctor Girard to meet the Du Bois at the Grand Duchess Hotel. What else do you need my girl?'

Scooping Henri up into her arms, Bella shook her head. 'Thank you, no, I need to get him cleaned up and into a warm bed.' She tapped Rene's arm to urge him to his feet. Sir Malcolm followed them down the stairs.

'If there is anything I can do for you Tony, day or night, send me a message.'

Touched by his offer, Bella paused to kiss the Ambassador on the cheek before following Rene into the carriage that had just pulled up outside the Embassy. It was a short but rather unpleasant drive.

Although Henri had stopped throwing up, the five year old had lost control of his bowels and his crying had been replaced by bouts of violent coughing. *The deep lung-destroying coughing. The imitation of a large hound barking coughing. It is painful to listen to and it tears at my heart as I know there is virtually little that I can do to ease the little man's suffering.* Rene was frustrated by his inability to help his family.

Bella kept Henri tightly bundled up against her, speaking soothingly as she rocked her son in her arms. *We're going to face a couple of very rough days ahead and I have none of my usual medical supplies to make Henri's illness easier to manage,* worried Bella.

How Can We Help You?

Drawing up outside their hotel, Rene, still holding Henri, jumped down and held out his hand to assist Bella out of the carriage. They hurried up the steps and paused for a brief moment as Victor, the Clerk, looked up startled by their abrupt entrance.

'Henri is very sick,' stated Bella, 'I'll need to see whoever is in charge of housekeeping and your kitchens as soon as possible please.'

Nodding to Hugo, Victor sent the Porter running into the back of house as he asked, 'Can I send for a Doctor, Madame Du Bois?'

Rene shook his head. 'One has already been sent for. What we will need is a hot bath and the bed warmed up.'

'Of course Captain. Your room has a newly installed ensuite and I'll see to it that you have additional fuel for the fire.'

'Thank you. Please send the Doctor and the other staff Bella wishes to speak to straight up to our room.'

'Of course Captain. I hope your little chap isn't too ill.' Victor added as Rene followed his family up the main staircase to their room.

'So do I,' sighed Rene. *I know next to nothing about tending to sick children and I suspect that with Henri's weak constitution this is not going to be a walk in the park.*

Pausing only long enough to guide Rene into an arm chair, Bella carried Henri through to the ensuite. She started to run the bath before stripping her son of all his clothes. She had managed to calm him down so that his coughing was only spasmodic but Henri was left with a wheeze as she wiped his bottom clean before popping him into the bath tub. Henri's fur rug and Bella's overcoat would need cleaning along with all Henri's clothes.

Remembering that she still carried Nigel's pistols in the pockets of her overcoat, Bella removed them and slipped them into the drawer on one side of the double bed before returning to her son. She had just stripped off her overcoat which had protected the rest of her clothing, when Madame Juliette Martin entered the bathroom.

'Now Madame Du Bois, what can we do to help you? One of my Chamber Maids is preparing a hot water bottle while another is passing a bed warmer through the sheets of the single bed that the Stewards have set up in front of the fire while you were out.' Juliette Martin picked up the soiled clothes, disposed of any waste before bundling the clothes up in the fur rug.

'Thank you that is most helpful. We'll need to keep Henri's fluids up. Lemonade, ginger ale, or peppermint tea. Tomorrow we can try clear soups,' Bella sponged Henri clean as she tried to think of everything she was going to need to keep her son alive.

'Pork jelly is highly recommended, Madame.'

Bella shook her head. 'He can't stomach pork or sea food. Chicken is our best option.'

Juliette left the room for a moment to look through the carpet bag for Henri's nightgown and fresh underwear, bringing them back to assist as Bella helped Henri out of the tub and towelled him dry.

'You probably won't have enough changes of clothes for the little man if you are kept here a little longer than you planned.' Juliette was trying to be tactful as the young family probably didn't have money to splash out on additional clothes. Bella withdrew from her jacket pocket the smaller purse and pulling out several notes, handed them to the Housekeeper.

'I may need someone to buy supplies to tide us over. I've a little extra money as I had intended to purchase a few items for the new baby.' Dressing Henri in a night shirt Bella permitted Juliette to pick him up and carry him into the bedroom.

Hugo was adding more kindling to the fire as the Chamber Maid, Rosemary, was passing the bed warmer between the sheets of the small bed that several of the hotel's staff had assembled in the room. Bella was grateful that they didn't have to lay Henri down on chair cushions, a cot or trundle bed.

Rosemary drew back the bedding as Juliette gently laid the boy under the covers. Bella picked up an extra blanket from the end of the single bed and spread it over the sheets and blanket already covering her son.

Hugo offered his assistance to Rene, who was trying to stay out of the way as he took off his overcoat. The sight of the numerous weapons Rene carried momentarily polarised the hotel staff. Juliette recovering first, waved the other staff out of the room.

'When the Doctor has been to see Master Henri, I'll organise some dinner to be sent up for you,' offered Juliette, ducking back into the ensuite to pick up the soiled clothes.

'Thank you,' said Rene, 'We truly appreciate all your help.' He undid his gun holsters, laying them over the arm of the chair behind him.

'Not at all Captain Du Bois. We're here to make life a little easier for you.' Juliette let herself out as Bella sat down on the edge of Henri's bed and brushed his hair out of his eyes.

I'm Not Deserting You Now!

Removing his sword and scabbard and laying it on the chair beside his pistols, Rene asked, 'Is there anything I can do to help you Bella?' Although Henri was no longer coughing all the time, his breathing was harsh and laboured. *It is hard to stand by and do nothing to ease the boy's suffering.*

Bella rose and glided across the room to sit her husband down on the double bed and pull off his boots as she knelt in front of him.

'There is not much more we can do until the Doctor has seen Henri. Do you want to see if there's another room available for you? There won't be too much restful sleep tonight.'

Capturing her hands and drawing Bella closer towards him, Rene was surprised by the offer. 'Now what sort of father would I be to desert my son when he needs us the most? Besides which I'd rather lose a little sleep than the possibility that either of you could be stolen away from me again. We stay together. That is how it should be.'

He traced his thumb against Bella's cheek before lowering his head to claim her lips. *Rene's dedication to our protection even when it means we're in for a really rough couple of days, is incredibly arousing for me.* She willingly leant into his embrace and met his lips with a hunger to match his own. His arms tightened around her and although her baby bump made that a little difficult, he appreciated a challenge. He drew Bella up onto the bed beside him without breaking the kiss.

They were both a little disappointed when they were interrupted by a knock at the door. Reluctantly Rene released her lips as he sighed.

'It's probably the Doctor or Phillippe.' He stated.

That broke the spell for Bella and she ran a nervous hand through her hair as she rose to her feet. While she crossed the room to open the door, Rene felt his way to the arm chair where his weapons lay and picked up one of his pistols. He moved to stand protectively beside Henri's bed but Bella's words of greeting relieved his mind.

'Doctor Girard? Thank you for coming so quickly. Oh Cousin Phillippe, I am so glad to see you.' Bella was not surprised that Phillippe Du Bois stared at her in disbelief.

'Sweet cousin, I had no idea your pregnancy was that far advanced.' Phillippe embraced Bella before entering the room. She closed the door behind them as Phillippe lightly laid his hand on Rene's arm. 'How are you Rene? I thought that you and I could wait outside while the good Doctor examines Henri.'

Rene didn't move. 'I don't like them to be out of my… protection.'

'We'll only be just outside the door. No one will be allowed in past us,' Phillippe reassured. Still Rene refused to move.

'I don't have any shoes on.'

Bella caressed her hand against her husband's cheek. 'It's all right Rene. You can explain our journey to your cousin while I assist the Doctor.' She led Phillippe and Rene to the door, closing it firmly behind them before focussing her attention on Doctor Girard.

Telling Their Story… Again

Sliding his pistol into the waistband of his trousers, Rene permitted Phillippe to guide him to the stairs leading upwards from their floor and they sat down on the steps. *I'm actually surprised by Phillippe, I had expected a much younger man of my own age but Phillippe's deep pleasant voice sounds like he is much older, at least in his 40's. His fatherly manner reassures me that Phillippe is no threat to our masquerade.*

'I should apologise for borrowing your family's name.' Rene's manner was a little stiff and formal which made Phillippe chuckle.

'Not at all. Actually it was a stroke of genius. You're just another Du Bois travelling to Paris for my father's funeral. How are you holding up under the strain?'

Trying to suppress a sigh, Rene shook his head. 'We could've done without Henri getting sick. That's going to delay our plans to get home safely.'

Phillippe reassuringly patted his arm. 'It'll be a long time to maintain the facade. Once I can clear the house of mourners you can stay with me and you'll be able to let the mask slip in private.'

Rene was quite touched by Phillippe's generosity. 'Thank you but I don't think Bella will sanction moving Henri even so short a distance until he is well again.'

Drawing a small decorative enamel case out of his breast pocket, Phillippe lit up a cigar. 'Tell me of your adventures.'

Running a hand lightly across his developing beard, Rene took Phillippe back to the start. It was barely a week ago but now seemed as though a life time had passed since that night he had arrived at the Stirling Arms Inn.

Doctor Girard's Diagnosis

With the whole story told, they had been sitting in companionable silence as Phillippe finished his cigar when Bella opened the door to call them back inside. Rene didn't refuse Phillippe's assistance to rise from the stairs. They'd been sitting for a while and he had become stiff.

'What's the verdict Doctor Girard?' Rene refused to be led to the arm chair but sat down on the end of Henri's bed and reached out to lay his hand over the boy's.

The Doctor was packing up his medical bag. 'You have a very sick little boy on your hands Captain Du Bois. I'm going to drop in and check up on him every day.'

Tutt-tutting, Phillippe shook his head. 'La la! It's as bad as that then? Would you like Louise to come and assist you nurse Henri?'

'That's a very generous offer,' stated Rene, 'I'm not going to be of any use to Bella.' Languishingly the small boy managed to raise his head from his pillow.

'Can I please have Nanny? It's' too much for Mama to cope alone.' No one immediately answered Henri as he broke into a fit of lung destroying, ear busting coughing and no one would have been heard for several minutes.

Rene took the small bottle of oil that Doctor Girard placed into his hand and he listened carefully to the instructions to slip his hand under Henri's nightshirt and rub the oil over the boy's chest. Knowing the routine better than his parent, Henri rolled onto his side so that Rene could also apply the oil to the boy's back. Slowly the coughing eased and Rene removed his hand to pull the blanket further over Henri.

'Of course Louise will be here by morning,' promised Phillippe, opening the door for the Doctor.

'The draught I've given Henri should see him sleep now for several hours. You'll have to wait six hours before he can have another dose. When he is awake, try to get him to drink as much as possible. I'll have more medicine made up for you when I return after my rounds tomorrow morning. If you're at all worried, have a message sent to me and I'll come immediately. Anytime of the day or night,' reassuringly Doctor Girard patted Bella on the shoulder.

'Thank you Doctor,' she managed to say.

He smiled down at her. 'Don't worry Madame Du Bois, we'll get you through this. Excessive stress will affect your unborn baby.'

A sigh escaped from Bella as a smile twisted on her lips. 'I'm a worrier Doctor. Especially when I have no control over the situation.'

Doctor Girard squeezed her shoulder. 'I won't pretend that Henri's condition isn't serious but it could've been a lot worse. Don't forget to have something to eat as you need to keep your strength up and try to get some sleep when Henri drops off.' Glancing across at Rene, he added, 'I'll check your burns tomorrow Captain Du Bois.'

Rene nodded. 'Thank you Doctor Girard.'

What Do You Need From Me?

Upon the Doctor's departure, Phillippe closed and locked the door. He placed a supportive arm around Bella's shoulders and led her back to Henri's bedside.

'You've all been very brave and resourceful to have gotten this far,' Phillippe said, sitting Bella down onto the edge of Henri's bed beside Rene before bending down to place more fuel on the fire. 'Apart from sending for Louise, how can I be of service to you? Do you need any money? I'm afraid you'll be in Paris a lot longer than you planned. Do you need me to contact the Earl?'

Shaking her head, Bella sighed. 'Sir Malcolm, the British Ambassador is contacting Papa and Rene brought a large sum across with him in case he needed it for a ransom payment.'

'Louise changed it into French currency for us,' Rene added, running his hand along the top of the blanket until he found Bella's hand. He entwined his fingers through hers. The gesture was not lost to Phillippe.

'Perhaps something a little more intimate? I could locate for you a Protestant priest so that you can be married immediately.'

Colour rushed across Bella's cheeks. 'There's no need for that cousin. Rene... Rene has been a perfect gentleman throughout all of this. He hasn't compromised my honour.'

A frown descended upon Phillippe's brow. 'But this whole adventure has compromised your honour, no matter how noble Lord Delacourt has been.'

Rene held up a warning finger. 'Please Phillippe, no titles here. The mask must remain in place until we're safely on English soil once more.'

Sighing Phillippe acknowledged the logic in Rene's answer. 'If you were married, you'd have less qualms about sharing a bed and having to control your desires.' Rene shook his head, certain his cheeks must be flushed as Bella's by this conversation.

'Henri is our main concern. Bella won't be able to focus on anything else until he is well. Besides which… I'm a little reluctant to get too amorous with Henri able to hear or see us.'

Refreshments

Even if Phillippe had any further argument to offer, it was to be left unsaid as they were interrupted by a knock on the door. Waving Bella back down into her seat, Phillippe strode across the room to unlock and hold open the door.

A trolley was wheeled inside by one of the hotel's Stewards Bruno, which held not only jugs of lemonade and peppermint tea, but also dinner for Bella and Rene. Bruno bowed to Bella.

'Madame Martin said to tell you that our head Chef is organising chicken soup and ginger ale for tomorrow. She hopes that you'll forgive her for ordering dinner for you but thought you had enough to worry about.' He placed the jugs on a side table set close to Henri's bed which already had a glass upon it.

Bella was impressed by their attention to detail and issued a message of thanks to be conveyed back to the Housekeeper. Bruno set up the trolley which folded out into a small table between the two arm chairs, far enough away from Henri so that the delicious smell did not upset his delicate stomach.

As the Steward bowed himself out of the room, Phillippe was preparing to follow him.

'Andre said he'll pick you up for the funeral tomorrow Rene. I doubt I'll have any free time to see you tomorrow Bella but if anything urgent arises, I'll drop everything and come to your aid.'

She followed Phillippe to the door as Rene made his way into the ensuite to wash the scented oil off his hands before they sat down to eat. 'Thank you Phillippe. It's a comfort to know that we're surrounded by so much love and protection.' She felt foolish as a stray tear fell down her cheek.

'Never doubt that, sweet child.' As Rene re-emerged, Phillippe added, 'Behave yourself cousin.'

Grinning wickedly, Rene flicked Phillippe a salute. 'Says the voice of experience?' He retorted. Phillippe acknowledged the hit and left them, chuckling as he ran down the stairs.

The Masquerade Becoming Reality

Bella locked the door before she slid her arm through Rene's and led him to their dinner. *The meal is well chosen, light and easily digestible,* mused Bella. *Once the draught takes effect upon Henri, we need to take advantage of the lull in coughing to also get some sleep.*

They conversed softly as they ate, about normal every day topics and for the first time, Bella could see the masquerade becoming a reality. *It all seems… so normal and if it wasn't for Henri being ill or all of us being in mortal danger, we could have enjoyed ourselves.*

But there was work to do before anyone could consider sleep. Bella knelt beside Henri's bed and using a cool damp sponge, wiped his sweating hands and face. To be helpful, Rene carefully wheeled their dinner trolley out of their room, ensuring the door was securely locked when he closed it again.

Feeling his way to the main bed and locating the carpet bag, Rene pulled the contents out. Naturally he was unable to be absolutely certain what items of clothing he had but as Bella lifted Henri up to allow him to drink, Rene separated two nightshirts from the other clothes. Sitting up had caused Henri to start coughing again. With incredible patience Bella soothed her son and Rene folded again the spare clothes.

There isn't anything I can do to assist Henri so I'll try to be useful and stay out of the way. I'm honest enough to admit that even if I had my sight, I'd not be much use in caring for the sick little boy. What Rene didn't realise was that his asset was his protection.

Best Offer All Day

'Papa?' Henri called out once his coughing had subsided. Rene moved cautiously across the room to sit on the edge of the boy's bed.

'What is it Little Bear?' Rene laid his hand over Henri's.

'You're going to protect Mama aren't you?'

'Of course Henri. I'm here to protect both of you. Try and get some sleep.' He brushed the hair out of Henri's eyes. 'Do you need to pee?'

Henri shook his head. 'No thank you. Take Mama to bed.' He yawned as Rene smirked at his answer.

'That's the best offer I've had all day!'

Henri raised quizzical eyes to Rene's face. 'Are you being naughty Papa? Phillippe said you needed to see a priest before you're allowed to be naughty.'

Having the grace to blush, Rene apologised. 'Sorry Little Bear but it was an offer too good to refuse.'

Bella chuckled. 'Perhaps I should sleep in the arm chair beside Henri's bed?'

'I promise as a gentleman that I'll try to be good.' Reaching across the bed to locate her hand, Rene assisted her to her feet.

Smiling Bella's eyebrows rose. 'Try to be good?'

Rene grinned. 'I'm only human Bella. Besides which…' He led her around the bed and drew her into his arms. 'When I'm bad I am very, very good!'

'You're being naughty again aren't you Papa?' Henri covered his mouth as he coughed again.

'Go to sleep Junior, we'll try to keep the noise down.' Rene led Bella over to the main bed. 'I need Bella to play nurse to me for a while.' He gestured to where he knew the medical bag sat on the bedside table because he had placed it there while unpacking the carpet bag. Bella slid her hand free from Rene's arm.

"I'll just wash my hands. I can't afford to have both of you sick.' She disappeared into the ensuite.

Just A Little Bit Naughty

Removing his jacket and undoing his cravat, Rene moved the folded clothes to make room on the bed for him to sit down. Thinking about being very naughty, a devilish smile twisted his lips as he stripped off his shirt and trousers. Feeling his way around the bed, Rene located the arm chair so that he could place his pistols in easy reach beside the bed. He had just enough time to school his expression to one of innocence as he sat down on the edge of the main bed.

Bella uttered a gasp as she re-entered the bedroom and as he tried to keep a straight face, Rene raised his eyebrows.

'Something wrong Bella?' He removed his dark glasses in preparation for her medical care. Picking up the medical bag, she chuckled as she stood directly in front of him.

'Now why didn't you say you wanted a complete physical?' A shiver ran through him as she caressed her fingers lightly down his naked chest. Trapping her hand beneath his, he raised it to his lips.

'Actually I was thinking of performing the examination.' Rene slipped his arms around her waist and drew her against him. Sliding her hands slowly up Rene's chest, Bella willingly met him in a passionate kiss. Giving into the pleasure as his hands trailed slowly up from her waist until he moulded his fingers around her breasts; Bella involuntarily purred.

As Rene lowered his head to press a searing kiss against her throat, he slid his hands up to her shoulders. His lips continued to glide down Bella's throat as he peeled her dress off her shoulders. Slow, hot kisses melted her defences as her husband caressed his fingers along the hemline of her bodice. While his lips followed his fingers, Rene gently undid the laces at the front of her dress to expose her breasts.

A shiver of desire ran through Bella, her body instinctively melting against him as Rene's warm breath whispered her name across her bare breasts. He didn't need to be able to see to know that as he placed tantalising kisses against the swell of Bella's breasts, that her nipples were hardening.

It had been three days since Rene had shaved and he was careful that his beard didn't cause a rash against Bella's sensitised breasts. A whimper of need escaped from Bella, *as I desperately want Rene to take my nipples into his mouth, to suckle strongly, to use his tongue to fan the flames of desire that are building inside of me.*

Betraying her, Bella's body arched towards him and she found herself begging as her fingers ran through his hair. 'Please!'

Rene continued to rain tender, gentle kisses across both Bella's breasts, not giving her exactly what she wanted but to relieve some of her need, his hands cupped beneath her breasts and he caressed his thumb lazily over her aroused nipples.

'Oh Caleb! Please! Take me into your mouth!'

A Slap Of Reality

Her words brought Rene to his senses. *She hadn't spoken very loudly, in fact I doubt that even Henri could have heard her but it raises a difficulty that I had not foreseen.* Reluctantly he raised his head from his sensual exploration of her delicious breasts. 'Although it pleases me that it is my real name on your lips in desire, but if you scream out that name when I bring you to climax, we'll be undone.'

'Do you... do you want to stop?' She found that the words tried to choke her as she said them.

'Hell no! But if you don't think you can remember to call me Rene, it would be easier to stop now than if we got to the point of no return.' Tenderly he caressed his hand along her arm.

A moan slipped passed Bella's lips. 'So close that I'm almost prepared to ask you... to complete us. To be... very, very naughty with me!'

It was Rene's turn to exhale very slowly. 'Wow! Perhaps... perhaps we'd better accomplish our medical duties before... before I'm tempted to accept your offer.' It wasn't easy but they managed to draw apart and regain control over their baser desires.

After several deep, steadying breaths Bella peeled away the pads over Rene's eyes and with shaking fingers managed to clean his burns. Neither spoke as she applied ointment then the smaller pads over his eyes, the larger pad over the whole burns area before bandaging them into place.

Keeping his hands clasped tightly into the blanket beneath him, Rene thought, *I cannot believe how hard it is to not just give into the desires burning deep inside of both of us. I'm trying to concentrate on the job at hand and not on the fact that Bella's naked flushed breasts are only inches away from me. Or the fact that as she winds the bandages around my head, she inadvertently brushes her naked flesh against mine.*

A Couple Of Hours Of Sleep

Stepping back from him, Bella cleared away the medical supplies before collecting the clothes off the bed so that Rene could turn down the covers. Shaking the clothes out, she hung them in the wardrobe in the corner of the room before finally slipping out of her dress and petticoat. He refused the nightgown she offered him, slipping between the sheets in just his underwear.

Bella hesitated about removing her baby bump. *Would I have enough time to put it on again if anyone came to our room?* Holding out his hand towards her, Rene made the decision for her.

'Take it off Bella, give your back a break for a while.'

Dropping the padding onto an arm chair, Bella threw her nightgown over her head and slipped into bed beside Rene. As he drew her down into his arms, she could still feel the tingle and flush of desire all over her skin.

'Rene... I ... we... we should try to sleep while Henri lets us. I'll probably have to get up to him about midnight.'

Rene pressed his lips against the top of her head. 'I understand. To be honest, I find our desires a little overwhelming and intense. I'd rather we were a little more alone... a little less in mortal peril when we... give into earth shattering pleasure.'

Bella sighed in relief. 'You do understand! It's not that I don't want to...'

Stroking his hand down her back, Rene chuckled, 'It's just that it's not the right time. Good night Bella.'

Snuggling in close to him, she allowed her body to relax as she contemplated a future of many, many nights in the arms of this very special man.

SUNDAY

Tending To Henri's Needs

Jerked out of a very enjoyable dream, Rene was forced up into a sitting position. It took him a few minutes to comprehend what woke him. As Henri coughed again, Rene's brain cleared and he reached out to shake Bella's shoulder.

'Bella, wake up. Henri needs us.' When his hand came up empty in the bed beside him, a note of panic entered his voice, 'Bella?'

'It's all right Rene, I'm already up. I'd hoped I could dose our son before we woke you.' Her soft voice came from across the room. 'Why don't you go back to sleep and I'll join you when Henri has settled again.'

Scrubbing his hand along his jaw, Rene threw back the bed covers and rose to his feet. 'What can I do to help?' He made his way cautiously across the room until he reached Henri's bed and sat down to take the boy's hand. Bella was moved by his offer and picked up the bottle of oil from the table beside Henri's bed and placed it into Rene's hands.

'If you can rub oil onto Henri's chest and his back again. I'm just trying to work out how to reheat the hot water bottle without burning the bottle or myself.'

Taking the oil bottle, Rene paused before he attempted to apply the oil to ask, 'Would you like me to ring for assistance?'

Wincing, Bella removed her hand from over the fire. 'I didn't want to disturb anyone.' Giving up on the hot water bottle, she massaged her sprained wrist.

All three of them jumped, startled, at a knock on the door. Bella started to rise but Rene waved her down.

'Stay there Bella. Do you need your padding?'

'No, I put it on when I got up.'

Rene moved swiftly across the room to locate the pistol on the bedside table before making his way to the door. He reached it just as there was a second knock.

'Oh dear! We've disturbed the other guests,' sighed Bella but Rene wasn't convinced, as the knock hadn't been made in anger. Even so as he reached out to open the door, Rene held the pistol ready to defend his family. On the other side of the door stood a nervous Bruno.

'It's Bruno, the Steward, Captain Du Bois.'

The tension left Rene's body as he stepped back to allow Bruno to enter. 'Complaints from the other guests?' Rene asked as he closed the door again.

'No sir, Madame Martin instructed us to have a hot water bottle ready at midnight and offer you any assistance when the young master woke.' Bruno handed the hot water bottle to Bella before bending down to stoke up the fire.

'That is very considerate,' said Bella. 'Are we disturbing anyone Bruno?'

Rene sat down on the edge of the bed to resume the oil rub while his wife gave the boy another dose of his medication.

'Oh no,' Bruno reassured, 'Monsieur Martin, our Manager arranged for the guests in the rooms either side of you to be moved to avoid that issue. He said you had enough to worry about and besides which the little chap can't control that sort of coughing.' Straightening, Bruno glanced around the room. 'Is there anything else I can do to be of service to you? Do you need any more blankets?' He picked up the cold hot water bottle.

Bella laid her hand gently against Henri's forehead. He was still shivering, hot and clammy. 'Another blanket is actually a good idea. Thank you.'

Nodding, Bruno headed for the door. 'Won't be a minute Madame Du Bois.' He slipped quietly out of the room.

Papa Bear Loves You

A chill ran through Rene, which didn't surprise Bella as he was sitting there in just his underwear. Removing the bottle of oil from his hands, she placed it back on the small table beside the bed before leading him into the bathroom to wash the oil off his hands. She was just urging her husband back into his own bed when Bruno returned.

The Steward was not unnerved by the appearance of the pistol in Rene's hand but did not move until Bella spoke words of reassurance and it was laid aside onto the bedside table. Bruno assisted Bella to throw the extra blanket over her son before he headed back to the door.

'Don't be embarrassed to ring the bell for assistance, Madame Du Bois. We're here to help you. Any time of the day or night.'

She followed him to the door. 'Thank you, everyone has been so kind.' She closed and locked the door behind Bruno and was surprised when she turned around to find that Rene was standing right behind her.

'Put the door catch across,' he instructed before making his way back to Henri's bed. 'Is there anything else we can do to make Henri more comfortable?' Rene added, and as his fingers located Henri's, he slid both the boy's hands under the blankets. Bella sat down on the other side of the bed.

'He should go back to sleep if we leave him.' She was overcome by the touching scene as Rene raised his hand to brush against Henri's cheek.

'My poem please Maman.' Henri broke off as he coughed. Bella massaged her hand against his chest until the coughing stopped.

'Happy Little Bear, sleepy Little Bear, safe and warm and fuzzy too. Mama Bear loves you,' Bella reached out to lay her hand on Rene's arm but he seemed to instinctively know what he had to say.

'Papa Bear loves you.'

A small croak came from Henri, 'Little Bear loves you too.'

Bella continued to stroke her son's chest until his coughing had subsided into a wheeze and he closed his eyes. Checking that there was enough fuel on the fire to keep it burning for several hours, Bella was surprised when she reached over to touch Rene's arm that he had already risen and was holding his hand out to her. A tingle ran through her as she placed her hand into his and allowed him to lead her back to their bed.

Removing her padding and extinguishing the candles Bella snugged into his embrace, *I love how natural, how stimulating is that simple gesture. If I want more, he is more than willing to give it to me; if it is all I need Rene seems content enough with that too. The wee hours of the morning are not time for grand gestures or fancy words especially with a sick child to attend.* As Bella drew the bed covers over both of them, Rene gently pressed his lips against the top of her hair.

'Papa Bear loves you too,' he whispered, tightening his arms around Bella as her body shook with silent laughter.

An Abrupt Awakening

It wasn't the light streaming into the room that woke Rene for naturally he couldn't see it. Nor the subtle sounds outside their room of trolleys being wheeled by the Stewards or voices of other guests descending to the dining room for an early breakfast. It wasn't even the wheeze and occasional cough from Henri that caused Rene to stir.

As the hairs on the back of his neck rose, he slid his hand under his pillow for his pistol and he sat up, wide awake and alert for danger. He had diagnosed the sound now; someone else was in their room. Throwing back the sheet, Rene sprang to his feet, the gun steady in his hand as he whispered, 'Bella?'

He was answered by a gasp and a nervous giggle and Bella's soothing voice. 'It's all right my love, Madame Martin sent

Rosemary to see if we needed anything before breakfast was brought up to our room.'

'Oh I see.' Rene lowered his weapon and felt a trifle underdressed. 'Sorry if I scared you Rosemary. Excuse me.' He placed the pistol back under his pillow and headed into the ensuite.

Leading Rosemary to the main door, Bella cast her a look of apology. 'Rene is extremely protectively of us at the moment. The loss of his sight has made him a touch paranoid.' The Maid bobbed a curtsy.

'I understand, Madame Du Bois, I have five older brothers. Jacques will be along with your breakfast unless...' Rosemary caught the sound of running water in the ensuite. 'You'd prefer to bathe first?'

Glancing mischievously across at Henri, Bella was reassured that he was all right for the moment. 'Andre won't be picking Rene up until 9.30 as the funeral is at 10 o'clock. Give us at least half an hour.'

Analysing the smile on Madame Du Bois' face, I'm not certain that will be long enough for what she has in mind, mused Rosemary. 'I'll tell Jacques an hour and if you're ready before that you can pull the bell.' An embarrassed flush streaked across Bella's cheeks that her thoughts of being naughty had been so transparent; a giggle escaped from Rosemary again. 'Bruno's wife was the same after he returned from battle. It was like they were newlyweds again.'

Bella chuckled. 'An hour then, thank you.' Shutting and locking the door behind the Maid, she took a deep breath and with the mischievous smile playing on her lips, she joined Rene in the bathroom.

An Intimate Bathing

Due to the water running into the spacious tub, he didn't hear Bella come in and so as not to startle him, she softly said his name. Straightening up from bending over the tub and turning around Rene was surprised but pleasantly so to find his arms suddenly full of his wife.

'Have you come to scrub my back elfling?' He teased, enjoying the way her fingers caressed reverently down his naked chest.

'And other things… if that is what pleases the Master of my heart.'

Images of a multitude of pleasurable possibilities rose in Rene's imagination, *but I want to get one practicality out of the way first. Well actually three practicalities.* 'Is Henri all right? Are we likely to be disturbed? How big is this bath?' The eagerness in his voice caused Bella to giggle as she stepped back to shed her nightgown and baby bump.

'Henri is fine, we have an hour before breakfast and this is the biggest bath I have ever seen in my life!' Running her hands down Rene's body, Bella dropped to her knees in front of him and slid his underwear to the floor.

He dragged in a sharp breath as Bella caressed her hand along his taut stomach and wrapped her fingers around his penis. As she stroked along his growing length, Rene swallowed hard as the words he wanted to say were trying to choke him and remain unsaid.

'Bella wait… I want to be clean before we…' His words faded into a moan as her tongue slid languishingly along his throbbing flesh. 'Bella…' As this seemed important to him, she released him and rising to her feet, slid out of her own underwear.

'I'll take your bandages off now so that I can wash your hair.' Bella checked on the running water before unwinding his bandages. *He is going to have to be good and keep his eyes closed no matter how tempting it becomes to see what we get up to; or his desire to see me naked.*

Securing her hair on top of her head, Bella turned off the taps and stepped cautiously into the hot water. Happy enough that the water wasn't about to burn either of them, she reached out to take Rene's hands and assisted him into the tub. Sighing as they sank into the water, a look of bliss appeared on his face.

'Oh, I'm going to enjoy this!' He sighed. Taking up a bar of soap and a wash cloth, Bella giggled at his enthusiasm and she started to scrub his back. The tender kisses that Bella placed against his neck only added to the smile of pleasure on Rene's lips.

Before she switched to washing the front of him, she carefully tilted his head back so that she didn't get any shampoo in his eyes as she washed his hair. The idyllic scenario tickled Rene's sense of humour and chuckling he suggested, 'Perhaps we should have Henri join us to complete this family scene.'

Having rinsed his hair, Bella laughed as she moved to sit across his lap and chewed playfully upon his ear. 'If he was well, he'd love all this water but I don't think that what I have in mind will be suitable for the eyes of children.' Her breath blew softly against his cheek as she soaped up her hands in a rich lather and focussed her complete attention on washing his arms and torso. Except for the fact that her hips moved subtly but rhythmically against his very responsive flesh.

It seems to me that Bella is paying far too much attention to the top half of my body when it is my lower half that is screaming out for her touch. When he captured her hand and tried guide it under the water to caress him more intimately, Bella tutt–tutted him and drawing her hand free, went back to rinsing off his arms and chest. Even so her hips continued to tease against his until Rene slid his hands under the water to clasp her bottom and attempted to pull her harder against his tormented flesh.

Instead of reprimanding him again, Bella lowered her head to languidly brush her tongue against his nipples as one of her hands slid between their bodies to curl around his engorged member. A moan of bliss was torn from Rene's throat as she slowly stroked her hand along his length.

That moan turned into a protest as she released him to soap up her hands once more, this time to clean down both of his strong, muscular legs. He was just wondering, *if I'm going to have to beg Bella to touch my throbbing cock. I am prepared to offer anything, promise everything if Bella stops tormenting me and gives me release.* When her hand slowed, Rene couldn't contain the protest that rose immediately to his lips.

'Bella please!' When she removed her hand completely, Rene had to bite his bottom lip to stop himself from crying out.

'Please don't laugh at my inexperience, Rene, but I can't become pregnant if you come in the bath can I? You have to actually be inside of me for that to happen, is that correct?' Her voice was full of doubt. His knuckles were white as he gripped the sides of the bath and tried to drag laboured breaths deep into his lungs.

'That is… correct my… my beautiful elfling. You won't fall pregnant… masturbating in a bath with me.' He managed to keep his voice light and reassuring, even though his body was screaming for action and not words.

When her hand encircled his throbbing penis once more Rene almost wept in relief. Instinctively Bella stroked him hard and fast pressing her lips firmly over his to smother his cry of joy as his body went rigid and he ejaculated over both their chests.

As Rene struggled to regain his control, Bella wiped them both down with the soapy face cloth while tenderly stroking his chest as he dragged in deep breaths. His slightly trembling fingers rose to locate her shoulder and then travelled up to cup her face.

She leant in to meet his kiss but drew back as she continued to study him, afraid that she had hurt him and tried to apologise. Having been granted his release, Rene was more forgiving than she was on herself. He silenced her apology with another kiss before turning her around so that she laid back against his chest.

With his arms protectively wrapped around her, they remained in comfortable silence as his breathing slowed to a more normal pace. When Rene's lips nuzzled against her neck, Bella placed the soap into one of his hands and the wash cloth in the other and edged away from him a fraction so that he could soap up her back. When she started to turn to face him, Rene drew her back against him.

'No, stay as you are for now.' He slid his hands around her and he took his time soaping up her front compared to the time spent on her back. By the time Rene had thoroughly, very thoroughly soaped up her chest and was moving down her stomach, Bella was already purring before his hand slid languidly between the apex of her thighs.

Instinctively her hips rose into his caress as his fingers traced teasingly against her sensitised flesh. A flush of pleasure swept over Rene as his name, his real name, was whispered breathlessly. When his hand left where she wanted him most, to caress the wash cloth along one of her thighs, Bella protested and reached down to place her hand over the top of his.

Her attempt to bring him back up to the dampness between her thighs had nothing to do with the water surrounding them; she was momentarily distracted as Rene moulded his other hand around one of her breasts and he whispered Gaelic words of love into her ear. Not until he had thoroughly washed down both her legs, did he return to caress her intimately once more.

The wash cloth was forgotten as Rene's long, sensitive fingers stroked and teased Bella's clitoris before sliding down to slowly enter her tight moist passage. A shudder of desire ran through Bella as Rene's fingers mimicked the slow enter and withdrawal that in a very short period of time, his penis would be making.

Although she didn't understand a thing he said, his Gaelic words equally heated her blood as his other hand caressed and fondled her breasts.

'Oh Caleb, I want you inside of me!' Bella bit her bottom lip to try to keep her voice down as Rene took her higher and higher towards ecstasy.

'Soon, my beautiful elfling!' He released her breast to caress his hand up her throat and tilted her head back so that he could take possession of her mouth with his own to smother her cry as her body twitched under his pumping fingers.

Rene continued to stroke inside of her until she went limp against him. He released her lips to allow her the chance to catch her breath and wrapped both his arms possessively around her waist until she had recovered.

Rene's Doubts

'How soon?' Bella's quiet question took him by surprise and he had to rack his brain back to what he had actually said. 'If we wait until we're married, Phillippe did offer to find us a priest,' she added, turning in his arms and straddling across his hips. Reaching up to caress his hand against her cheek, Rene smiled.

'In a couple of days, Henri will be well enough to travel. We'll take him home and Reverend Gray will marry us in that lovely little church you have there. I've every intention of returning you to your father's house as innocent as you left it.'

Bella's eyebrows rose as she gave a gurgle of laughter. 'Considering where we currently are, I don't think innocent is the correct word.'

A rueful blush crept across his skin. 'All right then, Virgo Intacta!' He brushed his thumb along Bella's throat. 'I desperately want to give in to my burning desire for you but a couple of things are holding me back from acting upon it right at this moment.'

Bella traced a distracting pattern across his bare chest. 'The fact that Henri is never far from us?' She suggested.

'Yes, he has enough to scare him, I don't want him to think I was hurting his beloved sister. You're also preoccupied with his illness and besides which...' Rene paused as he was close to what truly worried him. Bella caressed her hand up to cup his bearded chin.

'Is it... is it about your eyesight that worries you?' Her astuteness surprised him and he exhaled slowly.

'In part, I... I know the first time we make love will be a little scary for you. I don't want you to tell me everything is fine, that I'm not doing it badly or hurting you... I... I want to see, to know for myself that I'm making it as enjoyable as possible for you.'

Bella's eyes narrowed momentarily. 'Are you keeping an escape plan up your sleeve? Do you want an easy way out of our engagement?'

'No, but... I want you to have other options if I'm... if I can't be the man you... you need.'

Frowning now, Bella thought, *I feel I am standing on the edge of a cliff of truth. What really scares Rene?* 'Why? I think we've just proved that a certain part of you works very well. Oh, you're afraid that I'm shallow and won't want you if your blindness is permanent!' Taking both of her hands into his own, Rene raised one to his lips.

'You deserve only the very best Bella.'

'Sight or no sight, I won't love anyone the way I love you! No one else has ever made me so glad that I'm actually a woman. When Louise placed that baby padding on me for the first time, I could easily imagine your child inside of me.' Bella kissed him briefly. 'Something I've never done before!'

'My love!' Her voice became quite husky. 'My life!' Another kiss. 'My salvation!' This time the kiss lasted longer as their arms entwined around each other.

Even More Doubts

The water surrounding them was beginning to cool but with the heat their bodies generated, neither of them particularly noticed. What did distract them was Henri coughing and as Rene had already begun to release Bella, they heard, 'Maman?'

Breaking the kiss, Bella replied as she rose to her feet. 'Coming Henri,' Stepping out onto a bathmat, she wrapped a towel around her before bending down to kiss her husband once again. 'Do you want to soak or shall I help you out?'

Gripping the edges, Rene hauled himself to his feet. 'We'd better get dressed and have breakfast before Andre arrives.' He held out his hands so that she could assist him over the edge. Rene accepted the towel Bella handed him but retained a hold of her hand.

'Bella, I may not always be able to say what is in my heart but I hope that you know the truth all the same. I will endeavour to show how much I love you every single day for the rest of our lives. But if you do have any doubts…'

Her fingers tightened around his. 'I… I do have doubts…' He swallowed hard to try and keep the rising fear from choking him to death. 'Did you offer for me because of the scandal of the first abduction?' She asked, 'Do you want a hasty wedding because of the scandal of this flight through France from our second abduction? Are you doing this only out of obligation?'

A weary sigh escaped from Rene. 'It would seem that I'll need to overcome my inability to clearly state my feelings if you have such little faith in my motives.' Wrapping his towel around his waist, Rene took both her hands into his.

'I offered for you because I fell in love with you. I want a speedy wedding because I can't keep my hands off my future bride. I will not marry you out of any obligation and you will not marry me out of pity! You called me the Master of your heart, well you are the Mistress of mine. Now and always!'

Uttering a relieved sob, Bella threw her arms around Rene's neck and kissed him. As his arms tightened around her and the kiss deepened in intensity they were reminded of their other duties. "Maman?'

Don't You Think It A Little Odd?

Picking up her baby bump, Bella led Rene back into the bedroom. Satisfied by Rene's answer, she tended to Henri's need for a drink before assisting her husband to dress. She applied the ointment to his burns before placing fresh pads over his eyes and the dark lens glasses.

Retying her baby bump on again, Bella slipped into a clean dress. She needed Rene to do up the sash as her left wrist was still too painful to use. They had both managed to brush their hair before Jacques arrived with their breakfast. As the Steward assisted Rene to one of the arm chairs, Bella picked up their towels to return them to the ensuite and pick up their discarded underwear. She shoved them into the carpet bag, *I hope that when Louise arrives in Paris she will have thought to bring more clothes with her.*

Sitting down opposite Rene, Bella was puzzled by Jacques' ready acceptance of the pistol that sat openly on the arm of Rene's chair. Raising her eyes to meet the Steward's, he merely smiled as he lifted the covers keeping their plates warm, before he bowed himself out of the room. Rising to lock the door, she voiced her query to her husband.

'Don't you think it odd that no one has made any comment about your weapons being visible?'

Picking up his cutlery, Rene shook his head. 'Not really, but I'd bet the talk is running wild downstairs. Each new nugget of information eagerly shared and discussed. But unless I'm actually forced to fire my pistols, their presence will not be spoken of to us.'

Sighing as she poured out tea for them both, Bella stated, 'Oh you won't be able to take the pistols with you to the funeral.'

Rene nodded. 'I was going to leave them for you to protect yourself and Henri. I'm not happy about having to leave you alone even for a couple of hours. We've no idea what either Nigel Sutherland or your cousin Patrick is up to.' He used his fingers to find the edge of his plate so that he could judge where to place his knife and fork.

'I know, but you'll be back for the Doctor's visit so until then I'll just keep the door locked and the catch across.' Bella buttered a piece of toast for Rene and slid it into his hand. He didn't reply, knowing too well that a mountain like Sutherland could easily break down a locked door but he was not about to share that information with his beloved.

Rene's Weapons

They were in the bathroom, brushing their teeth when a knock came at their door. Rene's hand immediately descended to the pistol he had placed into the band of his trousers. Rinsing her mouth, Bella laid a reassuring hand on his arm.

'It's probably only Jacques for the trolley or Andre to pick you up.'

Rene did not move his hand from the weapon. 'We can't afford to become complacent Bella.' He accepted the glass she placed in his other hand to rinse his mouth before following her into the bedroom.

'Rene, its Andre,' came from the other side of the door as Bella went to open it. Stepping into the room, Andre Guillaume looked very dashing in his black suit as he embraced Bella and kissed her on both cheeks.

Knowing that Rene was not fond of stray kisses, the Author reached out to take Rene's hand instead. He assisted Rene into his jacket but drew out the pistol and handed it over to Bella.

'My dear Rene, if you wish to father any more children, refrain from thrusting a loaded pistol down the front of your trousers.' Affectionately he patted Rene's cheek.

'Bella wouldn't let me put on my gun holsters, she says they make me look like a pirate.' Rene did up the buttons of his jacket before finding the edge of Henri's bed to sit down.

'Especially with that beard,' Andre added provocatively. 'So how is this little man doing? I was concerned when Phillippe told me that Henri had fallen ill.' *Studying Bella's face, I can tell that she is worried and wondered how much has she told Rene about how serious was the situation?*

'We're in good hands with Doctor Girard,' Bella admitted, unknowingly pacing in front of the fireplace. 'My main concern is the trip home. Henri must maintain a certain temperature to prevent a relapse.' She didn't explain any further, probably to prevent scaring Henri but Andre, meeting her eyes, understood what she had left unsaid. *A relapse, so soon, could kill the boy.*

'We'll just have to ensure that you don't have to run around in the middle of the night.' Andre laid his hand on Rene's shoulder. 'You ready to go?'

Pressing a tender kiss against Henri's hot forehead, Rene rose to his feet. 'Bella...'

She interrupted him. 'One of your pistols on me at all times, another under Henri's pillow. The door locked and catch on. Ask who it is before opening the door. If anyone breaks down the door shoot to kill and we'll worry about the legal implications later.' Bella placed a reassuring kiss against Rene's cheek.

Andre's Admiration

Opening the door, Andre was startled to find a pretty young woman in hotel livery with her hand raised about to knock. 'My goodness, if I'd known this hotel had such pretty Chamber Maids, I would've stayed here too!' Andre smiled charmingly as Rosemary blushed.

'Madame Du Bois, Madame Martin has cleared my morning schedule so that I can sit with your son so that you can attend your uncle's funeral.' Rosemary dropped a curtsy, not unflattered by Andre's admiring gaze.

'Thank you Rosemary, that's very kind of you and Madame Martin but I won't be going to the funeral. Andre has kindly agreed to look after Rene until he too can be returned to my care.'

Large, awe filled eyes were raised to Andre's face. 'Andre? Not... not Andre Guillaume?' Rosemary breathed in disbelief.

The Author's eyebrows rose in question. 'I'm sorry, have we previously met?' Andre took the Maid's hand and raised it to his lips as Rosemary bobbed another curtsey.

'Oh no sir! But my brothers have all your books. They're such huge admirers of your stories.'

Andre bowed gallantly. 'It is always nice to meet any of my readers. Too often these days people just want to criticise my work.'

Then they are cretons! Oh my brothers will never believe that I actually met you!' Rosemary looked as though she were about to faint so Andre placed his hand under her elbow and leant her against the wall.

'I'll be returning here with Rene, so perhaps you could arrange a time for your brothers to come here. If they bring their books with them I'll sign them. Just your brothers, though; I am in Paris for a funeral rather than an official book tour.'

'Do you mean it sir?'

Andre smiled. 'Yes I do. Let Madame Du Bois know when your brothers can be here and I'll be happy to meet them.' Turning back to Bella, he kissed her on both cheeks. 'Stay safe, I'll keep Rene in line.'

A bark of a laugh came from Rene. 'Come on Andre before you start telling tales out of school!' He linked his arm through Andre's and they headed down the main staircase.

Rosemary's Errand

Pulling herself together Rosemary looked enquiringly at Bella. 'Is there anything I can do for you, Madame Du Bois?'

A flash of devilry lit up Bella's eyes. 'Actually yes there is Rosemary. Come inside for a moment.' Following her into the room, Rosemary wasn't worried that Bella locked the door before she went across to the medical bag and drew out the second purse.

'When will your brothers be free to meet Andre?'

'They are usually all home for supper at seven o'clock.'

Bella nodded. 'Good, now you need to let Madame Martin know about this informal meeting. She may have to inform your hotel's Manager to make sure that there are no problems. Send a message to your brothers to be here by eight this evening.'

Rosemary bobbed another curtsy. 'Yes ma'am.'

Removing several of the larger denominational notes from her purse, Bella handed them to Rosemary. 'I want you to go to the book store and purchase a copy of every book of Andre's that you can get your hands upon. If you can't get a complete collection then try his publishing house.'

Frowning in thought Bella didn't really register Rosemary's gasp of surprise. 'If you can, try for two copies of everything.' Bella drew out another couple of notes and added them to the money she had already pressed into the Maid's hands. 'If you need more money, have a message sent to me and I'll send the money back with the messenger. Can you do this Rosemary?'

The Maid looked at her stunned. 'I'll... I'll certainly do my best Madame Du Bois.' She tucked the money into the bodice of her dress for safe keeping. 'I'll go and speak with Madame Martin first, yes?'

Bella smiled, guiding the girl back to the door. 'Definitely! Don't do anything without letting Madame Martin know first. What is the name of the hotel's Manager? In case I need to speak with him.'

'Monsieur Martin.'

Opening the door, Bella's eyebrows rose. 'Any relation to...'

Rosemary nodded, 'Husband and wife run the hotel.'

'Thank you Rosemary. If you have any problems, please let me know immediately.'

Absolutely stunned at this strange turn of events, Rosemary bobbed another curtsy, before hurrying away to find her employer as Bella locked the door behind her.

Rene Seeks Andre's Counsel

During the drive to the cemetery, Rene was very quiet. For a brief time Andre kept up a general, rather one sided conversation but lapsed into thoughtful silence as he received little response from Rene. Laying his hand over Rene's, Andre finally asked, 'What's troubling you mon ami? Bella and Henri will be safe enough. Are you worried about any of Phillippe's relatives realising who you are? There are so many members of the Du Bois clan that even Phillippe has trouble naming them all.'

Uttering a small sigh, Rene shook his head. 'I said something to Bella but I don't know if it's actually true. At the time I would've said anything so that she didn't stop...' Blushing he broke off.

Andre's eyebrows rose. 'Have you two been naughty?'

Rene's blush deepened.

'Yes not the "send for a priest" naughty… well I'm not sure now.' He wondered if Andre was going to laugh and was reassured when he didn't.

'Tell me about it.'

Rene hesitated. 'Will it end up in your book?'

Smiling, Andre patted his hand. 'I don't think I'll be able to get it published if it ends up being that naughty.'

Deciding to take a chance, Rene described what took place between him and Bella in the bath.

'And now you think that you may have impregnated her due to your amorous activities?' asked Andre, once Rene had finished his story.

'No, I know that can't be possible, now that I've talked it through. It's just at that moment, I would've said anything. As far as I knew it wasn't a lie but could I have lied just to get release?'

Andre laid his hand on Rene's shoulder. 'I don't think you'd ever intentionally lie to Bella but I can assure you that the moment you're married and having regular intercourse, you won't feel so desperate for satisfaction. I get the feeling that isn't what is really worrying you.' Andre let the ensuing silence continue for a couple of minutes.

When Rene didn't answer, Andre sighed. 'Are you just going to ignore the issue?'

'What would you do?'

'You're afraid she'll marry you out of pity and Bella's afraid you'll marry her only out of obligation. Do you really think that the loss of your sight will make Bella love you less?'

Grinding his teeth, Rene finally admitted, 'This scandal, Andre, isn't going to be just a seven day wonder. It… it could haunt us forever. If it doesn't kill us, it could drive us apart.'

Andre shook his head. 'Or make you stronger. Were you just a little naughty as engaged couples might be or very naughty – something that could not be undone?'

'I did not compromise Bella. Although...' Doubt entered Rene's voice.

His host sighed, 'Not the bath tub again! Or are you worried about sharing the same bed? I thought you said most of the time Henri slept between you?'

'Not all the time and he's only a child, we can't guarantee that he remembers it the way it really happened.'

Patting Rene's hand reassuringly, Andre chuckled. 'My dear boy, what would you have done differently if you weren't in love with Bella?'

'If I wasn't in love with Belle then we probably wouldn't be in the situation we are now in.' A quick review of their adventures so far, Rene could not stop the goofy grin that appeared upon his face. 'I hope that I would have acted in a more gentlemanly manner. I'm glad, though, that we didn't have to do it differently. Fighting the burning need to make love to Bella is an effective distraction. From this infernal darkness. From the blood lusting locals. From the members of our own family who instigated this madness.'

'Are you sure that Patrick is the only one you have to worry about?' Andre stroked his chin, deep in thought.

'You mean apart from Sutherland and however many millions of your country men who would want our heads as ornaments?'

Glancing out the window as the carriage began to slow, Andre realised that there was no time to delicately tackle what was on his mind. He tapped Rene's arm. 'Later! Keep your wits about you, these are not ignorant peasants you're dealing with.'

Rene stretched out his hand to cover Andre's. 'I don't underestimate anyone, least of all you.' A cheeky grin appeared on his face as he could imagine the look of surprise that his words would have caused. It was also a cheap shot as they descended from the carriage. That made it impossible for Andre to retort as they joined the assembled mourners.

Interrupting The Wake

Even before the mourners had all reconvened at the Du Bois house, Rene had had enough. *I long to be back at the hotel with Bella and Henri but having taken on the personae of a Du Bois, I will have to remain true until I can get my loved ones safely home again.* Andre forced him to take a plate of food and a glass of champagne to look the part as they circulated through the room.

Rene was content enough to fade into the back ground as Andre dealt with his critics and admirers. Rene made his way to a settee close to the front door while he waited to go back to Bella. So he was in a good position when Louise blew into the house.

'Bring Captain Du Bois outside with you Monsieur Guillaume, I need both of you to help me with François.'

Rene was surprised that Andre was still keeping such a close eye upon him and he permitted Andre to take his arm as they trotted down the front steps after Louise. Phillippe had noticed Louise's abrupt arrival and managed to excuse himself to his guests to follow them outside.

'What's happened to François?' Phillippe demanded, as Andre jumped up into the carriage to assist Louise's brother.

'Two men broke into the house, two Englishmen! François refused to tell them what they wanted to know. They... they beat him.' Louise's voice broke and she could not continue.

Rene felt a cold hand tightened around his heart. 'Oh Louise, I am so sorry! You and François should never have been made to suffer for our escape from Sutherland.' *I had never thought that the French siblings would be in danger after we had left the Du Bois country house.* 'If François needs medical assistance, he should come back to the Grand Duchess Hotel with us. Doctor Girard can examine him when he comes to check up on Henri.'

Andre jumped down from the carriage. 'I think that would be best Rene. The boy doesn't look at all well. Sorry to desert you, Phillippe, bit I'm going to take these young people back to the hotel.'

Phillippe assisted Louise back into the carriage. 'I just wish I could go with you. Andre see that they have everything they need. Money no object.' Phillippe helped Rene into the carriage but as Andre was about to follow, Phillippe placed his hand on the Author's arm. 'Trouble is more than likely coming to town. I'll have one of my people send over any weapons we can discover.'

Andre laid his hand over Phillippe's. 'What… what do I do if Patrick tells the whole hotel who exactly our young friends really are? How do I protect them from a city full of angry or money hungry French citizens?'

Swallowing hard, Phillippe paled at the idea of a slaughter. 'Silence him! Anyway you have to!'

Nodding, Andre jumped up into the carriage, as he thought, *I'm not absolutely confident that I am going to be able to handle taking this much active participation in the adventure.*

Back To The Hotel

For the first time, Rene was glad that he could not see François and how much damage Nigel and Patrick had inflicted upon the young god. He had been placed next to François in the carriage and not asking any questions, Rene stretched out his hand to find François'. The younger man slid his closest hand out of Rene's grasp but allowed him to have his other hand. Louise was touched by Rene's gesture.

'They damaged that hand my Lord,' she explained.

Rene shook his head. 'No titles Louise.' He felt the young man beside him shiver in fear. 'I won't let anyone hurt you again François. You're safe now.' He slid his arm around François and did not recoil as the young man pressed his face into Rene's shoulder as a sob escaped from him.

Andre was surprised that such a promise from a blind man could cause relief in the battered god. 'It's all right François, you've been very brave and loyal. You don't have to bottle it all up.' Releasing François' hand, Rene stroked the young man's hair who immediately gave way to his over-wrought emotions. Andre cast a scrutinizing glance over Louise and noted that she was wearing a cape with a hood.

'Do you mind if we borrow your cape Louise?' Andre considered his next words carefully. 'I thought we shouldn't shock the guests of the hotel.'

François gave a watery laugh. 'The beauty has become the beast!' He wrapped his arms around Rene, accepting the handkerchief that Louise handed him but didn't raise his head from Rene's chest as he sobbed. Rene permitted this intimacy as they only had a short distance to travel and the young man had been made to suffer a great deal.

Bella's Shock

With Louise's cloak around François, Andre and Rene half carried the young god into the hotel and up the stairs. Louise raised her hand to the door knob but Rene stopped her.

'Wait! If you try to open the door, you could have your head blown off!' Rene knocked on the door. 'Bella, its Rene.' They heard the catch scrape across and the lock click before the door was finally opened.

'I wasn't expecting you back so soon. Oh Louise thank goodness you're here!'

As Andre and Rene carried François into the room and laid him gently upon the main bed, Bella added, 'François? What on earth has happened? No...' Realisation hit her hard as the hood of the cloak fell back from François' battered and bruised face. Andre shut the door behind them and locked it again. Louise rushed forward to place her arms around Bella as her knees began to buckle. Absently Bella laid the pistol in her hand down on the table beside her.

'Steady Bella, we're all safe now.' Rene made his way around the bed to assist Louise in lowering his wife into one of the arm chairs.

'Safe? We have to leave before anyone else gets hurt because of us! Everyone who helps us is in danger!' Bella tried to rise but Louise held her in her place.

'Now don't be silly, my Lady, Aidan can't be moved until his illness has passed.'

Rene sighed. 'Louise no titles and please use our assumed names until we can leave France. Andre, I know Bella abhors alcohol but she needs something to stabilise her nerves.'

Heading to the door, Andre was stopped by a command from Louise. 'No sir, no alcohol! It's not good for the baby.'

They all looked at each other in surprise. No one knew how to reply but it had been the shot in the arm that Bella needed. Dragging in a deep, steading breath, she pulled herself together.

'Sorry, I'm all right now. We're going to need another room.'

All ready at the door, Andre nodded. 'The rooms either side of you are empty. I'll go and talk to the Manager.' Opening the door the Author was once more startled to find Rosemary and Juliette Martin about to knock. Behind them was a young man with two boxes on a trolley as well as the Porter carrying up the luggage from the carriage. Bella gestured to Andre to allow them to enter.

'Madame Martin, just the person we need to speak to. Louise, Doctor Girard will need to examine François fully so strip him down and put him into a nightshirt.' Bella motioned for Juliette Martin to sit down in the arm chair opposite her. Rene entwined his fingers through Bella's.

'Be careful what you say Bella.'

'My protective beloved.' She reached up to caress her free hand against his bearded cheek. 'Go and rub some more oil over Henri's chest please.'

Bella's Tale

When the Porter and the young man with the trolley deposited their cargo, Madame Martin signalled them to leave and Rosemary shut the door behind them. She then went to the main bed and offered her assistance to Louise in undressing François. Madame Martin sat down beside Bella as Rene reluctantly moved to sit on the edge of Henri's bed.

'I think I know what this is about,' said Madame Martin. 'Trouble can easily arise when too many of the one family get together in the same place and emotions are running high.'

A rueful smile appeared on Bella's face. 'Actually it's my family that is the problem Madame Martin. It's probably well known by now that it was Sir Malcolm White, the English Ambassador who called Doctor Girard when Henri became ill. Sir Malcolm is my uncle. Rene is tolerant of me having English relatives.'

Juliette Martin sighed. 'I do understand Madame Du Bois, my... my sister married an Englishman. I'm torn between my loyalty to my family and my sister. That doesn't explain why that young man has been beaten.'

Glancing only briefly across to where Louise was re-dressing her brother into a nightshirt, Bella said, 'It's a little more complicated. Before I married Rene, I was arranged to marry my English cousin, Patrick. What with France taking side with the colony in America against England, the need for our family to flee France during the revolution and the various wars between France and England; the marriage plans fell through.'

Bella took a deep breath before continuing, 'Patrick never accepted my marriage to Rene, but there was nothing he could do about that until this latest conflict between our countries. Rene was reported missing, presumed dead at Waterloo. Patrick thought it was time for him to finally claim what he had always thought as his.'

Andre was impressed by how well Bella blended the truth with the personae they had adopted. 'You can imagine how angry Patrick was when he found out that Rene was only temporarily injured instead of dead,' he added.

Juliette Martin glanced across to where Louise was carefully laying her brother back down onto the bed. 'So Cousin Patrick is following you to Paris.' She surmised. 'He didn't catch up with you at the Du Bois country seat so he had the staff assaulted. What can we do to help you? I don't want you to feel that you have to run from our hotel.'

'The two rooms either side of us are empty, may we move François and Louise into one and Andre into the other? We'll naturally pay for the rooms,' Bella said. 'If... if Patrick comes to the hotel and asks for us... perhaps your staff can say that we're not staying here.' *I wonder if I am asking for too much.*

'Not a problem Madame Du Bois.' Juliette smiled. 'In fact I have an idea you might like to consider. I'm quite happy to have Rosemary's brothers come to the hotel to meet Monsieur Guillaume. In fact I feel it is a very generous offer but I think we could also ask the boys if they'll take on some security work.'

'Oh... I don't want to put anyone else in danger Madame Martin. If you can just deny our presence here. That would of immense help.'

Juliette smiled, 'Captain Du Bois, let Rosemary know if you would like her brothers to work as security guards.' She rose to her feet and smoothed her dress into place. Everyone looked at Juliette in surprise. Rene's eyebrows rose and he wondered, *is it a good idea to say anything but which woman is going to kill me if I do speak?* Juliette smiled, understanding his dilemma.

'Don't worry Captain, I've been that pregnant and crazy with hormones four times. Best if you don't say anything and you'll not die a horrible death.' She headed to the door and signalled for Rosemary to join her. 'We'll just make certain that the rooms next door are ready for occupation. I'll arrange for

124

luncheon to be brought up once Doctor Girard has been to see you.' Juliette smiled confidently at them all. 'You need to focus your energy upon taking care of your little boy Madame Du Bois. Leave everything else to us.' Nodding to the stunned occupants, the Housekeeper followed the Maid out of the room.

Bravo!

Locking the door, Andre stood staring at it for a moment as he fought to control the urge to shout, 'Bravo!' Trying to sit up, Henri started to cough violently and as both Louise and Bella made their way to his bed to tend to the boy, Rene got out of their way and went into the ensuite to wash his hands. Upon his return to the bedroom, he found his hand seized and he was drawn to sit on the edge of the bed beside François by Andre.

'That was amazing!' Andre whispered. 'I am in admiration at Bella's story-telling ability! I'm starting to think that she could write your story herself.'

Rubbing a weary hand across his chin, Rene sighed. 'Can we just get to the end of the story alive before we consider writing it? Don't think I have forgotten that we have something to discuss, Andre. You've given me something else to worry about!'

Andre was glad Rene couldn't see his guilty school boy grin. 'Sorry but as an Author I'd throw in a twist about now.'

'Well hold that thought until after the Doctor has seen us.' Rene rose to his feet and making his way across to Henri's bed, slid his hand under the pillow to retrieve his pistol. Andre looked worried as Rene attached his gun holsters to his hips.

'What is it Rene?' Andre rose slowly off the main bed.

Rene held up a warning finger, strode over to the door and flung it open. Rosemary gave a squeak of fear and her raised hand, to knock on the door, now pressed against her racing heart.

'Sorry Rosemary, can we help you?' Rene slipped his pistol into its holster. A nervous Porter stood behind Rosemary with a trolley.

'The rooms are ready and I was going to take Louise's bags and the boxes of books into their rooms. Someone from the Du Bois house has just delivered Monsieur Guillaume's luggage.' Rosemary bobbed a hasty, nervous curtsy.

Andre's eyebrows rose. 'Boxes of books? Is there something you want to tell us Bella?'

She looked up surprised and left the care of Henri to Louise as she realised she had to explain her crazy idea. 'The books to Monsieur Guillaume's room, Rosemary, thank you.' Bella ordered and did not say anything else until the Porter had loaded his trolley with the boxes as well as the luggage Louise had brought with her and taken it away. Bobbing another curtsy, Rosemary shut the door behind her and vanished, wondering, *am I ever going to actually knock on their door before it is opened first?*

Bella's Literary Idea

'I'm sorry Andre but I've taken a little liberty in your name. I sent Rosemary out to buy a couple of copies of your complete literary collection.' Bella laid her hand on Rene's arm and led him to one of the arm chairs.

'I'm flattered but that looks like more than just two copies of each book. I didn't think that drawing too much attention to this hotel was a good idea. A book signing is not a private activity.' Andre sat on the edge of the main bed as Bella sank into the other arm chair.

Taking a deep breath, she admitted, 'I do want you to sign all those books but they're not for the public. One set is for Rosemary's brothers; I must find out their names or we'll be forever calling them 'Rosemary's brothers'. It might also lessen their anger at your very obvious attraction to their sister and where your attraction must may lead you.' Andre had the grace to blush as ever since he had met Rosemary, his thoughts had been dwelling on what he would like to do with that pretty Maid.

'Touché!' His hand rose in a fencing gesture registering a hit.

'A second set for Monsieur and Madame Martin, who have been absolutely fantastic to us since the moment we arrived. One set for Louise and François for their assistance, and one set for when Henri is older.' As Bella concluded, Andre was doing the mathematics in his head.

'If those boxes are full, then there should be one more complete set. Would you like that fair cousin?' Andre reached over to gently flick his finger against her cheek.

'Most definitely! But to be honest I was keeping it in reserve just in case we need to bribe or reward anyone else.'

A delighted crack of laughter escaped from Andre. 'Oh Rene, if you don't marry this woman, I will! What a business woman you would make!'

Rene ran his hand along the arm of the chair until he located Bella's hand and entwined their fingers. 'Sorry Andre, take solace with your pretty Maid, as Bella has already made her choice.' Rene raised her hand to gently press his lips against her palm. Bella was pleased with his choice of words. *He isn't saying that I belong to him, but that he belongs to me.* She laid her free hand against Rene's cheek and kissed him passionately, rather surprising everyone in the room including Rene, not that he was going to stop her.

'Bella! Really! Not in front of your son!' admonished Louise, remembering to use her assumed name. As Henri hadn't even been interested in what the adults had been doing until Louise brought it to his attention, Andre laughed. Even so a highly flushed couple drew reluctantly apart. Henri only snorted in scorn.

'They're only kissing again. They're engaged now, they're allowed to do that! Not like what happened in the barn...' The boy yawned as the topic bored him.

Andre, though, leant forward, his eyes sparkling in curiosity. 'What happened in the barn Henri?' Bella had been rather sketchy about that in our discussion on the way to Paris.

Casting the Author a rather shrewd glance, Henri yawned again. The latest medicine has beginning to take effect. 'Nothing happened, I was asleep.' Deciding that was the end of the conversation, Henri turned over again and snuggled down with his hot water bottle. Louise tucked the blankets more securely around the child before moving away from the fireplace to check on her brother. François was awake and was listening to everything being said but was in too much pain to take part in the conversation.

Andre laid his hand on Rene's arm, 'When this is over, I want to know every little detail of this adventure. Even the naughty bits. Even if it can never be published.' For a moment Rene's imagination took him back to that very morning and the very stimulating bath that he had shared with Bella. He knew that Andre's eyes must be closely scrutinising his face as he blushed in pleasure of the memory. A sharp intake of breath by Andre was Rene's answer.

'Mon Dieu! You have been naughty children! Well I look forward to the full, unabridged story.' Andre released Rene's arm.

Watching her husband, Bella could just imagine where his thoughts had wandered and making certain that Louise wasn't watching, she leant forward to whisper into Rene's ear. His immediate, unrestrained laugh caused Andre's breath to catch in his chest as he tried to imagine what she had said to put such a sexy, irresistible smile upon Rene's face. Andre was about to ask for enlightenment when a knock came at the door.

More Than One Patient

Before Andre's eyes, the smile slid from Rene's face and his hand reached automatically for his pistol.

'Captain Du Bois, I have Doctor Girard with me.' Rosemary's voice on the other side of the door cause the tension to immediately leave Rene's body. Andre rose from the bed and opened the door. Rene's hand, though, still remained upon his pistol. Leading the Doctor into the room, Rosemary bobbed a curtsy.

'Doctor Girard this is Andre Guillaume,' she said. Andre bowed as the Doctor looked at him in surprise.

'The Author?' Doctor Girard asked.

Andre bowed again. 'I have that honour. I'm afraid we have one more patient for you to attend to Doctor.' He gestured to François on the double bed. 'Bella, I'm going to borrow this lovely young lady and discover for you the elusive names of her brothers and start signing all those books. I think we've found the recipient of your fifth set of books.' Andre's eyes travelled from Bella to Doctor Girard and back again.

Rising to her feet, she agreed but had a parting word of warning for the Author. 'Before you do anything, discover just how protective are Rosemary's brothers or better yet, how big are they.' Bowing elaborately to Bella, Andre took the puzzled Rosemary by the hand and led her out of the room, closing the door quietly behind them.

As Bella approached him, Doctor Girard opened his mouth to ask a question, but deciding it wasn't any of his business, opted to get down to the reason he was there.

'Well now, how is my youngest patient?' Placing his medical bag on the end of Henri's bed, Doctor Girard sat down beside the patient to take one of his hot, sweating hands into his own. Wheezing, Henri eyed the Doctor in dislike.

'I won't be poked and prodded!'

'Henri! That isn't very polite,' Bella said quietly as she knelt down beside his bed.

'That's all right, I don't need to do a full examination of Henri this time. How well is the current medicine working Madame Du Bois? Do I need to make it stronger?' Doctor Girard laid his hand upon Henri's forehead before checking his pulse against his fob watch.

'Oh no, he sleeps soundly for at least six hours, only waking once or twice close to the end of that time. The coughing isn't as drastic as it can be when he gets soaked through. The oil helps but not as well as what we have at home.' Bella brushed a wayward lock of hair out of Henri's eyes; her calming presence was enough to keep her son from misbehaving.

Slipping his watch back into his pocket, Doctor Girard sighed. 'Unfortunately I'm not as lucky as you to have a cousin in Australia to send me eucalyptus oil so I've made up an infusion of herbs in oil that may work just as well.' Out of his medicine bag, Doctor Girard handed Bella a bottle of oil and one of medicine.

'Finish the first bottle of medicine before starting on the next one,' he instructed, 'the second will make him sleep less heavily so you may be up to him a little more often.' Glancing around at Louise, the Doctor added, 'Don't refuse help if it is offered Madame Du Bois, if you run yourself into the ground it won't do the baby you're carrying any good.'

Louise bobbed a curtsy, 'I'll watch over Master Henri during the night so Madame Du Bois can sleep.'

'Good girl,' Doctor Girard rose from the bed and moving his medical bag to the table beside Rene, he disappeared into the ensuite to wash his hands.

Having felt the Doctor pass close to him, Rene removed his dark tinted glasses and the small pads that covered his eyes. *I'm nervous about the impending examination but hope that I am hiding it well.* Bella drew back the curtains to allow as much natural light into the room and placed a reassuring hand on Rene's shoulder. He was surprised that her fingers were actually trembling and reached up to lay his hand over hers.

'Well young man, let's see what we can do to give Madame Du Bois back her handsome husband.' Doctor Girard didn't speak again as he examined Rene's burns and the treatment Bella was giving him.

'Before you leave Paris, we should be able to determine whether you'll see again, Captain Du Bois. The odds are very much in your favour, but we must keep the burns sterile and covered when possible.' The Doctor supplied Bella with extra pads and bandages before placing fresh pads over Rene's eyes and allowing him to place the dark glasses on once more.

When Girard approached the double bed, Louise bobbed another curtsy. 'This is my brother François, Doctor.' She turned to assist a very stiff and sore François out of his night shirt. For the first time Bella saw the extent of the damage inflicted upon the young Frenchman and could not contain her gasp of horror.

As he carefully examined François, Doctor Girard agreed with Bella's revulsion. 'Yes Madame Du Bois, this fine specimen of manhood should never be treated with this much disrespect. I'm afraid it'll be several weeks before this young god is ready to dazzle anyone with his charms.'

A despairing groan was uttered by Rene. 'I really don't stand a chance keeping Bella if François is still god-like after a beating!' There followed a stunned silence and Rene silently cursed himself as he had not meant to have said that aloud. Bella caressed her hand against Rene's cheek.

'How many times do I have to tell you that as beautiful as François is, I still prefer my own god-like husband?' She pressed a reassuring kiss against his lips.

'François' injuries will fade, mine... mine might be permanent!' The pain in his voice ensured that Bella spoke gently to him as she urged him to his feet and asked him to help her up. The baby bump really was restricting her movement.

'Louise, pay close attention to the Doctor's instructions for looking after François. I need to borrow your room for a moment. Doctor Girard, thank you for your time and care,' Bella led a bemused Rene to the door. He managed to throw a command of his own over his shoulder as he was dragged form the room.

'Louise, there is another pistol somewhere in the room. Stand guard over our son.'

'Of course Captain.' They heard Louise's reassurance as the door closed behind them.

Disciplining Rene

Literally running into Rosemary, Rene reached out to steady the Maid.

'Sorry Rosemary, can you let us into Louise's room please?' Bella asked.

'Of course Madame Du Bois.' Rosemary didn't query why Bella was dragging her husband into another room but used her master key to open the door.

'Monsieur Guillaume is signing those books you bought but will join you for luncheon,' added the Maid.

Bella nodded. 'Good, just make sure that Doctor Girard is all right before he leaves. I'm afraid I need to discipline my husband.'

'Oh! Very well Madame.' Rosemary bobbed a hasty curtsy and retreated as Bella gave Rene a small push in the back and followed him into the room.

Closing and locking the door, Bella led him across the room before pushing him backwards so that he tumbled onto the bed.

'Bella…'

Ignoring his plea, Bella straddled his body and took possessive ownership of his mouth beneath her own. Her fingers undid his jacket and waist coat so that they could caress his torso through his shirt. When her exploring hand travelled lower and she drew a moan of pleasure from Rene, Bella finally released his lips.

'What do I have to do, to say, to make you realise I don't want any other man but you? Only you! Your lips, your hands all over my body. Only you inside of me, filling me, stretching me, pleasuring me. Only you teaching me the magic of that most intimate dance.' Bella undid the buttons of his breeches to draw out his penis, to stroke him to an erection.

'Only your seed filling me, creating your child... our child, completing us as a family. A handsome son like his father or a feisty daughter like her mother. All I want... all I will ever want is you!' She slid down Rene's responsive body to take his penis deep between her lips. He could not contain cry of pleasure as his erection filled her moist, warm mouth.

Words were beyond Rene for the moment, he could only cling to his sanity as Bella lavished her attention upon his throbbing flesh. It was hard, it was fast, and it was so damn hot! His brain was just catching up with his body when Bella's hand caressed his balls. As he exploded in ecstasy, Rene cried out, 'Bella!'

It was several minutes before Rene knew where he was and what had just happened. Bella had tidied him up and lay in his arms, her hand caressing lightly over his chest as he tried to catch his breath; when he was responsive enough to slide his arm around her waist, she spoke quietly.

'I can't imagine doing that with any other man, Caleb. I can't imagine a future with any other man. It looks like we both have trust issues.'

Slowly Rene expelled a breath of relief. 'I have only your word that I'm not a scarred, hideous monster.'

Sitting up, Bella shook her head. 'When the bandages come off permanently in couple of days, you'll be able to see for yourself that is far from the truth.' She did up the buttons of his waistcoat before hauling him into a sitting position.

'Such an optimist! Is the glass ever half empty in your world?' When his teasing words were met by silence, Rene realised he had put his foot in it again. 'Bella…'

She took one of his hands and held it between her own. 'When I saw you burst into flames, I… I thought that if God was going to take you away from me so soon, then I didn't want to live in a world without you.' Her voice was quite low and held more than a little tremble. Rene drew her into his arms and holding her tightly against his chest, he tenderly stroked her hair.

'I'm sorry Bella, it's easy to forget that I'm not the only one living in a nightmare.'

Raising her face Rene kissed her cheek, before finding her lips. Her hands slid up to encircle his neck but before they could really enjoy their kiss there was knock at the door.

Sighing Bella disentangled herself from her husband and rose to her feet.

'It's Rosemary, Madame Du Bois,' came from the other side of the door.

Rene quickly ran a hand down the front of his breeches to make certain that he was decent before sliding off the bed as Bella opened the door.

'Jacques is just bringing up your luncheon now. Doctor Girard said not to be too hard on the Captain, and he apologises if his comments made the Captain's doubts worse.' Rosemary was frowning as she tried to remember everything that various people had told her. 'Oh and Monsieur Guillaume said get over yourself, you lucky handsome young devil.' The Maid bobbed an embarrassed curtsy as Bella laughed. 'Sorry Sir,' she added.

Linking her arm through Rene's, Bella led him back to their room. 'Is that good enough for you, handsome young devil?'

Rene pulled them to a stop. 'When I get you alone Bella Du Bois…'

A chuckled answered him. 'Promises, promises my love. Come and have some lunch while you contemplate your revenge.'

A smile lingered on Rene's face as he allowed Bella to lead him into luncheon as he did indeed contemplate what he would do if he could get her alone.

Andre's Report

Not that was going to be any time soon. The smell of the adult's lunch had stirred up Henri's appetite. So after partaking of her own meal, Bella sat beside Henri and fed him a bowl of warm clear chicken soup. Andre and Rene assisted François to his room next door and made him comfortable in the bed. Louise was going to sleep now so that she could stay awake during the night to take care of Henri while Bella slept.

Aside from Andre's luggage, Phillippe had also sent over a couple of pistols and a spare sword. Andre made certain that one of the pistols was loaded before leaving it with Louise. *We are not going to let anything happen to François again,* Andre promised himself!

Back in Rene's room, he took the Author's hand and drew him down into the arm chair beside him.

'We need to talk,' Rene said quietly.

Glancing deep in thought at Henri, Andre said, 'Do you want to come to my room? I don't want to frighten Henri more than he already has been.'

Rene shook his head. 'No we need Bella if we're going to discuss other possible suspects.'

Looking up from settling Henri back against his pillows, Bella added, 'But first what information did you get from Rosemary?' Throwing a few more pieces of kindling onto the fire before joining the two men in the arm chairs, she would have sunk to the floor at Rene's feet but he drew her onto his lap. But she had to stand up again so that he could move his pistol to prevent her sitting on it.

'Hold onto your hats young lovers, as there is more to Rosemary's family than we first thought.' Andre leant back in his arm chair.

'Not uneducated peasants then?' drawled Rene.

Andre shot him a disgusted look which was pointless as Rene could not see it. 'It might be easier for me if they were! Papa Moreau is an export/import merchant. Rather successful one in fact. Eldest son Emile has become a partner in Papa's firm. Next son Isaac runs a warehouse that sells fabrics to the fashion houses of Paris and London and retail to those ladies forced to make their own clothes. Third son, Gilbert, is a rising politician; fourth son, Bruno, was a soldier until after Waterloo. He is working here as a Steward until he can determine what he wants to do now he has left the army. The youngest son, Theodore, is working his way up to management in a gentleman's club. Rosemary delicately suggested that Theo and François would get on well together.'

Rene let out a low whistle. 'Well that puts an end to any thoughts of dalliance with the pretty Rosemary. If it's more than lust Andre, it will have to be marriage.' There was a note of glee in his voice that was impossible to hide. Taking a deep breath Andre left unsaid the retort that readily rose to his lips.

'That will depend...' Andre reached over to take Bella's hand and raised it to his lips.

'On what?' Rene stretched out to take possession of her hand and drew it back onto her lap.

'If Bella has finally decided to take on a self-absorbed handsome young devil or if a slightly older less paranoid Author was to her taste.' *I know with that statement that I am skating on thin ice.*

'You do realise that I am currently armed Andre?' There was a hint of amusement in Rene's voice and yet underneath something harder.

'There are limits to even a besotted woman's patience dear boy,' Andre spoke flippantly.

'Well Bella?' Rene asked, 'Does the Author stand a chance?'

Her head tilted slightly to one side and a mischievous smile played across her face. 'Shall I describe to said Author what took place between us in the room next door?'

A deep flush raced across Rene's cheeks. 'Is that really necessary? I don't know if I want Andre to write down everything that we have done. What was said you can tell him but…'

Andre's eyebrows rose in excitement. 'Oh, now you've got to tell me!'

Giggling Bella rose from Rene's lap and leant forward on the arms of Andre's chair to whisper exactly what they had done in Louise's room. Andre dragged in a sudden intake of breath as lust flooded through his veins.

'Mon Dieu! Rene, I bow gracefully aside! Any woman prepared to do all that is beyond besotted.'

As Bella began to straighten up, Andre grasped hold of her undamaged wrist. 'Before I limp away with my tail between my legs, am I allowed a consolation prize?'

Bella glanced over her shoulder at Rene. 'Well Rene?'

He sighed, 'Really Andre you're starting to annoy me!'

Bella patted his cheek with her free hand, 'Don't shoot Andre, we can't afford to kill our friends.'

Immediately Andre released Bella's wrist, prepared to apologise for stepping over the line but he found for the first time in his life, that he was lost for words. As Bella caressed her hand across Rene's arm, the tension suddenly melted away from his body.

'One kiss,' he said, 'as your consolation prize.'

Andre could not believe his ears but he wasn't the only one to stare at Rene in surprise. Bella's eyebrows rose.

'You're not afraid that Andre could persuade me to change my mind with one kiss?'

A devilish smile appeared in answer, 'Not after what you said in Louise's room.'

Leaning on the arms of Andre's chair, Bella allowed him to cup her face with one hand as he drew her lips down to meet his. Certainly more experienced than her, and more skilful; Andre kissed very well. The moment Bella shyly responded, Andre sighed and raised his other hand to cup one of her breasts. That was a mistake as it made Bella immediately draw away from him.

'Sorry Andre only Rene is allowed to touch me like that,' she whispered, taking a step away from him and towards her husband.

Andre sighed wistfully. 'There's your answer then you handsome devil. She's all yours.'

Rene's searching hand reached out to find Bella's and drew her back onto his lap. 'As soon as we return to England we're going to be married. We'd like it if you, Phillippe, Louise and François could attend but we understand if it is difficult for you to leave France.' His offer surprised Andre.

'I'd be honoured to attend your wedding. I've no commitments at present. Naturally I cannot speak for the others.'

Entwining her fingers through Rene's, Bella said, 'There are a few minor details we need to deal with first. Getting Henri well again, and trying to not get killed. Little things like that!'

Andre's Alternative Scenarios

The two gentlemen grinned at her thinly veiled sarcasm.

'Which brings us to the topic I started in the carriage,' stated Andre, 'are you certain that Patrick and Sutherland are the only people you have to worry about?'

'You mean apart from an entire country full of French citizens?' drawled Rene.

Bella soothingly caressed her fingers against Rene's chest. 'Why Andre?'

He shrugged elegantly. 'If this was a novel I was writing...'

'But it isn't!' interrupted Rene.

Bella tapped him lightly on the nose. 'Behave my love, let Andre finish.'

'If this was a novel I was writing, my villain wouldn't be as obvious as Patrick. I'd also have thrown in a twist in the plot about now.'

'So you don't think that Patrick is the master mind behind our abduction?' asked Bella.

'I didn't say that.'

'But you do think someone else may be involved then,' she clarified.

Dropping his scepticism Rene stroked his beard. 'Patrick is so firmly in the frame as the bad guy that someone could have set him up to be the scapegoat if Nigel succeeded in killing us.' He wasn't completely convinced but Rene could see the possibility of Andre's theory. 'Who is next in line to be Earl if Henri and Patrick are out of the way?'

'Patrick has a younger brother, Edward. He's up at Oxford at the moment,' answered Bella.

Andre nodded. 'Then there's your step-mother's brother and mother. Could either of them have planned the second abduction to humiliate you?'

Thinking about Claude and Agnes, Bella shook her head. 'They'd never put Henri's life in jeopardy. There's no guarantee that the child Charlotte is carrying will be a boy.'

Leaning back in his chair, Andre steepled his fingers. 'What about you Rene, who is your successor?'

Without hesitation Rene said, 'My cousin Geoff.' A silence followed and Andre refused to break it. 'Hang on now! Geoff has told me that he never ever wanted to be in my place.' Rene rushed to defend his cousin. 'Patrick is still our most likely candidate.'

Bella, though, was no longer sure of that fact and frowning she tried to recall what they had overheard of Patrick's conversation with Nigel Sutherland and Captain Sheppard at the Inn in Hon Fleur.

'When I told Patrick that I had accepted your offer of marriage he warned me that someone wasn't what they seemed to be. That I should be careful who I trust. With Nigel, Patrick said, "I don't know what you were offered to kill them, just return them unharmed." That could suggest he wasn't the person who assisted Nigel to escape,' she suggested.

'So someone else may be involved,' accepted Rene. 'What do we do with that piece of information?'

'Not that I want to quote your cousin Patrick,' said Andre, 'but trust no one just yet.' A silence followed his words which Andre felt needed clarification. 'Phillippe, Louise, François and I have no ulterior motives if you do or do not live. Either way we gain nothing.'

A cheeky grin dimpled Bella's features. 'It's nice to know we don't have to question your loyalty, Andre. You have us questioning everyone else's!'

'Sorry about that.' Andre rose to his feet and straightened his jacket. 'Well I have two boxes of books to sign before this evening. Behave yourselves young lovers, we're not out of the woods just yet.'

Rene sighed. 'Being so cheerful keeps me going Andre!'

Chuckling, Bella laid her hand over Rene's. 'Before you disappear, André, you gave us additional suspects but you didn't get to your plot twist. Did you have anything particular in mind?'

Another sigh escaped from her beloved. 'Don't you think he's scared us enough for one afternoon? I thought the plot twist was Rosemary's family tree? Or was it the additional suspects?'

Andre scratched his head. 'The trouble is I'm not writing this story so I can't plan ahead any twists in the plot. I can give you a dozen scenarios but I don't know how probable they may be.'

'In any of these scenarios do we actually get home alive?' drawled Rene.

Reviewing the various scenarios took a couple of minutes. 'At least half of them.'

Bella felt Rene's body stiffen beneath her and jumped to her feet to hurry Andre towards the door. 'You'd better go before he punches you on the nose.'

A Pleasurable Cat Nap

Shutting and locking the door behind the departing Author, Bella bent down beside Henri's bed. She gave him his last dose of the original medicine which meant the boy should sleep until supper time. *I am pleased by how much soup Henri has drunk as well as the continuous glasses of drink he is consuming. It means a coughing fit every time he has to get up for the bathroom but it is a sure sign that he is improving.*

Tucking the blanket firmly around Henri, Bella slid around the bed and taking Rene's hand into her own, drew him to his feet.

'A cat nap is a good idea. It could be a rough night.' Sitting Rene on the edge of the bed, Bella assisted him out of his boots, his coat and waist coat.

'On one condition,' his hands surrounded Bella's waist and drew her closer.

'And what would that be?' Lacing her fingers together behind his head Bella placed an evocative kiss against his neck.

'Do I get my revenge for you calling me a handsome young devil?' His hands travelled up her torso to cup her breasts.

'Technically I was quoting Andre but you can have your revenge so long as we don't disturb Henri.' Bella's next kiss was against his willing lips.

'Draw the curtains and come to bed Bella.' Rene released her so that he could throw back the quilt as she did as he asked. With no regrets, she fell into Rene's arms on the bed, prepared for her punishment.

An Insurance Policy

As enjoyable as Rene's punishment actually was, when he finally drifted off to sleep Bella tenderly kissed his cheek before slipping out of his embrace. Trying to not disturb either of her boys, she sat down at the desk, a worried frown upon her face and carefully weighing up their options; Bella begun to write two letters. To two different people but basically the messages said the exact same thing.

Rene seems assured that Patrick is behind our abduction but after the discussion with Andre I am no longer confident that is indeed the case. I know that Rene and his cousin Geoff are close, perhaps as close as brothers but Andre had raised serious doubts in my mind about the people around us. It throws a different hue over whom I think I can trust with our lives. Thus these letters to Phillippe and Sir Malcolm White begging them to not reveal our whereabouts to anyone, except my father.

Rising to her feet to pull the bell for attendance, Bella slipped the letters into a pocket of her dress before checking that one of Rene's pistols had been replaced under Henri's pillow.

'Maman?' came a hoarse whisper. Bella moved around the bed so that Henri didn't have to turn to be able to see her.

'Yes baby?'

'You're worried about what Monsieur Andre said aren't you?' The boy started coughing and Bella sat down beside him to gently rub his chest.

'Yes baby. Don't you worry though, Papa will not let anyone, even if they are family, hurt us.' Calmly she soothed his fears, continuing to rub his chest until the coughing stopped.

'When we get home… can I have a puppy?'

Smiling Bella brushed the back of her hand against Henri's cheek. 'That'll be a nice companion for you but soon you'll have a new brother or sister to play with.'

Henri shook his head. 'I want to train the dog to bite anyone who tries to hurt me.'

'Oh I see.' Briefly Bella wondered, *how scarred is this abduction going to leave my fragile son?* 'So not a pug then?'

A giggle ended as a cough. 'Something a bit bigger Mama.'

'We'll talk it over with Papa when we get home.' She rose to her feet as there was a discreet knock at the door.

News From Phillippe

'It's Hugo, Madame Du Bois.' Bella verified the softly spoken statement through the peep hole in the door before opening up.

'Good afternoon Hugo,' she slipped out the door to talk to the Porter in the passageway so their conversation didn't disturb her boys. 'I've a couple of letters I'd like delivered as soon as possible.' Handing them over, Bella added a couple of coins.

'Of course Madame Du Bois. A letter from Phillippe Du Bois just arrived for you.' Hugo handed the letter to Bella before bowing and heading down the stairs again. Letting herself into the room she ensured the door was securely locked once more before she sat down at the desk. Slitting open the letter Bella couldn't contain her gasp as she scanned the message. The sound was loud enough to cause Rene to sit up.

'What is it? I thought I heard the door open.' He threw his legs over the side of the bed. With the letter in her hand, Bella moved across the room to sit down on the bed beside her husband.

'A note from Phillippe,' she explained, laying her hand over his. 'Not long after you left the wake, Nigel and Patrick forced their way into the Du Bois house.'

A smile touched Rene's lips. 'How did they fare? Phillippe's servants toss them out again?'

A giggle answered him. 'Actually, no. that must be a very elite guest list at the wake. According to Phillippe, they took great exception to the intrusion of two Englishmen to the solemn affair. They forced them back onto the street before they could even demand to know where we're hiding.'

Deep in thought, Rene stroked his chin. 'Yes it was an elite group. Andre told me there were politicians, Generals, Admirals and other high ranking military dignitaries. They wouldn't have taken kindly to an interruption of the funeral.' A moment later his hand tightened around hers.

'What is it?' The grip on her hand was actually painful.

'They are either absolutely stupid or incredibly brilliant!' Rene released her hand, much to her relief, before she had to ask him to. Glancing down at the letter in her hand, Bella gasped as she realised what Rene meant.

'They only had to wait for Phillippe to send a letter warning us that Patrick is in Paris and follow the messenger to discover our whereabouts. That is rather cunning.'

Rene reached across to lay his hand over the pistol on the bedside table. 'That also means that we're in even more immediate danger than before.'

144

'Except for one thing,' Bella re-read the letter, 'Phillippe said that he would send the messenger to four other hotels before coming to the Grand Duchess and three others after that. They'd have eight hotels to check out and not just ours.'

Rene's eyebrows rose in surprise. *I am actually impressed by Phillippe's clever idea.* 'We must never let our guard down now that Patrick has been sighted in Paris.'

Our Future Happiness

Laying the letter upon the bedside table, Bella wrapped her arms tightly around Rene's waist and pressed her cheek against his chest.

'Reality setting in elfling?' Rene encircled his arms around Bella and allowed her to draw him back down onto the bed.

'It's always felt real but with Henri sick we can't continue running. This time we'll have to stand and fight.'

Stroking his hand down her hair, Rene pressed a tender kiss against her forehead. 'No one is going to take away our future happiness. I'm so confident that I want you to go out tomorrow with Rosemary and Andre.'

Bella raised her head from his chest to look up at him in surprise. 'And what exactly are we going out to do? I thought we were supposed to be maintaining a low profile? Keep together? Until we leave Paris?' Bella kissed his cheek and when he turned his head, allowed her lips to linger against his.

'I've been thinking about our wedding,' Rene stole another kiss before he continued, 'we won't have time to arrange a wedding dress when we get home so I thought seeing that Rosemary's brother is the owner of a wholesale fabric warehouse, you could select some fabric for your future role as my wife.'

Allowing him another kiss Bella wasn't completely convinced. 'There isn't time to have a dress made from scratch before the wedding.'

Rene trailed another couple of kisses along her jaw and down her throat before he answered, 'That isn't why you're going to have Rosemary take you to one of the finest fashion houses here in Paris. I want our wedding to be one of the happiest days in our lives.'

Uttering a purr of pleasure, Bella laced her fingers through his hair as he continued to caress his lips along her shoulder.

'Only one of the happiest? I thought it is supposed to be the happiest day of our lives?'

He chuckled, 'It will only be one of the first of many.' Rene's nimble fingers undid the buttons at the front of her dress so that he could uncover more of her flesh to his sensual lips.

'Such as?' She was managing to hold onto her wits; just! His tantalising kisses and caressing hands were a very competent distraction.

'The first time we make love… when we make this a reality.' Rene caressed his hand across Bela's baby bump and his teasing lips continued to trail down her chest as he slowly uncovered more of her flesh. 'The birth of our first child,' he added, his tone low, mesmerising and evocative. 'Their first step, their first word, the first time we mount them on their own horse. The many, many, many nights of passion for the rest of our lives.' Rene's breath whispered across Bella's flesh causing her to shiver in desire.

Somehow she managed to add a note of regret to her voice. 'Oh? Only…?'

Pausing with his lips just hovering over one of her breasts, he asked, 'Only what my elfling?'

Bella giggled. 'Only nights?' She raised her hand to caress against his cheek as his laugh caused goose bumps to rise across her body.

'Oh my love, you're one very bad girl!' Rene's tongue flicked across her bare nipple.

Managing to retain a scrap of her sanity Bella laughed as she threw his own words back at him. 'When I'm bad, I'm very, very good!'

A wicked smile descended upon Rene's face. 'My beautiful elfling, I can hardly wait to discover just how wicked you can really be.' His lips traced hot, sizzling kisses across her bare breasts. Sighing in pleasure, Bella's body arched up into his caress as she thread her hand through his thick dark hair.

'If you keep doing what you're doing, you won't have long to wait!' Her other hand caressed lightly down his torso until Bella slid her fingers into the band of his trousers. The moan of pleasure that her teasing caress evoked from Rene was like music to her ears. As she curled her fingers around his growing erection and stroked lovingly along his length, Rene slid his hand languidly under Bella's dress to caress his fingers up her thigh as his lips suckled teasingly upon her nipples.

They were close, so very close to tearing the clothes from each other's bodies and giving into their carnal desires that Bella was already whispering his name, his real name in encouragement as their breathing quickened and their blood became overheated with lust.

A Slap Of Reality

They were so lost in the act of giving pleasure to each other that Bella actually cried out as a knock at the door made them jump startled. Rene cursed himself as he rolled off the bed, for allowing them to become distracted when they should have been on high alert. He seized his pistol from the bedside table as Bella struggled to put her clothes right again and moved cautiously across the room to the door.

'Who is it?' Bella asked, attempting to peer through the spy hole but it was suspiciously blacked out. She held her breath as she watched as the person on the other side of the door attempted to turn the door knob.

'Tony?' Bella bit down on her bottom lip to stop herself gasping aloud as she recognised her Cousin Patrick's voice.

'Non, non! No one here by that name!' Bella thickened her accent, hoping to disguise her voice. She could feel Rene pressed against her back, his pistol ready and she wished her heart would stop pounding in her ears. The door knob was tried once more but remained securely locked and on the catch. Taking her hand, Rene drew her behind him to protect her as he levelled his pistol at the door.

They didn't realise that they had both been holding their breath until they let it out slowly in relief as they heard footsteps move down the passageway. Bella felt her knees shake uncontrollably beneath her and was grateful for the supportive arm that Rene placed around her waist. He eased her onto the edge of the bed. They faintly heard a tattoo on Andre's door and the question, 'Tony?' Andre's answer was rather rude and very graphic, using words Bella was unfamiliar with. It caused Rene to chuckle but he refused to enlighten her with a translation.

Hugo, delivering medicine sent by Doctor Girard to François' room, upon hearing Andre's explosive language, grasped Patrick Stirling by the collar.

'Now then, Sir, we'll have to ask you to leave. Our guests do not like their privacy intruded upon in this manner!' Patrick wasn't given the opportunity to explain his actions as Hugo marched him rather forcefully out of the hotel.

A sob escaped from Bella before she could contain it. Sitting down onto the bed beside her, Rene slid his arm around her shoulders and tenderly kissed her forehead.

'It's all right. We won't let our guard down again. It's just that…' His words trailed into a deep sigh.

A hiccup of a laugh answered him as Bella lovingly caressed her fingers against his bearded cheek. 'It's just that once I am in your arms, nothing else exists,' she completed his sentence. Rene didn't deny it, nor did he resist as she kissed him but with regret he put a little distance between them.

'You are too tempting to my resolve to behave. Why don't you read to me for a while? Louise packed those novels into the carpet bag didn't she?' Laying his pistol back onto the table beside the bed, Rene stretched out once more upon the bed. Bella wasn't in the least insulted by the suggestion as she slid off the bed to locate the books placed in a neat pile in the wardrobe. Choosing one she came back to the bed and sitting propped up against her pillows she opened the book and began to read aloud "Sense and Sensibility".

Is He A Little Better?

Later Bella took a break to pour them a drink and check on Henri. Rene had been lying on his back, his hands folded across his chest as he listened to Bella read aloud. As she stretched her aching muscles before placing a glass of ginger ale on the bedside table closest to Rene, he sighed deeply.

'Bella, my love.' He sounded so serious that she was afraid that he was in pain.

'Yes Rene?'

Sitting up and holding out his hand for her to put the glass into it, he said, 'We'd better stick to the newspaper or even Henri's books. I don't think I can handle anyone else's drama at the moment.'

Laughing in relief that it wasn't something more serious, Bella kissed him before guiding his drink to his lips.

'I'm not sorry to stop. I wish the Dashwood sisters everything their hearts desire but I think there will be a lot more pain before they finally achieve it.' She moved away to sit down beside Henri to assist him to sit up and have a drink. As usual it meant a coughing fit but it seemed to Rene that these were less severe than before. *I am certainly no expert in childhood illnesses so I am not prepared to openly declare my hope that Henri is on the road to recovery.*

When Bella led Rene and his drink to the arm chair to sit opposite her, he asked if his hope was wrong. Taking a long drink of her ginger ale, Bella didn't immediately answer.

'He is better, certainly compared to yesterday. The trouble is a bout like this weakens his immunity. If we were to move him too soon or if he were to suffer a relapse, his… his constitution couldn't cope. Tomorrow or the next day Henri might be bouncing off the walls and going stir crazy but it would be even worse to have to move him then than right now.'

Reaching out to locate her hand, Rene admired that although she spoke softly to keep Henri from overhearing, there was no fear, no quivering in her voice. *It is a simple fact, no matter what this adventure is going to throw at us next, leaving before it is safe for Henri to do so just is not an option. This tigress is going to be the mother of my children and I know that they are going to be in very capable hands. My heart is so full of love and pride for this woman but now isn't the time to reveal all I feel.*

'We won't leave here until you and Doctor Girard are satisfied Henri is ready. No one will be allowed to jeopardise our son's life.' Sighing in relief, a lot of the tension left Bella's body as she returned the pressure of his fingers and leant forward to kiss her husband.

'You're going to make an excellent father.'

A nervous laugh escaped from Rene. 'Well if Henri doesn't mind if I practice with him until our own come along, I hope that may become true.'

Putting his glass down on the table, Rene eased Bella out of her chair and across to his lap. She took another sip of her drink before placing her glass down beside his. She picked up his hand and laid it over her baby bump.

'Do you think your Mama will mind if we start practicing as soon as we're married to make this real?' Bella sighed as Rene pressed his lips against the nape of her neck.

'She'll be delighted! My sister, Georgiana, already has two little ones so Mama is not afraid of becoming a grandmother.'

Bella leant back into his shoulder. 'I'd like Mary to come with me after we're married but I don't want to separate her from William.'

'Not a problem, my Butler is getting on in years. Mama has been suggesting an additional Footman to help him and possibly train him up to eventually take over once the Butler retires. So William can transfer with Mary if they both wish to leave the Manor when you do.' Rene linked his hands around Bella's waist, enjoying the normal discussion about everyday problems. *We could be any young married couple, discussing servant issues and the running of the estate.*

Henri's Declarations

A knock at the door broke the illusion as the sense of the danger that hung over them re-emerged. Bella slid off Rene's lap as his hand reached for his pistol.

'It's Andre with Bruno and our dinner,' came from the other side of the door. As they both relaxed, Bella went to open the door once Rene had nodded his approval. Andre followed Bruno into the room and Henri raised his head as the trolley of hot food wheeled past his bed.

'Maman.'

'Yes baby?' Bella moved around the single bed as she picked up a bowl of soup from the trolley. 'Is your appetite starting to come back?'

'Yes Mama.'

Placing the bowl onto the side table, Bella assisted Henri to sit up. 'Andre before you sit down can you butter one of the rolls for Henri please?' She sat down beside her son and started feeding him soup.

'Mama, I can feed myself!' Henri took the spoon out of Bella's hand but let her continue to hold the bowl. Bruno took the buttered roll from Andre and handed it to Bella on his way out of the room. She thanked him and Bruno shut the door behind him.

'Since you're being so obliging Andre,' said Rene, 'you can butter one for me too.'

Andre sighed, 'I think you might be over-working a poor underappreciated Author.' Even so he cut open another bun and lavished it with butter.

'Better than me cutting off my thumb if I tried to cut open a roll myself,' drawled Rene as he used his fingers to judge the edge of the plate so that he could try to navigate through his dinner without embarrassing himself.

'Oh yes, sorry. It's easy to forget with those glasses.' Andre blushed in embarrassment.

'Mama.'

'Yes Henri?' Bella broke the roll in half before offering it to her son.

'I think that now that there's a new baby on the way that you'll have to stop calling me baby.'

Placing the buttered roll into Rene's hand, Andre choked back a laugh. 'That's a logical point Bella.'

She smiled. 'Fair enough Little Bear. Am I still allowed to use that endearment?' She brushed the hair out of Henri's eyes.

A light filled the boy's eyes as he looked up at her. 'Even when we're old and grey you'll always be able to call me Little Bear.'

Going very still, Rene slowly lowered the bun he had been raising to his lips. 'Oh, I called you Little Bear last night. Is it… is it only Mama's pet name for you?'

Bella had to reply as Henri had his mouth full of bun. 'Answer impending Rene, as Henri has just taken a bite of roll.

'Sorry,' apologised Rene.

Bella smiled. 'I just didn't want you to be crushed by the lengthy silence as Henri tries to finish his mouthful; without him choking on it. Henri please chew, there's no need to hurry.'

Sitting down in the other arm chair, Andre had picked up his cutlery but was staring at Bella and Henri as if he had been hit over the head with a mallet.

'What is it Andre? What's wrong?' Bella was a little startled by the curious expression on the Author's face. It took a moment for Andre to pull himself together.

'In six years' time, I want to see this exact same picture. Your five year old son, another on the way, the perfect family; healthy, happy, content.

Clearing his throat, Rene's eyebrows rose. 'Exact same picture?' There was no disguising the sarcasm in his voice.

Andre laughed in embarrassment. 'All right! Not exactly! Rene won't be blind, Henri won't be sick and you won't be in a foreign country running for your life!' There was a significant silence and Andre sighed. 'I meant this idyllic family gathering. It's just so…' Bella giggled as Andre floundered.

'The wordsmith is lost for words Rene.'

A devilish smile descended onto Rene's face. 'Nice, my beautiful elfling! What do we need to do to make him a drooling idiot?'

Don't do it Rene, I can't handle any more patients at the moment.'

'Mama?' Henri had managed to finish his bun.

'Yes Henri?' They all returned their attention to the five year old.

'Can I answer Papa's question?'

'Of course,' Bella wiped a dab of butter off her son's chin. 'The floor's all yours.' Rene lowered his bun down onto his plate as he swallowed hard.

'When you called me Little Bear and joined in with our bear poem, it made me feel warm and fuzzy. It was as if we were really a family. That you and Bella were really my parents. The family that I've always wanted.'

Andre pressed his hand to his heart, moved by Henri's words. 'That is so poetic.'

Equally touched, Rene had to be realistic about the future. 'Thank you Henri, but you know we will have to return you to your real parents once we're home. I'm looking forward to becoming your big brother and probably for a while we'll remain very close to you until you're over the shock of this adventure.' *Even as the words came out of my mouth, I wonder if this is not the right time for a reality check for the young boy.* Henri surprised Rene by agreeing.

'I know, but I'll still be able to visit you won't I?'

Rene sighed in relief. 'Of course. Delacourt Hall will always be open to you whenever you wish to visit us or even stay for a little while.' When Henri didn't seem upset, Rene felt that perhaps he had managed to navigate safely through rocky waters. Andre's reassuring pat on his shoulder meant they could resume their dinner as Bella helped her son finish his soup before she joined the men to eat her own meal.

The Moreau Brothers

When Bruno arrived to clear the trolley, Rosemary had come up with her brother. Although Andre smiled up at the pretty Maid, he looked a little worried.

'Is it time to meet all your brothers?' He asked, as he rose to his feet and unconsciously straightened his jacket and cravat.

Rosemary smiled, 'Not quite, I thought I'd just check to make certain that you had everything you need before the boys arrive.' She indicated that Andre should precede her out of the room.

'Are you going to back me up?' Andre threw over his shoulder as his feet reluctantly led him to his fate.

Rene grinned. 'Surely you're big enough to handle a few admirers?'

A giggle escaped from Rosemary. 'They would like to meet you as well Captain Du Bois.'

'We can't leave Henri,' countered Rene.

As Rosemary opened the door, Louise appeared on the threshold, ready to take over looking after Henri for the night. Bella bit her bottom lip to contain her laugh but Andre did not refrain from gloating.

'No excuses now Rene! You can retire after you've been hospitable.' Andre refused to leave the room until Bella had dragged a reluctant Rene to his feet.

'Will you be all right Louise? We'll only be next door?' Bella linked her arm through her husband's as she led him to the door.

'I'm fine thank you. I'll lock the door as soon as you've left.' Louise bobbed a curtsy before she shut the door behind them.

Suppressing a sigh, Rene allowed himself to be dragged into the next room. As Bella seated him in one of the arm chairs, his restraint in being a martyr meant he was rewarded with a kiss. His hand reached out to latch onto Bella's wrist and drew her back for another kiss. A little more tender, a little more passionate and it may have developed further but Andre cleared his throat.

'Enough you naughty children, or someone will get a spanking.'

Reluctantly releasing Bella, Rene drew her onto his lap. 'Don't forget I am still armed, Andre!'

The Author laughed. 'I didn't say you were the one I was going to spank!'

Rene surprised them by laughing. 'You'd try the patience of a saint, Andre, but I do admire your courage.' A wicked smile twisted his lips. 'Tell me Rosemary, just how big are your brothers?'

Andre groaned and the Maid looked startled as she had been tidying up the room and not really paying attention to the others.

'Well Theodore is the shortest and lightest at six foot and 140 pounds. Are you considering Madame Martin's suggestion to hire my brothers as security guards?'

Rene's smile widened as he comfortably laid his hands upon Bella's baby bump. 'No, I can take care of my family, I just wanted to remind Andre that angering me might be the least of his problems.'

Glancing from Rene's smiling countenance to Andre's obvious embarrassment. Rosemary added, 'I don't understand what that has to do with my brothers' height and weight.'

Taking pity on Andre's plight, Bella put an end to Rene's torture. 'Rene feels that your brothers may take exception to Andre's admiration of you.'

Bella!' Both men protested at the same time. Although Rosemary blushed, she wasn't offended by Bella's frankness.

'Well they could be equally annoyed by my admiration of Monsieur Guillaume,' she said boldly.

Andre's jaw dropped and Bella raised a mocking eyebrow. 'A straight forward answer if you ask a straight forward question,' she said. 'What you do with that answer is up to you.'

A chuckle from Rene answered her. 'You know you're beautiful when you're being devious.'

Andre snorted. 'That's not hard, she's always beautiful!' He sat down in the high backed chair at the desk.

Sighing, Rosemary agreed. 'I know what you mean; Theodore received more than his fair share of beauty in our family.'

A laugh from the doorway caused Rene's hand to fly to his pistol but at the sight of Bruno and his brothers, Bella laid her hand over her husband's. 'It's all right Rene. Oh my...' She slid off his lap, hampered by her baby bump.

'What is it?' asked Rene, rising to his feet as five young men entered the room.

'They really are quite tall and good looking. Oh, you must be Theodore,' Bella said to the youngest Moreau. He bowed with an elegant flourish and Andre, although left speechless, had to agree. *I can easily see why Rosemary has delicately hinted that Theodore would get along very well with François. They were both young gods so perfect in looks that they appeared almost effeminate.* Straightening his jacket, Andre rose nervously to his feet.

'Monsieur Guillaume, may I present to you my brothers?' said Rosemary. 'Emile is Papa's right hand man in the import/export business, Isaac has a flourishing fabric warehouse, Gilbert is our budding politician; you've already made the acquaintance of Bruno and Theodore is working in an exclusive gentleman's club.'

Bowing, Andre said, 'Very pleased to meet all of you. It is a delight to meet avid readers who aren't going to criticise every single word I put on the page.' This wasn't the first time that Andre had made mention of critics and Rene wondered, *is Andre more wounded than he is prepared to admit by criticism?*

'We didn't believe it at first when Rosy said she had met the Andre Guillaume,' stated Emile, 'or that we were to be granted an audience.'

Slightly embarrassed by the eldest Moreau's formal praise, Andre blushed. 'May I introduce two young friends of mine? Captain Rene Du Bois and his wife Bella.'

The brothers bowed in greeting and as Rene and Bella responded in kind, Rene took her hand. 'A great pleasure gentlemen. Mr Isaac, I need to discuss with you later a little shopping expedition that I have in mind for my wife.'

'I am at Madame Du Bois' disposal,' offered Isaac.

'Thank you. We'll leave you for now as it's really Andre that you wish to speak with. Rosemary, are there enough chairs to go around?' asked Rene as he sidled towards the open door.

Rosemary bobbed a curtsy. 'Extra chairs are on their way along with refreshments, Captain, but don't feel that you and Madame Du Bois have to leave.'

Shaking his head, Rene would not be persuaded to stay. 'Thank you Rosemary but I think it may become a little crowded if we all remain. Besides which we should check on François and Henri.' Rene nodded in the direction of the five brothers.' Nice to have met you; hope we can see you again before we depart Paris.' The brothers replied something suitable but weren't sorry they were going to have the Author to themselves for a while.

Bella quietly chuckled as Rene led her back to their room. 'Andre is going to skin you alive for deserting him!'

He shook his head. 'He has Rosemary there for support.' He knocked on their own door and said, 'Louise, its Rene.' They heard the scrape of the chain being drawn back and the click as Louise unlocked the door.

'That was quick.' She stepped back to allow them to enter.

Bella pulled a face. 'Rene thought Andre needed some alone time with his readers. Do you want us to check on François before we settle down?' She halted Rene from crossing the room to one of the arm chairs until Louise had answered.

'No, he's actually a little better now that he's seen Doctor Girard and had some medicine.'

Satisfied Bella closed and locked the door before lowering Rene into a chair. She allowed him to draw her down onto his lap and they all settled unto a companionable silence.

Rene Enlists The Help Of Isaac Moreau

It was over two hours later that there was a knock at the door.

'Captain Du Bois? It's Rosemary.' All the hotel staff had quickly accepted that it was safer for their own health if they announced their presence. Bella rose with reluctance from Rene's lap and approached the door. She was a little surprised to find not just Rosemary but also her brothers Isaac and Theodore waiting outside.

'A delegation?' Bella enquired standing back to allow them to enter.

Rosemary giggled. 'Actually I thought Theo would like to meet François, if Louise feels he is up to visitors.'

Rising from her chair beside the fireplace, Louise cast a careful, scrutinizing glance over Theodore. She must have liked what she saw because she smiled. 'I don't see the harm; I'll come with you.' Louise bobbed a curtsy to Bella before leading Theodore out of the room once more.

'Please be seated Monsieur Moreau,' Bella offered as she shut the door.

'Thank you Madame Du Bois.' Once he was seated opposite Rene, Isaac added, 'how can I be of service to you Captain Du Bois?'

Reaching out his hand to secure Bella's wrist, Rene drew her back down onto his lap. 'I'm interested in sending Bella along with Rosemary to your establishment for a shopping spree.' Before she could protest about needlessly spending money on herself, he added, 'I thought it would also be a good opportunity for you to get some material for that girl in the village who makes dolls.'

A thoughtful look settled on Bella's face. 'Bridget? That is actually a good idea.'

'I do have them occasionally my elfling!' Rene drawled. 'Then Monsieur Moreau, I'd like you to recommend an excellent establishment where Bella can get a dress made for a very special occasion.'

Tilting his head slightly to one side, Isaac cast an appraising glance down Bella's figure but when he spoke it was to ask, 'Do you have a budget figure for me?'

'No restrictions,' Rene immediately answered.

'Rene!' Bella's protest only caused him to smile.

'It will need to be done in a very short period of time.' Rene added.

Isaac nodded as he stroked his chin. 'Do you mind if we keep this a family affair?'

Puzzled Rene agreed. 'Not at all. Do you have a relative in the trade?'

A gasp came from Rosemary. 'Oh! Are you thinking of Cousin Susanna?' When her brother nodded, she added to Bella, 'having worked for ten years with Madame George's boutique, Susanna has just opened her own establishment. She does excellent work.'

'Wonderful!' Rene caressed his hand along Bella's arm. 'You'll understand I hope that I want Bella to be accompanied by Rosemary and Andre at all times.'

Isaac nodded. 'Rosy told us Madame Du Bois is having trouble with a cousin. We'll look after her as if she is our own sister.'

Both of Bella's eyebrows rose in surprise. *Such loyalty and consideration for total strangers is unusual. I wonder what on earth Rosemary has told her family about us and how will they react if they ever discover our masquerade?* A shiver of fear swept over Bella and Rene tightened his arms around her.

'What is it?' Trying to shrug off the coldness that had suddenly descended over her, she pulled herself together.

'It's all right my love. Someone just walked over my grave. That is all.' The imagery that was conjured up for Rene caused the blood to drain out of his face. 'It's just a saying.' Bella hastened to reassure him as she wondered if he were about to collapse in shock.

Swallowing hard he managed to answer, 'A little too close to reality for comfort. Be a good girl and fetch me a drink please.'

Immediately slipping off his lap, Bella went across to the table beside Henri's bed and poured a glass of peppermint tea. Placing it into Rene's hand, she guided it to his lips. Slowly the colour returned to his cheeks and he lowered the glass towards the table beside him.

Rising to take his departure, Isaac was momentarily startled as Louise made the mistake of entering the room without announcing herself and shrieked as Rene's pistol had risen at the sound of the door opening. Bella laid her hand upon Rene's shoulder and gently massaged his tense muscles.

'It's all right Rene, Louise just forgot to call out before she returned.' Slowly she caressed her hand along his arm to encourage him to lower his weapon.

'Sorry Louise,' there was a slight tremor of poorly concealed emotion in Rene's voice.

Louise lowered the hand that she had raised to press against her racing heart. 'No Captain Du Bois, it's my fault. I was still thinking what an attractive pair those two boys make.'

As she linked her arm through those of her brothers, Rosemary smiled. 'I thought they might have a lot in common.' She paused at the door to glance back at Bella. 'We'll be ready whenever you wish to go shopping Madame Du Bois.'

'Thank you Rosemary, good night.' Bella nodded to Louise to close the door behind the siblings.

You Naughty Children!

Bella knelt down in front of Rene and cupped his face between her hands. 'My love, what can I do to help you?' Tenderly she placed a kiss on his lips.

His arms wrapped around her waist and drew her into another kiss. 'Don't make offers you can't deliver... at least not yet anyway.' Rene eased Bella off the floor and onto his lap. 'Oh my beautiful elfling... I want you naked and beneath me... I want to hear you scream my name in ecstasy.' His husky voice whispered against her ear.

There was an underlying need, beyond the sexual, that caused his mouth to seek Bella's in a sense of urgency. She submitted willingly, eagerly, to the desperate need in his kiss. Louise tolerated their kissing but when Bella slid her hand inside Rene's waistcoat to caress his chest, Louise brought the love making to an end.

'That is not going to happen, belle enfants!' Louise drew Bella up from Rene's lap and eased her into the opposite chair. He uttered a deep sigh.

'Can we at least still get naked?' He managed to immediately conceal a mischievous grin but Nanny had sharp eyes.

'No Captain! You must be clothed at all times!' Louise fell easily into the role of authoritarian.

This time Rene had less success in hiding his smile. 'Even in the bath?' He heard Bella's gasp and could easily imagine her flush as she couldn't help but recall their naughty behaviour in the tub that morning. Louise cast a shrewd glance between the two of them.

'It looks like I'm going to have to chaperone you naughty children more closely! Would your Papa approve of what you've been up to? Louise glanced behind her to make certain that Henri wasn't paying attention.

Rene grinned. 'If we give him grandchildren I don't think he'll have any reason to complain.'

'Rene!' protested Bella. 'Honestly Louise, we haven't done anything to be ashamed of.'

'Yet!' Rene wasn't helping to satisfy Louise's concerns but it was too much fun winding Bella up.

Laying her hand upon his shoulder, Louise said, 'One more word Captain and you'll be sleeping in the room next door with François.'

All the teasing immediately deserted Rene. 'I'm not leaving my family unprotected.' There was a mulish set to his jaw that reassured Louise that there was one thing Rene was deadly serious about. Exhaling slowly Louise patted his cheek.

'Good boy! Focus on your mission and when you're safe and married you may be as naughty as you desire and create beautiful babies.'

Rene laughed. 'Thank you Nanny.'

'Now if you can be trusted to behave yourselves for five minutes, I'll just check upon François before I help you get ready for bed.' Louise headed towards the door but, holding it open, awaited Rene's answer.

'We are capable of undressing ourselves Nanny.'

Louise was quick to retort, 'And too capable of undressing each other!

Bella sighed. 'Don't you trust us Nanny?' Her voice was filled with such innocence that Rene couldn't help grinning as she reached across to lay her hand over his.

'No I don't! Once upon a time, not that long ago, you were more a boy than a girl but with this young man you are neither… you're a woman! The trouble is that no one has prepared you for what that will involve!'

Upon the older woman's words, Bella's voice became almost childlike. 'We haven't done anything that either of us have to regret or raise censorship. Rene is a true gentleman, he hasn't compromised my virtue.'

'I intend to keep it that way my Lady!' Louise didn't wait for an answer but closed the door behind her.

What Is Worrying You?

Uttering a deep sigh Rene raised Bella's hand to his lips. 'I don't think Nanny trusts us.' Tenderly he placed a kiss against her wrist causing her heart to skip a beat.

'I don't blame her, my love. It would be so easy to be very, very naughty with you.' With an incredible show of will power Bella drew her hand from his and placed it under his elbow. 'Why don't you get ready for bed while I check on Henri?'

Another sigh answered her, 'Fighting shy my love?'

Bella allowed him one tender kiss as she helped him to his feet. 'No fighting safe! You're just too irresistible!'

Claiming one more kiss, Rene resolvedly put her at arm's length. 'You're afraid of Nanny.'

She shook her head. 'No I'm afraid that in her anger she could unintentionally betray us.'

'Yes, I heard the "my Lady" jibe as Louise departed. We'll all have to be careful about what we say or do over the next few days.'

Bella had been moving around the single bed but paused as his words brought back to her why she had shivered in fear. 'The Moreau family are good people...' *I'm not certain how to complete that sentence or whether I should even reveal my fear to him. He has enough to worry about and I don't want to needlessly burden him with problems that haven't arisen yet.* Stretching his muscles, Rene silently considered her words, or more accurately what she wasn't saying.

'If you feel it necessary, I think it would be safe to reveal the truth to Rosemary and the Martins. I get the feeling that they wouldn't betray us.' Rene stated.

Glancing down at Henri to see if he was listening, Bella replied, 'That has me puzzled. Are we going to slip up assuming we can trust people not to hunt us down? Or have we been extremely lucky to have met really decent people? Or is our luck running out?'

Stripping out of his jacket and waistcoat, Rene threw them onto the end of the double bed. 'Are you worried about this shopping expedition with Rosemary tomorrow?'

'Shopping for material is fine but trying on dresses… if Andre is forced to protect me, it will betray him as being compliant with our masquerade.' Bella sank down onto the bed beside her young son to administer his next dose of medicine.

Rene paused in undoing his cravat. 'I hadn't thought of that. Go ahead with the fabric shopping but discuss the dress idea with Andre as it is his neck on the line.' He sighed before adding, 'I just had a vision of you on our wedding day in a stunning new dress rather than a hand me down from your step-mother.'

Tucking Henri's bedding more firmly around him, Bella rose to her feet and approached Rene as he slipped out of his shirt. Tenderly caressing her fingers down his muscular chest, she sighed. 'Remind me to ask Louise if she brought us any additional clothing.' She permitted Rene one slow tender kiss before she eased him down onto the bed to remove his footwear.

Bella had just undone the gun holster on Rene's hips when Louise announced her return. She had a bundle of male and female attire in her arms which answered Bella's previous concern over fresh clothes. Louise paused to study their actions but was satisfied that they weren't doing anything untoward. Ignoring them as Bella drew down Rene's trousers before throwing a nightshirt over his head, Louise shook out and hung the additional attire. Rene placed his pistols on the bedside table as Bella turned down the sheet. While Louise assisted Bella out of her dress and padding and into a night gown, Rene located the medical bag and placed it on the bed beside him. With his burns anointed and bandaged once more, he made no protest as Louise efficiently tucked them up into bed. Bella curled into his arms and Louise snuffed out all the candles before adding a few more pieces of kindling onto the fire as she settled down on the chair beside Henri's bed.

MONDAY
An Early Morning Intruder

Apart from the occasional coughing from Henri, it was a fairly quiet night. A soft knocking woke Bella but as she raised herself onto an elbow, she frowned in confusion as it hadn't sounded like a knock on the door. Rising out of her chair, Louise quietly crossed the room to bend down beside Bella.

'That's François. I'll just go and help him. The bottle of medicine Doctor Girard gave him is difficult for him to open with one damaged hand.'

Bella slid out of the bed and accepted the shawl that Louise draped around her shoulders. 'Take our room key and lock the door from the outside. You can let yourself back in when you've finished with François. Has Henri had his next dose of medicine?' Picking up the room key from the bedside table, Bella pressed it into Louse's hand but paused to put on her baby bump once more.

'No, I was just about to give it to him.'

Bella urged her towards the door. 'I'll tend to my patient while you tend to yours.' Preparing the boy's medicine, Bella unconsciously waited until she heard the key turn in the lock as Louise departed before sitting down on the edge of Henri's bed.

His coughing has increased the closer we approached the next dose of medicine so I'm not completely surprised that Henri is actually awake. Well awake enough for him to protest that the medicine I tipped down his throat is yucky but not awake enough to make giving him the dose too difficult. Bella allowed him a sip of peppermint tea to wash away the taste of the medicine. As she caressed her hand against his chest and he fell back to sleep, she heard a key clumsily enter the lock of their door. The only thought that entered her head was that perhaps there wasn't a great deal of light in the passageway. When she heard the lock click open and the door knob turn the hairs on the back of her neck began to rise as there was no whispered words announcing Louise's return.

Fighting a rising panic, Bella slid her hand under Henri's pillow for Rene's second pistol and moved out of the faint glow emitted from the fireplace. 'Rene?' She barely breathed the word but was answered briefly.

'Shh Bella!'

It could simply be that Louise, thinking that they were both asleep, didn't want to disturb them. Bella tried to listen to every foreign sound as the door slowly began to open but her heart was pounding so loudly that she could barely hear anything else. Her fingers tightened around the handle of the pistol as she raised her arm. She tried to use the dim light from the fire to watch a figure quietly close the door behind them as they entered. There was no gentle swoosh, swoosh of a woman's dress as this figure moved surreptitiously towards the double bed.

Bella dug her finger nails of her free hand into her palm to contain her fear, her wish to scream at this intruder, to tackle him before he reached Rene. *I need to stay where I am, protected by the darkness but more importantly stand protectively over my son.* Neither Bella nor the intruder had seen or heard Rene slip noiselessly out of their bed; to him the darkness of the room was not a hamper to his movements. By focussing on the intruder's breathing, Rene easily located him before he could reach the bed.

Calmly Rene pressed the muzzle of his pistol against the intruder's head. 'Move and I will kill you!' It had become second nature to speak only in French so although his voice, so close to the intruder, had startled him, he didn't understand what Rene had said. An oath, in English, was uttered by the intruder as he made a grab for Rene and the pistol was knocked out of his hand. As the two men wrestled in the dark, the intruder tried to punch Rene in the face but missing, struck a blow to his still healing shoulder. Fighting blacking out, Rene swore in French.

Even though Bella didn't understand what he said, it reminded her of Andre. For some unfathomable reason that made her laugh. Making sure that she spoke only in French Bella ordered, 'Drop to the floor Rene!' She gave him 30 seconds to obey and taking a deep breath, Bella steadied her shaking arm and shot at the figure who she could dimly see had turned at the sound of her voice.

An oath in English told Bella that she had struck someone and she prayed that Rene had done as she had told him and wasn't the one injured. In fact as the intruder took a step towards her, Rene's hand fell upon his pistol on the floor. Andre, having been woken by the gun shot, threw open the door as Rene rose to his feet and used his hearing to triangulate the intruder's whereabouts as he raised his pistol to halt the bleeding man's path toward Bella and Henri.

'Touch my wife and I will blow your head off!' This time Rene remembered to speak in English, stopping the intruder in his tracks. Andre had raised his own pistol and the intruder glancing from Rene to Andre, decided to push passed Andre as he ran out of the room. The Author made an attempt to grab the intruder but was thrown off balance and ended up on his backside on the ground.

François and Louise had rushed out of their own room at the sound of the gun shot and Louise bent down to assist Andre off the ground. François paused in the doorway as Rene's pistol was trained upon him.

'Captain Du Bois, it's François, the intruder has fled the hotel.' He stepped warily into the room as Rene slowly lowered his weapon. François slid the pistol out of Bella's hand and encouraged her shaking frame towards one of the arm chairs.

'Louise, Bella's in shock, she could do with something to drink. I don't think she's ever shot another human before.' François instructed his sister, who went over to the table beside Henri's bed and poured a glass of ginger ale before placing it into Bella's shaking hands.

François lit a few candles around the room as Rene sank onto the edge of Henri's bed and opened his arms to comfort the frightened boy. Andre bent down to examine the pool of blood on the floor just as the Night Porter staggered into the room, clutching his arm and covered in blood.

Rene's pistol rose defensively towards the door but Andre hastily reassured him as he rushed forward to support the wounded Porter to the other arm chair

'I'm Stephen,' gasped the Night Porter, 'I tried to grab the man fleeing after we heard the gunshot but he stuck his knife into me.'

Louise stopped Andre from removing the blade from the Porter's arm. 'Leave it in until a Doctor has seen him.'

'Alain, the Night Clerk, has sent for a Doctor, I'm supposed to check that no one else has been wounded.' Stephen accepted the drink that Louise poured for him and gulped it down, wishing it was something a little stronger to dull the pain.

Glancing back at the blood on the floor, Andre said, 'Well it looks like Bella wounded the intruder but I don't think anyone else was injured. Rene, did he manage to hurt you?'

With his arms still around Henri, Rene grimaced. 'He struck my injured shoulder. Another bruise to add to the collection but I'll live. I must say, my love, that was a fine shot but how did you know in the dark that you were firing at the right man?' Rene took the glass Louise placed into his hand and assisted Henri to drink before using the sleeve of his own night shirt to dry the boy's tears.

Wearily Bella shrugged her shoulders. 'I hoped that you would do as I told you and that the intruder wouldn't understand me and follow suit.'

So Who Was It?

There was a question burning on Andre's tongue and he was rather impatient to get answers. 'Well? Was that Cousin Patrick?'

Bella, laying her empty glass down onto the table beside her, shook her head. 'I don't know. All I saw was a silhouette. It certainly wasn't big enough to have been Sutherland.'

As he laid Henri back down, Rene absently massaged his damaged shoulder. 'I don't think it was Patrick, the intruder was certainly much shorter than me. Was there enough light Andre for you or Stephen to be able to describe the attacker? Bella, what is Patrick's fluency in French?'

'Limited school boy French. Certainly enough to have understood what either of us had said,' replied Bella.

Stephen agreed, a little pale around the gills due to the loss of blood but Louise used some of Rene's dressings to stop the bleeding. 'He certainly didn't understand when I told him to stop. The fleeting impression I got was a dark little weasel.' Stephen was a strapping young man well over six foot.

Bella stiffened and shot a warning glance across at François who had gasped in recognition of that description.

'Not Patrick then,' Bella said quietly, 'He isn't short or dark. It looks like you may have been right about someone else being involved in all of this, Andre. That description perfectly describes my… step-uncle Claude.'

Having taken to pacing the room, Andre absently stroked his chin, deep in thought. 'Is Henri in danger from Uncle Claude or does he just want the two of you dead? Or does Uncle Claude want to marry you too?' His sarcasm brought a blush to Bella's cheeks and her reluctance to answer him caused Andre to stop pacing and look at her quizzically. 'Really? Does anyone not want to marry you Bella?'

A harsh laugh escaped from Rene. 'Et tu, Andre?'

The novelist had the grace to stutter in embarrassment. 'S…so can Uncle Claude speak French?'

Bella giggled. 'Nice save Andre! No Claude is barely able to speak English let alone another language!' The unusual venom in Bella's voice caused Andre to look at her in surprise.

'Put your claws away tigress! That was a little sharp, even if he is a moron.'

She shook her head. 'He just tried to kill my husband and perhaps intended to murder us all! When the ones I love are under threat, I attack!' Noticing the way her eyes blazed in anger, Andre didn't push the issue but turned as a hastily dressed Doctor Girard appeared in the doorway.

More Patients For The Doctor

Faced with Rene's raised weapon the Doctor halted on the threshold until Bella's calm reassurance meant that the pistol was lowered again.

'What has been going on? I feared Henri had relapsed but the Night Clerk, Alain said that a shot had been fired and someone hurt in a knife fight.' Scanning the room, which was rather full of people, the Doctor's eyes settled upon Stephen and the blade still stuck in his arm.

'Bella shot an intruder and when Stephen tried to stop the wounded intruder fleeing the hotel he ended up being stabbed,' explained Rene, so calmly that Doctor Girard wondered what it would take to shake his equilibrium.

Undoing the makeshift bandages around the knife, he said, 'I saw Marcelle downstairs cleaning up the trail of blood, I assume she'll be up soon to stop the blood ruining the carpet.

She won't be able to announce her presence to you Captain, so please don't frighten her by pointing your pistol at her.'

Stephen gritted his teeth as the Doctor cut off the sleeve of his shirt and jacket.

'Marcelle can't speak,' Stephen explained, 'Robespierre's soldiers cut out her tongue when she refused to tell them if her master and mistress were hiding somewhere in the house, or had already escaped to England.'

'That's horrible!' Bella exclaimed. 'But… I would never have left my servants behind. I shouldn't judge as I wasn't even born then so I don't know what it was like during the Reign of Terror.' *Even so, I can't imagine leaving my beloved Mary or Louise behind.*

Marcelle

Noticing Rene's hand unconsciously twitch towards his weapon, Andre glanced up at the open doorway. He bit back the gasp that rose to his throat as he looked at a woman, well past her prime, who in her youth would have been quite pretty, but life had been unkind and unfair to Marcelle. Her hair, once golden curls, was now just grey and pulled back into a severe bun. She walked with a permanent limp and her long-sleeved, high-necked dress managed to cover most of her scars, but there was no hiding the scars of slashed flesh upon her face. Obviously cutting out her tongue had been only one of the tortures Robespierre's men had inflicted upon this woman.

As everyone else seemed bereft of speech and Rene's hand still hovered over his pistol, Bella cleared her throat. 'Marcelle?' The woman nodded in acknowledgement but didn't enter the room until Bella addressed her husband.

'It's all right Rene.'

When he removed his hand from his weapon, Marcelle carried her bucket of water and sponge across to the pool of blood beside the double bed. As Marcelle dropped awkwardly to her knees, Bella instinctively rose from her chair. *It seems wrong that this poor, misused woman should be scrubbing floors.* As Bella was about to offer her assistance, Doctor Girard firmly grasped hold of her arm.

'Don't Madame Du Bois, you'll inadvertently insult a very proud woman. Come and take Stephen's other hand as it's going to hurt as I pull out this knife.' The Doctor drew Bella back down into her chair and she automatically took Stephen's hand as ordered.

Andre placed one hand on Stephen's shoulder, the other on his wrist to hold him still so he didn't jerk as the blade was withdrawn and cause further damage. Dragging in several deep breaths, Stephen looked away, not wanting to watch what was going to happen next. Doctor Girard's movements were slow and steady as he determined how much internal damage had been done. *The blade isn't an overly large weapon. It has certainly not penetrated the whole way through Stephen's arm but it is razor sharp. It has miraculously missed the bone so damage is minimal.* As Stephen's face became quite grey, Doctor Girard cleansed, padded and bound the wound. *I won't close the wound until I can be certain that the muscle has not been affected.* Both Bella and Andre were relieved when they could relinquish their hold on Stephen and Louise cleaned away the blood-soaked clothes and dressings.

'Now then,' the Doctor came back from the ensuite where he had washed his hands. 'I suggest you try and get some sleep. Monsieur Guillaume if I could trouble you to assist me helping Stephen downstairs.' Retrieving a small flask from his medical bag, he tipped a nip of neat spirits down Stephen's throat. A little colour returned to his features and with Andre's assistance, he managed to get to his feet.

Shock Sets In.

As the Doctor followed Andre and Stephen out of the room, Louise bent down to press a kiss against Bella's cheek as she and François prepared to also leave.

'We'll reload your pistol in the morning,' said François. 'Your intruder won't dare return until he has had his own wound seen to.'

Shaking her head, Bella pulled herself together. 'I still have the pistols I took from Sutherland, but I agree we're safe enough for now. They'll have to rethink their strategy of attack.'

Louise chuckled as she patted Rene lightly on the shoulder as she passed him. 'No one can match the Captain if they attack in the dark. I'll just see François settled before I return to sit with Henri. I will naturally announce my return.'

'Leave the door open Louise, I'm sure Andre will have something to say before he retires to his room.' Rene rose from Henri's bed but hesitated in taking a step. 'I don't want to accidently tread on Mademoiselle Marcelle.'

Bella reached out to take his outstretched hands and guided him to the arm chair recently occupied by Stephen.

'Bella?' Rene could feel her fingers trembling in his hold.

She uttered an unsteady laugh. 'I know Louise will be cross but will you hold me?' As he squeezed her fingers reassuringly, she was already rising out of her chair and onto his lap. His arms surrounded her as she pressed her cheek against his chest. Bella didn't burst into tears but a fine tremble existed throughout her whole body.

Although a teasing quip quivered on Andre's lips as he paused on the threshold of the room, it remained unsaid as he could easily see that Bella was shaking, not in desire but fear.

'Rene, its Andre. Is there anything I can do before I go back to bed?'

Caressing one hand slowly down Bella's hair, Rene shook his head. 'No, thank you. Sorry we must have disturbed the whole hotel.'

Andre stroked his chin. 'I suppose that's why the intruder had a knife rather than a pistol.' As a shudder of horror ran through Bella, Andre quickly changed the subject.

'Try to not dwell upon it my dear. You will get home safely, no matter what they throw at us.' Andre was about to leave them when Rene spoke again.

'Just give Marcelle a hand up before you leave, Andre.'

Doing as he was instructed, Andre was surprised by just how acute Rene's hearing had become. Rene had heard Marcelle struggling to get to her feet, whereas Andre seeing her, had not really seen her. Uncurling herself from Rene's lap, Bella drew a note of francs from her purse before approaching the older woman. Taking one of Marcelle's hands, Bella looked deep into her eyes as she pressed the money into her hand.

'Thank you Marcelle.' Bella said nothing else and a ghost of a smile appeared on Marcelle's scarred face as she reached up to tenderly pat Bella's cheek.

This Is My Fault

Andre waited until Marcelle had left the room before quietly closing the door behind him. Seeing Louise hurrying towards him, Andre's frown suddenly lifted.

'François settled back into his bed?'

This polite enquiry caused Louise to sigh. 'This is all my fault isn't it? If I hadn't left the room to help my brother, that… that man would never have got so close to those precious enfants.'

Andre grasped her firmly by the shoulders, not certain if he should hug Louise or slap her. He decided on a comforting bear hug. 'You locked the door Louise. These people don't care what they have to do or who they have to hurt to get what they want.'

Slightly muffled as her face was pressed into Andre's shoulder, Louise said, 'But the door would have been locked and the security latch across if I had still been in the room.'

'And Rene and Bella would have been fast asleep and unprepared for an attack. Look at this.' Andre released Louise and turned her to look at the outside of the door. 'See these long scratches corresponding to where the catch is located on the inside of the door?'

Raising her hand to touch the fresh scratches, Louise raised questioning eyes to the Author. 'I don't remember seeing these before. What caused them?'

Andre took hold of both her hands between his. 'If I was to hazard a guess. I'd say a very powerful magnet was used to move the catch to gain entry.'

'Oh!' Louise gasped in horror. 'Then my babies aren't safe at all!'

Soothingly Andre patted her hands. 'They still have to get past Rene. Don't beat yourself up over this Louise. Perhaps if Bella does have a spare pistol, you should keep it close to you at night.'

Breathing a sigh of relief, Louise nodded. 'Yes sir, thank you.' Putting aside any feelings of guilt, Louise opened the door, announcing herself, as Andre returned to his own room to attempt to get a few more hours sleep.

Automatically Louise locked and put the catch across the door but with Andre's revelations still ringing in her ears she shuddered in fear. Bella had retrieved Sutherland's pistols from the drawer of her bedside table and paused as she placed one of the pair under Henri's pillow to look up at Louise.

'François is probably right, they won't try anything else tonight.'

Moving swiftly across the room, Louise wrapped her arms around Bella. 'My brave darling! For so long more a boy than a girl! And now…' Louise released her to wrap a hand over Bella's baby bump. 'I want to see this become a reality.'

Laughing at Louise's earnest expression, Bella kissed the older woman's cheek. 'It will happen, Nanny. Just…' She fondly recalled Mary's words when they had been experimenting in his room at Stirling Manor. 'Just not tonight.'

Louise tucked both Bella and, to his embarrassment, Rene into bed before extinguishing all the candles and returning to her chair beside Henri's bed and the fireplace. Curling up in Rene's arms, Bella wondered, *will we be able to fall asleep again?* As the adrenalin rush left their bodies, exhaustion swept them into slumber.

Rosemary's Doubts

Later that morning when Juliette Martin heard about the early hour attack, she made certain that the Du Bois entourage were allowed to sleep in with a later breakfast. Then she insisted upon being present when Doctor Girard returned to check Stephen's arm. Madame Martin then sent Stephen home to rest for a couple of days before Rosemary sought out her counsel.

The previous evening, Rosemary had informed Juliette of the proposed shopping expedition but now, with the recent attempt on their lives, the Maid was in doubt that it was such a wise idea. Contemplating the question as they sat in Juliette's office, the older woman poured tea for both of them.

'I think the Captain is right,' Juliette finally admitted, 'precautions naturally will have to be taken but now that Henri is a little better and Louise is there to nurse him, a shopping trip will be therapeutic for Bella.'

Taking a sip of her tea, Rosemary saw what her boss meant. 'It's been rather intense with the Senator's funeral, the Captain's injuries and now attack from the family, they need some… joy… distraction to release those on the edge nerves.'

Juliette smiled. 'Exactly. Monsieur Guillaume will be armed of course and your brother Isaac will ensure that you're safe in his establishment.'

'I was wondering,' Rosemary placed her cup down on the table before continuing, 'if you would like to join us?'

Juliette chuckled. 'Don't tempt me, my dear, but I do have a shopping list that you might be able to fill while you're there.' Handing over quite an extensive list, Juliette blushed. 'It's not all for me, word spread through the hotel about your planned shopping trip and requests began to mount up from the staff. You're to focus on helping Bella but perhaps one of your brother's people can fill the list when they're not too busy.'

Folding the list, Rosemary slipped it into the sleeve of her dress and finished her tea. 'Not a problem Madame Martin. Thank you for the tea.' Bobbing a curtsy she headed upstairs to see if she needed to convince Bella of the benefits of a little retail therapy.

Rosemary's Surprise Admission

The Du Bois entourage had had their breakfast, dressed and Louise was styling Bella's hair when Rosemary announced her presence. As expected Bella was loath to leave her son, especially as he was at the bouncing off the walls stage. Henri was still coughing spasmodically but had managed tea and toast for breakfast and was being a handful over having to remain in bed.

Rene's burns had been cleaned, anointed and he wore his dark glasses once more. He was rather silent about Bella's reluctance to leave the hotel but that may have simply been because Louise was very vocal about her disappointment that Bella didn't feel that they could manage without her for a few hours.

Andre had borrowed Rene's holsters and was slipping in Sutherland's pistols while François, out of bed but still moving cautiously, was reloading the weapon Bella had discharged earlier that morning.

When she turned besieged eyes towards Rosemary, the Maid smiled sympathetically but couldn't offer her the back-up Bella wanted.

'I think it'll be therapeutic for you to do something far removed from your current worries.'

Sighing Bella conceded her defeat. 'Dress shopping though…' She unconsciously laid her hands over her swollen abdomen.

'No one else need see you when you undress and I won't betray your secret, Lady Stirling.' Rosemary's words were met by sudden, deafening silence. Bella felt her breath catch in her throat.

'You know who we really are? How?' Rene was the only one who could find their voice.

'Ever since I learnt of the escape from the second abduction, I've been looking out for anyone who could fit the profile. My apologies Madame Du Bois but you don't quite have the movements of an eight month pregnant woman. You should support your lower back more.'

Rosemary took a deep breath before continuing, 'When you told Madame Martin about Cousin Patrick, one of the reasons you gave for the marriage between you not happening was your family having to leave France during the Reign of Terror that confirmed for me that you are aristocracy.'

'Then there is your French, it's too perfect. Every region will contain its own idiosyncrasies or dialect variations. Your French is that learnt from a Tutor or Governess rather than that used every day with family and friends.' Rosemary blushed as all eyes in the room were focussed upon her.

Andre uttered a nervous laugh. 'Brains as well as beauty! What do you think Rene, do I have to ask Papa Moreau or her brothers for her hand?'

Stroking his hand along his bearded chin, Rene didn't immediately answer. 'First we need to know what Rosemary intends to do with this information.'

The Maid shook her head. 'Nothing my Lord, I promise. I presume that what had captured Andre… Monsieur Guillaume's interest is the adventure, the danger, the mystery. For me, it's the romance. The hero who is prepared to risk everything, do anything to keep his love safe. To get them home so that they can be married and start a life together.' Rosemary sighed wistfully but Rene brought her back down to earth.

'Why isn't anyone interested in turning us in to our enemies or hand us over to the French people?'

Andre's eyes lit up as he thought he knew the answer to this question. 'You haven't been found out be anyone in desperate need for the reward money. None of us has to worry about where our next meal is coming from.'

Agreeing, Rosemary added, 'Inside all of us we can understand and relate to the need to return home. Whether we leave home voluntarily or not, there is that need to return to complete us. Close the circle.'

'Maman.' When Henri spoke, everyone in the room jumped as they hadn't realised that the boy had been awake.

'Yes Little Bear.' Bella moved from the chair to sit on the edge of his bed.

'Can we go home soon?' He laid emphasis on the "we" which caused Rene to chuckle.

'Very soon,' Rene said, 'when Doctor Girard says it is safe for you to make the journey.'

'Can I at least get out of bed today?' Henri reached out to lay his hand over the top of his mother's. It was no longer clammy but it was Louise who answered.

'You will get out of bed Master Henri. I'm going to give you a bath while your bedding is changed. Then you can play a couple of card games with François.'

As Henri cheered, Rene grinned. *I know all too well that playing games with Henri is not to be undertaken by the faint of heart.*

The Porter, Hugo, knocked on the door and called out, 'Your carriage is waiting Monsieur Guillaume.'

Resigned to her fate, Bella permitted Louise to place a hat on her head and took both purses, sliding them into Andre's hand.

'If I get too carried away, you may pull on the reins.' Bella told the bemused Author. She placed her hand under Rene's chin and lifted his head so that she didn't have to bend too much to kiss him. His hands instinctively rose to encircle her waist but he managed to control the urge to draw her down onto his lap.

'Try and enjoy yourself, my love.' Rene drawled softly and turned Bella towards the door. She laughed as she linked her arm through Rosemary's.

'You have no idea what you've unleashed when you give a woman permission to go wild when shopping.'

'Just remember to come back to us and maybe a little something sweet for our son.' Henri's eyes lit up at Rene's suggestion.

Yes please Maman,' the puppy dog eyes seemed to becoming a regular weapon in Henri's arsenal; it certainly worked on Rosemary who tousled the boy's hair.

'I know the perfect little Patisserie! It has the most exquisite delicacies.'

Holding the door open for the ladies, Andre chuckled. 'It's not also run by a member of the family is it?'

Rosemary blushed. 'Actually it belongs to the parents of a girl I grew up with and there's nothing wrong with promoting the businesses of friends and family so long as they live up to the praise!'

Bella laughed as Andre closed the door behind them. 'No fighting now children or I'll have to put you into separate corners.'

As they traipsed down the stairs Rosemary and Andre exchanged a cheeky grin. 'Oui Madame Du Bois,' they said in unison.

Retail Therapy

The fabric warehouse was enormous and would have been overwhelming but Rosemary knew the business so well that she easily guided Bella and their bewildered bodyguard through the extensive range of materials available. Into her brother's hand, Rosemary placed the shopping list from the hotel's staff. That could be dealt with during a quiet period. Looking around Bella wondered, *Is there such a thing as a quiet period; the establishment is packed with ladies from all walks of life.*

One elderly employee, who was being buffeted by the wash of women trying to be served next, was collared by Rosemary and sent out the back for a nice quiet job of collecting end of rolls and off cuts of material as well as a whole roll of calico. Rosemary explained to the puzzled Bella that this was for the young girl who makes dolls.

Being almost next to useless for making adult clothes, Isaac might even be talked into giving the remnants to Bella for free. Bella tried to protest and stated that she was prepared to pay for all her purchases but was silenced by a look from the business savvy Rosemary. After that Bella and Andre followed meekly in Rosemary's wake.

She decided that what Bella needed most was dresses for formal occasions so several different types of material were chosen and luckily Rosemary knew how many yards of each was needed as Bella didn't have a clue. As the employee assigned to them carted away the rolls of material to be cut and packed into a box, Rosemary headed to the section that carried material suitable for children.

Bella had explained how Bridget made not just dolls and dresses for the dolls but also dresses for herself and her younger sisters. So when they found a roll of material they liked and it contained maybe a yard or two left on the roll, Rosemary added it to the other rolls the employee took away.

By the time Rosemary headed for the aisle of accessories, she lost not just Andre to fatigue but also Bella. A sympathetic employee showed them to a couple of chairs as Rosemary decided that Isaac's old stock of accessories could do with a drastic cull.

When the poor Clerk in charge of adding up the total tried to charge the marked down price for the accessories, she was vaporised by a look from Rosemary. The Clerk hurried off to confer with Isaac and he agreed to another 25% reduction as he carried a box full of the off-cuts for which he wasn't charging Bella.

Rosemary opened her mouth to argue for a further discount but Bella, holding her back, agreed to Isaac's total. Even with the free off-cuts, the accessories at 25% of their original price and Rosemary's family discount, the total left Andre speechless as he drew out one of Bella's purses from his jacket pocket. As an employee carried out the boxes to Andre's awaiting carriage and Isaac personally handed the ladies into the vehicle, Bella had a quiet word in Andre's ear and he ensured that each of the employees who had assisted them had a nice tip

Before they headed for Rosemary's cousin Susanna's establishment to try on dresses, Andre decided they needed a little sustenance. Rosemary directed the driver to her friend's patisserie where they had a refreshing cup of tea and little custard tarts. Bella selected an assortment of delicious little cakes and pastries that they would pick up on their way back to the hotel. Rosemary tried to protest when Bella insisted on paying for their teas as well as the section of delights that would make Henri's mouth gape in awe but when Bella said this shopping expedition had turned out to be exactly what she needed, Rosemary didn't persist.

A Perfect Wedding Dress

One of the newest up and coming names in haute couturier was a fairly small shop but decorated in elegance and quiet assurance of quality. It was called simply, "Susanna" and employed five staff including the owner and her sister, Babette. Susanna greeted them and led them to a plush couch to peruse through her catalogue of fashions. As they flicked through the sketched designs, Rosemary started to get a sinking feeling as Bella liked several of the dresses but nothing had jumped off the page and said, 'I'm the dress you're looking for!'

They looked up from the catalogue as Babette, the Seamstress came out of her domain holding a medieval costume in ivory splendour.

'Madame M just informed me that her husband has cancelled their fancy dress ball and I have already finished her dress!' Babette hung up the costume on a rack to display the fine and detailed beading that had taken many hours to complete.

'That is very last minute, Babette, Madame M must still pay for the costume! It's not like anyone else is going to want a medieval dress.' Susanna was just as annoyed as the Seamstress that all that work would be for nothing and it was an exquisite work of art.

Bella gasped in pleasure as she beheld what she really, really wanted for her wedding dress. 'Oh Rosemary! That is perfect!' Bella said, a little breathlessly and Rosemary looked at her in surprise.

'It is beautiful Madame Du Bois but is it suitable for the occasion you're planning?'

'Oh yes! A fairy tale dress for a fairy tale ending to our adventure.'

Rising to her feet, Rosemary took a closer look at the costume as the sisters, Susanna and Babette turned to look at Bella. They were as surprised as Rosemary by Bella's choice. Babette held out her hand to assist Bella to her feet to quickly run a measuring tape over her.

This action caught Andre by surprise and his hand instinctively slid inside his jacket to one of the pistols that lay beneath. Babette looked startled at Andre over the top of her half-moon glasses and took a step back.

'It's all right Andre,' soothed Bella. 'I don't think these ladies mean any harm to us.' As Andre relaxed Babette was able to make her measurements.

'Normally it would be a perfect fit but…' Babette wondered how to complete that sentence.

Understanding what she meant, Bella laid her hand over her baby bump. Rosemary glanced away from examining the dress and caught the simple gesture.

'Is it truly the only dress you want Madame Du Bois?'

Bella nodded but didn't know how they could proceed without raising the suspicions of the dress making sisters. Taking a deep breath Rosemary let it out slowly before she finally spoke.

'Susanna, you and Babette must swear that what I'm about to tell you will never be repeated until I give you permission to do so.'

Andre protested, 'Rosemary no! The fewer people who know the truth until they're home again the safer it will be.'

Rosemary shook her head. 'I grew up with Susanna and Babette like they were my sisters. If I ask them to keep a secret, they'll never break that promise.'

Susanna's eyes lit up as realisation hit her. 'Oh! Of course we'll keep quiet! Oh Rosy, you actually found your romantic runaways.' She hugged her cousin in delight.

Embarrassed by such a starry eyed description of their plight, Bella's features became flushed. 'Not runaways, that makes us sound like star crossed lovers fleeing to the Scottish border to be married in secret at Gretna Green.'

Clasping her hands together over her bosom, Babette giggled. 'Oh this is perfect! This gown is meant to be worn by a princess but the daughter of an Earl is close enough.' The Seamstress gently removed the costume off the hanger and draped it across her arm. 'Come, we must try this on immediately,' she added.

Susanna looked a little doubtfully up at Andre. 'You don't have to keep that close an eye on Madame Du Bois do you?'

Although he opened his mouth, Andre had no idea what to say. Taking Bella's hand Rosemary gently eased Andre down onto the couch with her free hand.

'I'll help Madame Du Bois to change. Is there anything we have to worry about Babette? Pins, tacked together, anything like that?'

'No it is complete,' Babette replied.

There was a floor to ceiling curtain that cut off a section of the salon for privacy and Rosemary led Bella in the guise of a heavily pregnant married woman. When they re-emerged five minutes later the vision of a medieval princess took Andre's breath away. The dressmaking sisters stood with their hands pressed admiringly against their breasts as this was how they had envisioned their creation should look.

The entire costume was a symphony of ivory with the bodice, sleeves and underskirt in brocade. The overskirt and the long flowing over sleeves were tulle and lace also in ivory which accentuated Bella's trim waist while the v neckline highlighted her perfectly shaped supple breasts. All she needed was a wreath of flowers in her hair or one of those cone hats with more tulle streaming down from the point.

Andre wasn't sure that he hadn't stopped breathing; he was sure his heart had begun to beat faster and when Rosemary slid around from behind Bella to close his mouth, he then realised that his jaw had dropped in disbelief. Recovering from her own stunned state, Babette turned Bella so that she could see herself in the full length mirror on the wall.

'Well?' Rosemary was the only one able to find voice.

Bella wore a slight frown as she slowly scanned her eyes down the image reflected back at her. 'It's absolutely beautiful! It... it isn't too theatrical is it?' At the first part of statement the sisters breathed a sigh of relief. Whereas Rosemary seriously considered Bella's question.

'I think... I think it is as you said earlier that it befits a fairy tale and that is what you deserve... a perfect wedding.'

Relieved Bella embraced Rosemary but as she transferred her gaze back to the mirror another query, actually two arose.

'How much? And what about Madame M? What if she still wants her costume?'

From one of the pockets of her smock, Babette removed a letter that clearly stated that Madame M was cancelling the order of her medieval costume.

'As for how much...' The two sisters looked at each other before Susanna continued, 'what can you afford? We will still charge Madame M half the costs for a late cancellation.' They too wanted to see this beautiful woman in the dress that seemed to have been made just for her. Susanna went to her desk and wrote down an amount, showing it to her sister who nodded before handing it to Bella.

'Do we have enough funds for this heavenly creation?' Bella asked Andre as she handed him the slip of paper. His jaw dropped again in shock.

'That is a lot of money for just one dress,' Andre said, when he finally was able to get his mouth to work.

'Actually,' Bella admitted, as Andre handed the piece of paper to Rosemary, 'I've seen worse.' Rosemary nodded but still privately she agreed with Andre that was a lot of money to spend on one item of clothing.

As Andre emptied the contents of Bella's two purses to count how much they still had, Bella went back behind the curtain to change back into her baby bump and Louise's borrowed dress. Babette carried the medieval costume into the back room to pack it into a box while Susanna wrote out an invoice.

Re-emerging pregnant once again, Bella thanked both sisters for their service as Andre paid over the required money and took the box out to his awaiting carriage. Having assisted Bella and Rosemary back into the carriage they made a short detour to pick up the delicacies from the Patisserie before heading back to the Grand Duchess Hotel.

Patrick's Warning

Descending from the carriage, Bella had to admit that going shopping had in fact made her feel more relaxed and she even managed to laugh as Andre said he dreaded having to tell Rene how much money they had actually spent. Hugo, the Porter, had just collected the boxes from the carriage and they were about to follow him into the hotel when a hand suddenly grasped Bella by the arm and spun her around. As Andre reached under his jacket to draw a pistol to protect Bella, she found herself face to face with her Cousin Patrick.

'Tony! You must listen to me! You're in grave danger!' Patrick said.

Andre raised his pistol to just inches away from Patrick's face. 'Release Madame Du Bois or I will shoot you.'

Never removing his eyes from Bella's face, Patrick shook his head. 'I'm not armed, you can search me but I must warn you!'

Obedient to the nod from Andre, Rosemary did a quick search of the Englishman for any weapons. Finally she shook her head. 'He's not carrying any weapons.'

Andre stepped back but didn't lower his pistol. 'Say what you have to say,' he ordered.

Releasing Bella's arm, Patrick nodded. 'You must leave Paris before Sutherland or the others find you! Please Tony, you have to believe me I had nothing to do with Sutherland abducting you again!'

'I saw you with him in the Inn at Hon Fleur! You've always hated that I made Papa marry again to produce a direct heir and you hated the fact that I'm in love with another man. If you're not behind all of this, then who is? Why are you here in Paris?' Bella's chest heaved as she dragged in a deep breath to try and keep control over her rising anger.

'I have never hated you. I'd never do anything to bring harm to you or anyone you love. I'm here to try and prevent Sutherland from carrying out his orders. I can't tell you who is behind all this, they'd kill me.'

Curiosity got the better of Andre. 'They as in more than one person or is it your way of not having to say he or she and therefore giving away possible suspects?'

Bella had to repeat the query in English as Patrick could not follow Andre in French. Finally Patrick shook his head. 'Both actually. There's something else you need to know, I'm not the only one here in Paris. Claude Henry is here.'

Bella's lips thinned as her thoughts flitted back to the early hours of that morning. 'We know! We've already seen Claude.'

Reaching out to caress his hand down Bella's arm, Patrick was momentarily distracted a he was taking in the extent of her disguise. His eyes lingered upon her baby bump but when it looked like his hand was about to move away from her arm towards her swollen abdomen; Andre cleared his throat.

'Look but don't touch Monsieur Stirling. The Lady's husband will not take kindly to anyone touching his wife!' Andre spoke in English to make certain that Patrick perfectly understood his warning. Patrick's eyes flickered up to Bella's face and then down to her left hand where she wore the borrowed wedding ring from Louise.

The colour drained swiftly from Patrick's face. 'You're already married? Have you consummated it yet? Then you could already be pregnant!'

Bella shook her head. 'No to all three questions. What difference would it make if we had already tied the knot? We were going to be married anyway. Having us abducted has only sped up the necessity to have the wedding sooner rather than later.'

Rosemary didn't think it was possible but Bella's cousin actually became paler.

'Delacourt compromised your virtue?'

Bella uttered a hard laugh. 'Being abducted again and running for our lives in a foreign and hostile country has compromised my virtue! Doctor Masters will be able to verify that I am still a virgin but what will that matter as my reputation will be in shreds? Society raised an eyebrow but was tolerant of me running around in male attire, and the first abduction would have been a two day wonder. Caleb asking me to marry him may have extended the Ton's interest to make it a seven day wonder.'

'But **this**,' Bella swept her hand around her, 'we'll have to live with the stories about this probably for the rest of lives! One day, maybe Caleb and I will be able to laugh about this adventure but right now we're trapped, we don't know who we can trust and there's a good possibility that any of us may not come out of this alive!'

Andre drank in Bella's impassioned speech and hoped that he could remember it perfectly later for the book. *Her range of emotions – anger, fear, pride, her love for the two most important men in her life*. The more practical Rosemary realised that Bella was close to emotional collapse.

'Then why are you lingering in Paris? Sutherland said he had wounded Delacourt...' Patrick's hand tightened upon Bella's arm. She shook her head as she interrupted.

'It's Aidan, he's too sick to travel yet. Otherwise we would probably have left yesterday.' There were tears in Bella's eyes and Rosemary placed her hand supportively under Bella's elbow.

Andre had a question of his own as he removed Patrick's hand in preparation of getting Bella into the hotel before she collapsed. 'Why did you have to brutalise François? Was it really necessary to break him?'

Shaking his head as he ran an unsteady hand through his hair, Patrick said, 'That was Sutherland! I tried to get him to cool down but he was just so angry about you escaping again.'

Andre and Rosemary on either side of Bella were starting to distance themselves from Patrick.

'There is something else you need to know Tony, I've seen Delacourt's cousin here in Paris.'

Desperate for answers Bella paused, 'Is Geoff... is he behind all of this?'

Patrick lowered his eyes from the hard, searching glance that his cousin bent down upon him. 'I... I don't know. Tony...' Patrick called out as the French couple continued to lead Bella towards the steps of the hotel. She glanced over her shoulder at the urgency in his voice as he said her name. 'Stay safe.'

They Have Found Us!

Just returning from having delivered the boxes up to the Du Bois room, Hugo was stunned to witness Andre and Rosemary support inside Bella who looked like she was either going to burst into tears or utter an unladylike oath. The sight of the pistol still held in Andre's free hand snapped Hugo out of his polarised state and he hurried forward.

'What's happened Monsieur Guillaume? Do you need me to call for several of the boys?' Hugo caught Bella as her knees started to buckle and scooped her up into his arms.

'No, the danger has gone away. Madame Du Bois is emotionally exhausted,' said Andre. 'Rosemary run up and let the Captain know we're about to enter.'

Rosemary looked a little doubtfully down at the lack of colour in Bella's cheeks. 'Should I send for Doctor Girard?'

'No, no.' The feeble answer came from Bella who managed to wrap her arms around Hugo's neck as they headed up the stairs. Rosemary picked up her skirts and ran on ahead, calling out her name as she knocked on the door.

Rising out of his chair, Rene automatically picked up the pistol on the table beside him as Louise opened the door to Rosemary's nervous voice.

'What is it? Where's Bella?' demanded Rene as he strode across the room to the doorway.

It was Andre who answered, 'Step back Rene. Hugo, lay Madame Du Bois down on the bed.'

Doing as he was told, Rene felt Hugo brush past him with his arms full and as Andre entered the room, Rene grabbed him by the arm and dragged him into a corner of the room.

'What happened Andre? Hugo said you were all happy and laughing when he collected the boxes from your carriage. Was Bella attacked?'

Accepting the glass of something cool from Louise, Andre took a deep drink before he answered, 'Cousin Patrick.' Andre laid a finger against Rene's lips as he was about to demand the full story. 'Thank you Hugo.'

Andre slipped his pistol back into its holster before retrieving a few coins from one of his jacket pockets and pressed them into Hugo's hand. Andre closed and locked the door behind the Porter and led Rene over to the double bed where Rosemary was removing Bella's shoes and assisting her to sit up and also drink from the glass offered by Louise.

'I'm all right! Really Rene! Just for a moment I thought I was going to pass out.' Bella reached out to take Rene's hand and made him sit down on the bed beside her.

'Mama?' Henri had been sitting in one of the arm chairs with Louise as they read one of his books. He slipped off the chair and came to the edge of the main bed.

'Yes Little Bear?' Bella patted the bed, inviting the boy to climb up beside her.

'Did Cousin Patrick hurt you or threaten you?' Henri asked.

Bella shook her head. 'No, actually he wanted to warn us that we're in danger if we remain in Paris.'

A snort of derision came from her son, 'Well we already knew that!' *Sarcasm is going to come very easily to that young man,* reflected Rene. 'That didn't upset you though did it?' added Henri.

Taking another sip of her drink, Bella didn't immediately answer. 'No, not that. It's not easy to explain. If Patrick could find us, and Claude Henry, how long will we be able to keep our true identities a secret from everyone else in the city? We… we can't run and there's nowhere to hide. After such a lovely morning shopping it all seemed too overwhelming to deal with.'

One lone tear trailed down Henri's cheek. 'If it wasn't for me becoming sick, we could've been home by now.'

Rene stretched out his hand until he found Henri and drew him into his arms. 'You're going to have to tell me how you manage to make yourself sick whenever you want to.'

Henri choked on a laugh as he snuggled into Rene's hug. 'Don't be silly Papa, I can't make myself sick by wishing it!'

Rene brushed his hand against the boy's hair. 'Then you're not to blame for us still being in France. Now are you?'

There was a moment of silence as Henri thought through what Rene was telling him. 'No, but…'

Rene interrupted, 'Do you think its Bella's fault for being kidnapped again? I know she feels guilty that we've been dragged into this adventure through France. Do you blame her for what has happened?'

'Definitely not!' Henri immediately answered. 'If it wasn't for you and Mama, we couldn't have escaped that pig man, or got this far! Oh! I see what you're trying to show me Papa. Even so I bet it doesn't lessen any of Mama's feelings of guilt all the same.'

Chuckling, Rene gave Henri a quick squeeze. 'That's one smart boy you have Madame Du Bois!'

Leaning forward to kiss Rene's cheek, Bella retorted, 'Yes he takes after his Papa!' Removing one arm from around Henri, Rene drew her closer for a proper kiss.

Do You Believe Him?

Rolling his eyes at Rosemary who giggled, Andre took occupation of the arm chair vacated by Henri. As the kiss looked like it was about to develop into something more passionate, Louise rapped them both across their hands.

'Now then, what did your cousin have to say for himself?' asked Louise.

Reluctantly Bella drew away from her husband but Louise had just opened the box of pastries and was using its contents as an inducement for getting information.

'Oh yum!' Henri slid out of Rene's arms and off the bed as Louise cut one of the sweets into quarters before offering a small section to the recovering boy. He eagerly sat down on the floor beside Rosemary's chair and accepted a napkin and his sweets. For a couple of minutes there was no other sound but eventually

Andre wiped crumbs from his face and as accurately as he could recall told of their meeting with Patrick Stirling.

There followed another couple of minutes of silence as Rene processed the information. 'Did you believe him Andre?' Rene's question directed to Andre and not Bella surprised everyone in the room.

'I felt he was sincerely distressed about the danger Bella is in… to be honest with you Rene, if Patrick is the mastermind behind your abduction then he's a damn good actor.'

Exhaling slowly there was a momentary silence before Rene asked, 'He said he's seen Geoff in Paris… if cretins like Patrick and Claude Henry can track us down, why wouldn't Geoff have made contact with us by now?' There was no disguising the note of doubt that entered his voice. *I had been so certain that my cousin could have had nothing to do with our abduction.*

Laying her hand over Rene's, Bella said quietly, 'Patrick may have been lying about that. He could have been lying about everything! Is Geoff fluent in French? That could hamper his enquiries.'

Entwining his fingers through hers, Rene shook his head. 'No his Tutor taught Geoff Italian rather than French.'

The Italian

A surprised gasp came from Rosemary, 'Oh! The last couple of nights an Italian gentleman seemingly down on his luck has appeared at the service entrance of the hotel. Bruno speaks some Italian and said he was an ex-solider like him. Bruno gave him a hot meal and in return the Italian offered his services. One of the jobs may have taken him to the foyer and enabled him to read the registry.'

Rene had stiffened. 'What sort of work did this Italian offer do?' The fingers of his free hand were clenched so tightly that his knuckles turned white. Rosemary looked a little alarmed at the sternness of Rene's expression.

'I believe one task was fixing the squeaking wheels on the trolleys, another was mending a couple of broken chairs. Do you really think that may have been your cousin all along? Shall I get Bruno to inform you if the Italian returns again this evening?' Rosemary rose to her feet and brushed the crumbs of pastry from the front of her dress. *As pleasant as the morning has been it is time to return to work.*

Andre also rose out of his arm chair. 'Do you have to go?' He took possession of Rosemary's hand and everyone else in the room looked somewhere else.

'I must get on with my real job. Jacques will probably be up with your luncheon soon, if you have any room after those delicious pastries.'

Sliding off the main bed, Bella approached the Maid and kissed her cheek. 'I want to thank you for this morning Rosemary. Up until we were accosted outside the hotel; I really did enjoy shopping with you.'

A little embarrassed by all this attention, a blushing Rosemary sighed. 'I'm just sorry I won't get to see you married in that dress.'

'Oh I don't know,' Andre linked his arm through Rosemary's as she headed for the door. 'I think that might be easily arranged.'

Rosemary looked up at the Author in surprise but following them, Louise chuckled. 'Be careful what promises he makes you young lady. His smooth way with words is, after all, his trade.'

Opening the door, Andre managed to look hurt. 'You make me out to be a philanderer!'

Affectionately patting his cheek, Louise said, 'If your tongue was any smoother I'd swear you had Irish blood in you!' Glancing back at Bella, Louise added, 'Now that you're back I'll join François for luncheon and then have a nap until you need me tonight. That does not mean you and the Captain can start misbehaving!'

Looking as grave as a judge, Rene laid his hand over his heart. 'On our best behaviour Nanny. Especially now. I'm not going to let anyone hurt my family!'

Louise smiled. 'Good boy. Soon, all will be over and then you can practice making babies to your heart's content.'

Blushing, Bella closed the door behind the departing Louise, Rosemary and Andre. Cleaning up the used napkins and closing the lid of the pastry box, Bella was dreading the question she knew must be burning its way from Henri's brain to his lips.

'Mama?'

'Yes Little Bear?' Dropping the rubbish into a bin, Bella reached down to help Henri to his feet and back into bed until it was time to eat.

'Why do adults have to practice making babies? Is it hard to do, like when I first began to learn to read?'

Sitting down on the edge of Henri's bed, Bella cast an imploring glance at Rene but he naturally was unable to see it. *Even so, by the way he is grinning, I doubt I am going to get any help from that quarter.*

'Having never actually done it before, Henri, it's not easy for me to answer. I believe that sometimes it is possible to become pregnant the first time a woman has intercourse but sometimes there can be a variety of factors that make it more difficult to become with child.'

'Oh!' Henri digested this information for a couple of minutes.

Louise's Story

With his curiosity satisfied, Bella drew up the bedding around Henri before sitting down into one of the arm chairs opposite Rene who had moved from the bed to a chair.

'I have a question,' Rene stated quietly as he leant towards Bella and stretched out his hand to locate hers.

'Yes?' *Considering his enjoyment at my discomfort while answering Henri's question, I am naturally feeling a little apprehensive about what he will ask.*

'Why does Louise dislike the Irish?'

Bella exhaled slowly. 'It's a long story.'

Raising her hand to press his lips against her palm, Rene murmured, 'Good, it might keep me amused so that I stop thinking about how I'd like to kiss you from the top of your head and work my way down, slowly, to your toes.'

Bella could feel a blush spread over her entire body by the sensual tone of his voice. 'I though you promised Nanny that you'd behave?' She could feel her pulse quicken in excitement.

'At the moment I'm only thinking about it! Distract me until lunch arrives; afterwards we can have a little nap to make up for our abrupt wakening this morning.'

Feeling a little breathless, Bella picked up a glass of fruit juice and gulped it down before she began to explain Louise's dislike for the Irish.

'During the Reign of Terror, Senator Luke Du Bois felt it necessary to remove his family and staff from France as he and Robespierre had several differences of opinions. Louise would have been 16 at the time and Papa offered them sanctuary until they could safely return to Paris after Robespierre himself went to the guillotine.'

Rene interrupted the story, 'What was the link between the Earl of Stirling and the Senator?' His eyebrows rose in surprise as Bella giggled.

'Senator Du Bois' wife, Monique, is Papa's maternal Aunt. Lady Margarette's sister.'

'Wow! So this is really a family affair!'

Bella agreed before continuing. 'Staying in Stirling village was an impoverished Irish Lord, the impoverished part was not known until much later. Well Lord Sean… I won't mention his last name, laid on the charm and set about seducing the, then naïve, young Louise. Phillippe tried to warn Louise about Sean but she was hopelessly, deeply, madly in love and Sean could do no wrong in her eyes.'

'He promised her marriage and a life together in the Emerald Isle so Louise saw no reason to wait until after the wedding to share Sean's bed. He charmed information out of her about the running of Stirling Manor and more importantly, where Mama's jewellery and any valuables were kept in the house.'

'When he gave a family heirloom brooch as an engagement present, Sean asked Louise to get Papa to put it in the safe for her. Sean later admitted that he had been outside the study window to get the combination of the safe as the brooch was locked away for safe keeping.'

'So when did Louise begin to realise the truth about the cad?'

Bella paused to have another drink. 'When she discovered she was pregnant. Sean was quite angry at her. Said she was trying to trap him, to force him to marry her immediately. Louise was shocked by his hostility as she thought that they were actually engaged and therefore going to be married soon anyway. When he tried to force Louise to terminate the pregnancy she started to see the cracks in all his lies.'

'One day Louise was up very early due to morning sickness and overhead Sean talking in his sleep. Inadvertently he told her everything, his plan to burgle the Manor and flee back to Ireland, leaving her behind to take the blame for the thefts.'

'Did she kill him?' Rene asked casually.

Bella laughed. 'No, she thought about it but decided to go to my father and tell him everything. A trap was set to capture Sean in the act of ransacking the safe and he was hauled away to prison.'

'What happened to the baby? Oh!' For a brief moment Rene's fingers tightened around Bella's as realisation struck him. 'François isn't Louise's brother; he's her son!'

Acknowledging that his guess was correct, Bella added, 'After the trial but before Sean went to prison, Papa persuaded him to marry Louise so François was born in wedlock.'

'Therefore he is heir to an impoverished title in Ireland? No wonder Louise brought him back to France.'

Bella giggled again. 'Not so impoverished actually. Papa has been managing the estate ever since Sean went to prison. When François turns five and twenty he can claim the title, the estate, the revenue or he can allow Papa's Irish Manager to continue running everything and do what he wants with the income generated.'

'Why five and twenty? When did Sean die?' Rene was caught up in the story even so he noticed that someone had arrived outside their room with a trolley.

'Sean died in prison when François was about ten. On a different sentence, apparently. Sean's stealing habit was a hard one to break. At first Louise didn't want anything to do with the inheritance. Then there was a massive legal battle from the Irish cousins who did not want a Frenchman lording it over them. Papa wanted time to make something sustainable for François to inherit when he was old enough to make that decision for himself.'

Bella rose to her feet to open the door as Jacques knocked and announced himself. Even so Rene's hand lay casually over the pistol on the arm of the chair as their lunch was wheeled into the room. Sniffing the delicious scent, Henri threw back his bedding as he sat up in bed.

'Mama? Can I join you and Papa at the table for luncheon?' Puppy dog eyes were raised to Bella's face as Jacques removed the covers off their plates.

'You may, Little Bear, but the moment you feel a chill you'll go straight back in front of the fire.' Bella smiled at Jacques who picked up the desk chair and brought it around for Henri to climb up onto. Bella waited by the door to tip Jacques and locked the door after he had left.

Joining her boys, Bella made a mental note, *I need to retrieve my purses from Andre and pay for the additional nights' meals and board. For now, though I need to focus upon assisting my boys to eat their meal without eating too quickly or too much and either making himself sick, or making too much mess as he struggles to manage his cutlery despite his blindness.*

The Eye Of The Storm

The afternoon was spent relatively quietly. After lunch, Henri returned to his bed, without a fight, to take a nap. When Bella returned to her chair after Jacques had collected their trolley, Rene reached out his hand to locate Bella's.

'That isn't a good sign is it?' He nodded his head towards Henri's bed. 'Being that docile means that he's still far from fully recovered doesn't it?'

His concern always moved Bella. 'When Henri starts throwing his medicine back at us, we'll know he's on the road to recovery.'

Oh joy! Something to look forward to!' Rene drawled, causing her to giggle. When Jacques had entered to collect their trolley, Rosemary had slipped in briefly to give Bella that day's and the previous day's London newspapers as well as to return her purses from Andre. He also sent the masqueraders a message that he had gone down to reception to settle their bill for another couple of nights.

Spreading out the newspapers, Bella read aloud any of the articles that interested her husband. She was actually surprised that the London papers seemed to be really well informed about their plight. She wondered, *from where are they getting their information and does that place us in even more danger?*

Rene was less disturbed by the printed account of their adventure. 'Although the newspaper presumes we must be in Paris, it isn't a stated fact. Also there is no report of Henri's illness which rules out the informant being anyone intimately connected to us.'

Bella uttered an un-ladylike oath which surprised Rene but didn't shock him. 'I told Patrick, when he accosted us outside, that Henri is the reason we haven't left Paris yet.'

Soothingly Rene caressed his hand over hers. 'Well if that information ends up in the newspaper in the next two days, we'll know Patrick is the contact with the newspapers. Don't fret about it my love. No harm done.'

She shook her head. 'Unless Patrick uses it as an opportunity to force natural causes to clear his way to inherit.' A sudden thought made Bella reconsider the conversation she had with her cousin. 'When Andre told Patrick that my husband wouldn't like anyone touching me, all the colour drained from Patrick's face. He asked me if we were already married, whether we had consummated our marriage and could I possibly already be pregnant. At the time I thought it odd Patrick should ask me such intimate questions but now… Rene… who would it affect if I was in fact all of those things? Surely it would be at least a month before we would know if I was carrying your child?'

The thought of our child growing inside of Bella is a very pleasant image but the Lady has asked me a question. 'Would Cousin Patrick know that? If you were married, it rules him out as being able to marry you. Unless he intends to kill me and marry my widow. If we had already had our wedding night, or if you were pregnant then he'd be faced with the problem that your first born child may not be his.'

'Surely Claude Henry has by now informed Patrick that Lady Charlotte is pregnant again and that puts further jeopardy on Patrick becoming the next Earl?' He paused and Bella remained silent as he carefully contemplated his next words. *I acknowledge the truth behind the fact but I still find it hard to accept that my cousin has anything to do with our current predicament.* Seeing the struggle upon his face, Bella didn't speak or force him to accept this possibility as a fact just yet.

Slowly Rene exhaled. 'The other person affected by our marriage and a conception of an heir is Geoff.' He spoke slowly, carefully weighing each word before they left his mouth. 'Oh Bella! I can't believe Geoff has anything at all to do with our abduction! He has never shown any indication of jealously or ill will towards me.' His tone was begging her to offer him the reassurance that she just could not give him.

'Up until a very short time ago you had shown no indication that you were ready to settle down and start a family.' Bella didn't resist as Rene slid his hand out of hers to run both his hands through his hair.

'I know! But until I can… look Geoff in the eyes, I have to give him the benefit of the doubt. I thought… I thought we were as close as brothers.' Kneeling down in front of him, she took both his hands between her own to stop him pulling his hair out.

Very softly Bella said, 'Cain and Abel.'

The room was filled with stunned silence and then Rene drew her into his lap as he threw back his head and laughed. 'Oh Bella! One of these days that wicked tongue of yours is going to get you into deep, deep trouble!'

Wrapping her arms around his neck as he drew her into a kiss, she asked, 'Do you promise?' Bella eagerly met his lips with a passion to match his own.

A Surprise Arrival

A knock fell upon the door just as Rene's hand had released Bella's hand to seek out the pistol on the table beside him.

'Captain Du Bois, it's Rosemary. Ambassador White is here to see you.'

Although Rene's grip on his pistol eased as Bella rose from his lap, he kept his hand laying lightly over the weapon, just in case. Crossing the room, Bella unconsciously tidied her hair. Opening the door to their visitors, she let out a gasp of surprise and reacting immediately, Rene was on his feet, his pistol in his hand.

'Bella? What is it?' There was no hiding the fear in Rene's voice and Bella struggled to find the ability to speak as she launched herself at Sir Malcolm White's companion.

'Papa!' She sobbed from her bemused parent's arms and the tension drained out of Rene.

'Now then baby girl, you'll make me believe this young man hasn't been taking good care of you.' Kissing her on the forehead, the Earl of Stirling placed his handkerchief into his daughter's hand before observing her at arm's length.

Lowering his weapon, Rene bowed. 'It's more like your daughter has been taking care of us, my Lord.' He was taken by surprise as his future father-in-law embraced him. Being English and not French, Earl Stirling did not kiss him, for which consideration Rene was grateful.

'I'll wager it was more a partnership. I knew I was right that I could trust you to look after my children.'

A little embarrassed, Rene was relieved when the Earl released him. He heard Rosemary quietly shut the door as she left them to their family reunion.

'If I'd been doing my job properly Sutherland would never have managed to get into Stirling Manor!'

The Earl gently eased Rene back into his arm chair. 'I absolve you of any guilt my son! You're all alive and... I was going to say well but you've had another bout of bronchitis haven't you?"

Hearing the springs squeak slightly as the Earl sat down on Henri's bed, Rene realised that Lord Stirling wasn't still addressing him. A spasmodic cough answered the Earl as Henri sat up and held out his arms.

'Can we go home now Grandpapa?' Henri would not give up the masquerade until Bella gave him permission. *My slip up in revealing her true gender to Sutherland at the On the Rocks Inn had nearly cost Bella her virginity. I am determined to not make that mistake again.*

Being called "Grandpapa" by Henri had caused a fleeting look of pain to cross his face but the Earl was quick to conceal it as he brushed Henri's hair out of his eyes.

'As soon as your Doctor says it is safe baby boy.' Earl Stirling glanced up at Bella. 'You did call in a Doctor didn't you Tony? You've not been trying to deal with this on your own?'

Bella shook her head. 'No Papa, Uncle Inky sent for the top man in Paris. What... what news do you bring from home?'

As he had already heard both sides of the story, Sir Malcolm excused himself. Closing the door, the Ambassador was not surprised to hear it lock behind him. *As surprised and pleased as the masqueraders may be to see the arrival of the Earl, they are still not safe just yet.*

By the time the tea tray arrived, the Earl had persuaded Rene to detail their adventure. *It is an abridged version as there are just some facts I don't want to share with my future father-in-law.* Bella noticed this deliberate editing of their story and could not help smiling as Rene carefully chose his words. She sat on the edge of Henri's bed while the Earl sat in an arm chair beside Rene.

Earl Stirling wasn't oblivious to the silent messages that were being communicated between husband and wife but he was prepared to ignore it. *I am just so relieved to have found them alive and relatively unharmed that I'm not going to force the loving couple to elaborate upon the obvious gaps in Caleb's story.* Bella had just poured the tea and handed out the cups when she asked again about news from home. Taking a sip of his tea the Earl cast his mind back to the night of his daughter's engagement.

News From Home'

'I don't know what Preston, the Butler, said but he cleared that ballroom in no time flat. Only Heather Gray refused to leave until she learnt what had caused Caleb to tear out of the ballroom as if the devil himself was on his heels. When Preston explained that my children had been abducted again and Caleb was hot on their heels, Charlotte fainted. Luckily Doctor Masters was still outside and we carried Charlotte up to her room.'

'Geoff was a little startled that Caleb had driven off to the rescue without him. There was nothing we could do until morning when I prayed you'd all walk back through our doors, so I sent everyone off to bed. I paced in the morning room as I knew you could return at any time.' The Earl paused to sip his tea before continuing.

'Just after midnight I heard a vehicle pull up. Doctor Stevenson brought the news that Sutherland had blinded Caleb and was carting all three of you across to France. In the hope that the Pirate managed to bring you back on his ship, I travelled to Birling Gap with Doctor Stevenson. I was very disappointed when the Pirate stepped off his ship without you.'

'Captain Sheppard, Papa.' Bella had been silent when her father had said, "Pirate" the first time but felt she needed to correct the Earl when he said it again. He cast her an indulgent look.

'Oh Tony, you know I'm shocking with names.'

Rene chuckled as he could just imagine the naughty school boy expression on his father-in-law's face. 'Go on, please, my Lord.'

'The Pirate,' the Earl cast a defiant look at his daughter but when Bella refused to take the bait he continued, 'explained his plans to return the next evening to Hon Fleur; after that he said you would head for Paris. When I returned home, Patrick decided to head across to France to rescue you.'

'The Pirate delivered a note from Patrick the next day, stating that Sutherland had made the French seaside village of Hon Fleur too hot for you to enter and Patrick was going to Paris. With that news Geoff Delacourt packed up his bags and also headed to Paris. About midday on the third day I received the letter from Sir Malcolm.'

'I told Charlotte that you were all safe in Paris, for now, but I didn't add that Aidan had become sick. I knew she'd only worry and make herself ill. Knowing Aidan couldn't be moved yet, I didn't hurry over here as I didn't want to jeopardise your masquerade. Which by the way son-in-law isn't helped by you continuously referring to me as "my Lord"!'

Bella remained silent as she only half believed her father's reason for staying away. *Papa has never been very good when it came to dealing with sickness. To be fair, it is still too soon to contemplate moving Henri.* An amused grin covered Rene's face as he chuckled.

'Bella has already let slip that your family had to flee France during the Reign of Terror so you can keep your title of Lord. In turn you're not helping by referring to us by our real names.'

The Earl showed mild interest. 'Did you give our side of the family a fake name or can we use our own?

Rolling her eyes, Bella rose to place her empty cup onto the tea tray. 'Just be careful Papa, these are not fools we're dealing with.'

A hurt expression replaced the mild interest. 'Your great grandmother was French Tony. I'm not unfamiliar with our maternal cousins.'

'Speaking of relatives,' Rene was reminded of a question he had for the Earl. 'Did you or Lady Charlotte let her mother know about the second abduction? We've also been wondering who has been keeping the London newspapers up to date with our adventure.'

Both of the Earls' eyebrows rose. 'Charlotte did write to Agnes but… the Henrys can't be involved in this abduction attempt. Their desire for revenge against you can't be greater than having a Henry heir to the title of Stirling.'

'Then what was Claude Henry doing breaking into our room in the early hours of this morning?' asked Rene.

Stroking his chin, the Earl considered the problem. 'He may have intended killing the two of you and taking Aidan back to England.'

Bella slipped Rene's empty cup out of his hands. 'It is possible. I just wonder if we'll ever discover who is really behind all of this.' She sighed deeply as she placed the cup onto the tray. Rene reached out his hand to locate hers and gave it a reassuring squeeze.

'We will solve this Bella. In the meantime why don't you take your father down to Reception and book him into a room.'

The Earl's Regret

When the Earl didn't move, it appeared that he had fallen into a deep contemplation. A little alarmed by the forlorn expression on his face, Bella placed her hand upon his arm.

'Papa? What is it?'

'Hum? I was thinking how all of this could have been prevented if only Caleb had killed Sutherland when he had first attacked you on the way home from the Stirling Arms.' A flush swept across Rene's cheeks but it was Bella who protested.

'Papa, it's not fair to lay that upon Rene's shoulders. How could he... could any of us know that Sutherland would abduct us not once but twice? Well maybe Andre would have had a dozen different scenarios already plotted out in his head but that is after all his trade.'

Shaking his head, Rene squeezed Bella's hand soothingly. 'Do you think I haven't already abused myself for not utilising the various opportunities I had to rid us of this blight on our lives? But the sin of taking another human's life even in self-defence would weigh heavily upon me.'

The Earl waved a dismissive hand. 'Have I not already absolved you of your sins?'

Seeing that her father did not understand Rene, Bella added, 'I think it would be the need for absolution from a higher power that worries Rene.'

Puzzled, the Earl asked, 'The King?'

Bella sighed. 'No Papa, God! When...when you take away another person's life, a part of your soul is torn from you. Only God can absolve you of that guilt and make you whole again.'

'Even in self-defence or if it is justified? What about war?' queried the Earl as if this was one of Bella's philosophical lessons.

'Even then, my Lord.' Rene answered, *I'm not really surprised that my own ideology matches Bella's.* 'In each instance Sutherland was neutralised enough so that I could get Bella and Henri safely away.'

'Also,' Bella added, 'if we eliminate him too soon we may never learn who planned this second abduction with the intention to kill us.'

'Do you trust what Patrick told you?'

Bella shook her head. 'No Papa, we trust no one until we can expose the one or the many involved. The French people entrusted with our secret have nothing to gain or lose by us living or dying.'

Rene chuckled. 'I suppose Andre would still have his story regardless of the outcome. Although the romantic in Rosemary will hope that we both live happily ever after.'

'Oh so do I!' Bella tilted up Rene's face so that she could briefly kiss him. He grinned at the desperate need behind her teasing tone but he didn't reach to capture her and draw her down onto his lap.

She needs to escort her father down to organise a room for him for the night and besides which it really doesn't seem the appropriate moment to become passionate in front of the Earl. We aren't married yet and I don't fancy having to kidnap Bella and race off to Gretna Green if the Earl withdraws his approval of our match.

The very idea made Rene's blood run cold as he followed father and daughter to the door to lock it again upon their departure. With his pistol held loosely in his hand he leant backwards against the wall beside the door as he waited for their return.

Henri's Wisdom

Rene didn't want to start brooding over Earl Stirling's words, so he focussed upon what his ears were telling him. There was a rustling as Henri moved restlessly in his bed.

'Papa?'

'Yes Little Bear? Are you cold?' Rene heard the clink of glassware. 'Thirsty?'

'Thirsty but the jug is too heavy.'

He pushed himself off the wall and made his way carefully around the single bed. Laying his pistol down on the other side of the boy as he sat on Henri's bed, Rene picked up the jug of cordial.

'You'll have to help me, Little Bear, raise your glass to the lip of the jug.' Rene waited until he heard the clink of glass on glass before he gently tipped the jug just enough for the liquid to pour out. When the glass was just over half full, Henri said, 'Stop.' As the boy gulped down the drink, Rene held on to the jug in case he needed another top up.

'Yum! Fruity! More please.' Henri brought his glass back up to meet the jug as Rene raised it again. Henri didn't drink anymore but placed his glass onto the table once Rene had managed to put the jug safely back down.

Locating his pistol again, Rene was about to rise from the bed when he felt a small hand lay over the top of his.

'Papa, Mama said that hindsight is a flowering tool.'

A reluctant grin spread across Rene's features. 'Not flowering but flawed Little Bear.'

Frowning in concentration Henri tried to understand. 'I thought floored was when one boxer knocks out another boxer.'

Rene chuckled. 'Same sounding word but different spelling and definitely different meaning. A flaw, f-l-a-w, is an imperfection often found in people's personalities or jewels.'

'So what Mama was saying is that hindsight isn't a good measurement of events?'

Rene smiled. 'Yes Little Bear.'

'Do you... do you think you would kill the pig man if you had to?'

'Very easily! If he hurt you or your mother... if he had violated her in anyway... yes I would've immediately slit Sutherland's throat without a single regret.' Rene paused to drag in a deep calming breath. 'But killing is wrong Henri. That is why I neutralised the threat and got you and Bella to somewhere safe.'

'That was the logical and rational decision. I couldn't afford to let my emotions or anger get out of control. If I started stabbing Sutherland I wouldn't stop until there was nothing left but an unrecognisable pile of body parts!' Rene was forced to take another shuddering breath and tried to remember that he was talking to a five year old boy.

In sympathy, Henri patted Rene's hand. 'We can't change the past, Papa, but we can learn from our mistakes. You must stay focussed upon the present and the danger that may be closer than you're aware. Grandpapa doesn't understand as he hasn't been here with us. As you and Mama have struggled to get us safely to this point.'

Rene turned his hand over so that the boy's hand fitted snugly into his palm. 'Bella has tried to shield you as much as possible from the danger but you've been aware of how serious our situation has been haven't you?'

'And it still is serious Papa.' Henri yawned, raising his hand to cover his mouth. A spate of coughing brought an end to their conversation as Rene slid his hand around Henri to gently pat his back until the coughing eased.

'Are you due more medicine yet?' *I'm loath to handle that side of Henri's care as the bottles of oil and the medicine are sitting side by side on the table and I can't tell which is which.*

Henri pulled a face. 'Probably, but that's Mama coming back isn't it?'

Picking up his pistol Rene had already begun to rise as he too had heard Bella returning. He waited until she had confirmed that she was Bella before he opened the door. Although she was alone, Bella carried a pile of freshly laundered clothes and Henri's fur rug. Placing the clothes on the end of their bed, she threw the rug over the top of Henri.

Bella Becomes Restless

Closing and locking the door again, Rene asked, 'Where's your father?' He tried to sound light and unconcerned but the Earl's arrival in Paris meant one more person for him to be worried about. For his safety, not that Rene considered his future father-in-law a suspect in their abduction. Bella looked up from measuring a dose of medicine for her son.

'He's gone to see Phillippe to pay his respects. Grandmama sent a letter of condolences to the Senator's widow, her sister, Monique.' Tipping the medicine swiftly down Henri's throat, she briefly patted him on the back before moving around the bed to take Rene's hand to lead him to the arm chair.

'About what Papa said…' Bella's gentle reassuring tone was interrupted by Rene.

'Henri and I have discussed it and we've decided to focus on the here and now.' Although his tone was jovial, there was a hint of something hard beneath it and that he didn't want to discuss it anymore.

'Well then…' She was a little lost for words at how this temporary father and son had bonded.

As Henri snuggled down under his favourite rug, Bella emptied the medical bag onto the double bed and sorted and reorganised her supplies. She also made a note of anything that was running low. Collecting up any of the medical supplies that had spread around the room, she brought it all together in the bag.

From where he sat in his arm chair, Rene sensed Bella's activities. He didn't say anything as she finished packing the medical bag before placing it on the bedside table on her side. When she drew out of the wardrobe the carpet bag and started sorting their clean and dirty clothes, he finally spoke.

'Nervous energy, my elfling or do you know something is about to happen?' He kept his voice light and teasing but Rene could feel the tension radiating from her.

An exasperated sigh escaped. 'Andre has me thinking about how he might have thrown a plot twist into the story about now. I just… I just want to be ready to leave at a moment's notice if it becomes absolutely necessary.' With the additional clothes

Louise had brought up to Paris for them, Bella set aside a clean set of attire for each of them before folding all the other clean clothes and packing them into the carpet bag. The used clothes she packed into an additional bag Louise had supplied. The material and her wedding dress, she was going to leave in their boxes.

'I thought we had to stay here until the Doctor says it is safe for Henri to travel?' It was a question and not an accusation.

'That is still true,' Bella paused as she glanced at her son but Henri was warmly wrapped up in his fur rug and fast asleep. 'But this safe haven is starting to feel like a trap waiting to snap shut around us.'

'But we can't risk moving Henri...'

Bella interrupted, 'I know... I know! We can't move my Little Bear but we can't stay here for too long either.' There was a desperate edge to her voice that brought Rene out of his chair and made his way across the room to take Bella into his arms.

'Be calm Bella. What are our options? How can we move Henri without causing a relapse? Hot water bottles? Heated bricks? Wrapping him up in several blankets? Even if we could ensure a constant temperature for him, Du Bois' house would be no safer a haven than this hotel. Once we leave here we have to be heading for home. But if Henri cannot make that trip then we can't leave.'

Bella was fighting back frustrated tears. 'I know, I know! That's what's setting my teeth on edge! I thought for a moment that with Papa's arrival some of the pressure would be lifted from our shoulders but you're the only one I trust to help me make the right decisions.'

A tremor of deep emotion ran through her as Rene stroked his hand down her hair. *I had already begun to feel that the Earl was going to be more a liability in Paris than an asset but to hear Bella have to admit her doubts about her father is heart wrenching. At the same time my heart sings at her confidence that together we can deal with anything that life throws at us.*

'How about another cup of tea, my love? You need to calm down or you're going to collapse in exhaustion.'

Nestling her head against his shoulder, Bella gave a gurgle of laughter as she nodded. 'Next you'll be saying that the stress isn't good for the baby.'

'Well it certainly isn't good for your husband!' Rene tilted her face up so that he could find her lips and turned her laugh into a sigh of pleasure as Bella willingly met him in a tender kiss. It could have easily developed into something more passionate but he deliberately drew back and pressed another kiss, this time against her forehead as he removed his arms from around her.

'Tea is a good idea.' Bella took a deep breath and let it out slowly before moving towards bell-pull to summon service. 'I like the sound of that!' She returned to Rene's side and taking his arm, led him back to the arm chairs, sitting down beside him.

'Tea?' He was a little surprised by the tone of excitement in her voice. Reaching over to take his hand, she uttered her delightful gurgle of a laugh.

'No, I mean when you referred to yourself as my husband. I hope... I hope that we can make it a reality.'

Rene's eyebrows rose in surprise. 'You're not doubting us getting home are you? I thought you had more faith in us than that?'

Sighing Bella shook her head. 'I do but... there are so many obstacles still ahead of us. I'm... I'm afraid that what I really want is just in reach but someone or something won't let us get there.'

'Then I'll just have to remove that someone or something from our path.' Rene squeezed her hand. 'Perhaps you need something a little stronger than tea? What about a brandy? For medicinal purposes?' His other hand moved to cover the pistol on the table beside him as a knock sounded on their door.

'No!' Bella said very firmly, but immediately softened her tone, 'No, I'm all right. Really.' She rose to open the door as Bruno announced his presence.

Don't Say Hormones Again!

'How can I help you Madame Du Bois?' Bruno stepped into the room and picked up the tea tray to remove it.

'Rene and I were contemplating another cup of tea but I'm thinking that an early dinner may be a better idea,' answered Bella.

Placing the tray down again, Bruno took out his fob watch from his waist coat pocket to check the time. 'We've been serving dinner for you at six o'clock. Would you prefer to eat at five o'clock tonight?'

Laying her hand on Rene's arm, Bella asked, 'What do you think? It means I can settle Henri down with his next dose of medicine at six and he might sleep then.'

Rene nodded, 'What time is it now Bruno?'

'Just after four, Captain.'

'After a disturbed night perhaps an early bed time is a good idea. It's not going to cause a problem in the kitchens Bruno?' enquired Rene.

'Not at all Sir. Now is this just for yourselves or does it include Monsieur Guillaume and your father-in-law?' Bruno picked up the tray again.

'Oh! I hadn't thought about that!' Bella was a little upset at how easy it was to disregard the needs of anyone but her two boys.

Bruno smiled. 'It's all right Madame Du Bois. I'll check with the rest of your party if they'd also prefer an earlier dinner.'

'Thank you Bruno.' She smiled impishly. 'I'm afraid my brain isn't working too well today and if anyone says hormones again, I think I'll scream.' She directed the statement to both men.

Bruno looked shocked as he had no intention of saying anything so rude but Rene grinned and was prepared to accept the blame for Bella's warning. *It is something a husband would say to gently suggest that his pregnant wife is acting a little irrationally.*

'It's all right Bruno,' soothed Rene, 'its' been a long and tiring day.'

'Yes Captain, I'll just see that your dinner is started right away.' Bobbing his head to Bella, Bruno carried out their tea tray and she shut and locked the door behind him.

Planning For Our Future

'Actually I wouldn't dismiss it Bella. I'm sure that excuse of over sensitive hormones could get you out of all sorts of trouble.' Rene suggested lightly as he drew Bella back onto his lap.

Placing her arms around his neck, she chuckled. 'I'll remember you said that when we make this a real pregnancy.' She placed a kiss against his cheek as his hand slid lovingly over her baby bump. 'Do you know what I'm not going to miss when we get home?' She placed another kiss, this time, against Rene's neck.

'Let me guess... you don't like the beard?' There was considerable amusement in his voice.

'Not really. I hope you don't mind but once we're married and free to give into our wildest desires, I think the beard will cause an abrasive rash... all over my body.' Rene could almost hear Bella blushing as she spoke. 'Which might make it too uncomfortable to be making love again and again and again.'

His breath hitched suddenly at the erotic image of the hours they would spend in each other's arms in their marital bed and elsewhere.

'The second we're home, it's coming off!' Rene promised.

Bella giggled and trailed one hand down from his neck to caress against his chest. 'The only problem with that plan… to spend hours making love, is that Henri will still be with us.'

Raising his hand to cup her face, Rene sought her lips beneath his own as he thought about the problem. Although it would be very easy to forget everything else as Bella eagerly met his passion and her hand, caressing his chest, slid tantalisingly lower down his taut stomach. Reluctantly Rene broke the kiss and captured her hand before it swept too much lower and he lost the ability to think at all.

'Would it be better for Henri if we spent the first two weeks at Stirling Manor so that he is surrounded by all that is familiar to him? Then when we get caught up in the need to get naked perhaps Henri can be in the next room with Mary and William? He trusts them doesn't he? And we'd only be a door away from him.'

Bella sighed deeply, drawing his hand up to her lips. 'It's not much of a honeymoon for you. Won't you be longing for your own home?'

'We can ride with Henri over there a couple times during the week and as Henri's confidence grows we can all then spend a night or two there. We're not going to rush this Bella. How we deal with Henri's return to a normal life will determine whether or not this adventure scars him for life. I'm looking forward to being his big brother and it is a role that I'll take very seriously.'

Bella looked at him stunned for several seconds before she could find her voice. 'Do you know how irresistibly sexy you are right at this moment?' Her words were low and just a little husky which brought a rueful smile to Rene's lips.

'I meant every word of it but if it makes you want to drag me off to yonder bed and make sweet delicious love to me, then who am I to go against the wishes of a lady?'

Laughing, Bella removed herself from his lap just in case he followed through on that thought. 'Unfortunately until this is your ring on my finger and we're somewhere less hazardous to our health, then you'll have to take a raincheck.' Regardless of her words, she leant forward to claim his mouth beneath her own. 'We'd better head home soon, Rene, it's getting so much harder to keep my hands off you.'

He grinned but didn't reach out to grasp her round the waist and drag her back onto his lap. 'Same here, my beautiful elfling! Just keep that dream alive as we survive the next couple of days and then...' Rene's breath caught in his throat as his chest tightened in anticipation. 'Then we will make it a reality.'

As Bella's body flushed in lust for their future erotic adventure, she smiled as she realised that her anxiety and edgy nerves had been swept aside. 'Oh Caleb,' she sighed. 'I look forward to it!'

No Longer A Safe Haven

Dinner was a quiet and uneventful affair, for which Bella was grateful. *Henri is managing to eat a little more at each meal and even asked for some left over pastries for his sweets. What does surprise me is the acceptance of the earlier time for our dinner by the other members of our entourage.* The Earl hadn't been sleeping very well as he worried about his children. Also like Henri, he wasn't much of a sailor and had not enjoyed the voyage across the Channel.

The French contingent of their party were looking forward to what might prove to be an uneventful evening. Seeing that Bella was packed ready for flight, Louise instructed Andre and the Earl to also be ready for anything. The Earl could not imagine what their enemies could possibly do to them while they remained inside the Grand Duchess Hotel. Even so no one dared to argue with Nanny.

When Bella settled Henri back into his bed and gave him his next dose of medicine, she was rather surprised that when two hot water bottles were brought up to their room, it was Rosemary who delivered them.

'Surely you should have gone home by now Rosemary?' asked Bella, thanking the Maid as she slipped a hot water bottle on Henri's chest and the other on his back before tucking the blankets securely around him.

'Madame Martin is a little worried that as Cousin Patrick saw me with you, then Andre and I are also in danger. She thinks that we may have to leave Paris for a little while.'

Mortified, Bella took Rosemary's hand. 'I'm so sorry! I didn't realise that we'd be endangering even more of our friends!'

Rosemary squeezed her hand. 'That's all right, I might just get to see you married in your perfect dress.' Releasing Bella's hand, Rosemary stepped towards the door when the sounding of a siren made them all jump.

'What does the siren mean, Rosemary?' Rene was already rising out of his arm chair and reaching for his pistols.

'The only time the siren is used is for fire. Stay here while I find out what's going on. There's a second but different siren if we need to evacuate the hotel.' Rosemary tore open the door and picking up the skirts of her dress, ran down the stairs to the reception desk.

This was what I have been waiting for, mused Bella. *Some way for our pursuers to force us into leaving the safety of our hotel room.* Wrapping his fur rug around Henri to keep his hot water bottles securely against him, Bella then wrapped one blanket around the boy's shoulders and head before wrapping a third blanket to keep all of his layers in place.

Leaving Henri all bundled up on his bed in front of the fire, Bella moved the boxes containing her wedding dress and material to the double bed before completing packing the carpet bags with clothes. Placing the medical bag onto the bed beside the carpet bags, Bella threw on her jacket and overcoat, slipping Nigel Sutherland's pistols into the pockets of the overcoat. Rene put on his holsters and loaded up his pistols. At the sound of the siren Andre, Louise and the Earl had appeared in Bella's room to find out what was happening.

Pausing to catch her breath as she ran back into the room, Rosemary remembered to announce herself as Rene's pistol had risen to train upon her. 'There are fires on the second, fifth and seventh floors. Not out of control yet but Monsieur Martin will be evacuating the hotel while our men get the blazes under control. The second siren should sound any second now.' Rosemary had barely finished explaining when that was exactly what happened.

'Go and get your belongings,' Bella ordered as she bent down to pick up Henri. 'We'll meet you downstairs.'

Andre had just stepped over the threshold when Madame Martin grabbed his arm and urged him back into the room.

'You can't go out the front door,' said Juliette Martin. 'There's an ugly mob waiting to cut you into a million pieces the moment you set foot out there. Come down to my rooms and you'll be safe there until the fires are contained.'

Under Madame Martin's guidance, they dispersed, picked up their luggage and followed her downstairs to the back of house area where Monsieur and Madame Martin had their own apartment.

'We won't be able to remain here, Madame Martin,' Bella said, carrying the bundled up Henri and leading Rene by the hand. In his other hand, he held one of his pistols ready. 'That mob will tell your guests who we are and we won't be able to go back to our rooms again. We must leave you or those people will burn this hotel down around you.'

Geoff's Strange Behaviour

Juliette Martin ushered them into her parlour and would have answered but a voice, from one of the two arm chairs beside the fire place, made them jump.

'An interesting predicament, Lady Tony, step out the front door and you'll be instantly killed, stay inside the hotel and you'll become trapped by the very walls that had once granted you sanctuary!' The man spoke in English and caused Rene to slip his hand free from Bella's as he took a step forward, hesitantly, in the unfamiliar room.

'You have no idea how pleased I am to hear your voice cousin!' Speaking in English, his hand was already returning his pistol to his holster as he reached out to embrace Geoff Delacourt who rose to his feet and closed the distance between them.

'I'm glad to hear you say that coz. I did wonder if you thought I had turned traitor like Patrick and Claude.' As the two men embraced, Bella slid around them and placed Henri down onto the floor before the lit fire place.

'Never!' declared Rene. 'If you'd been with me when I confronted Sutherland at the Anchor Inn, he'd never have got away with blinding me. You'd have shot him dead and we would've been back at the Manor before dawn!'

'Well I was a little hurt that you'd gone without me but honestly I thought you'd be rolling back in triumph two hours later.' Geoff patted Rene on the shoulder as he took a step back to look more closely into his cousin's face. 'You're looking old coz. I thought married life would be better suited to you.'

Geoff glanced across at Bella and his eyebrows rose as his eyes went from her changed hair colour, to her wedding ring and then to her baby bump. 'Well you obviously didn't waste any time getting your wife pregnant but I didn't think she would be that advanced.'

Almost instinctively Rene moved cautiously around the arm chairs to stand protectively in front of Bella and Henri. 'Technically we're not married. The ring Tony's wearing is purely to sell our masquerade.' Rene took Bella's hand as his cousin's tone had been a little off centre and just a touch forced.

'Really? In your shoes the first thing I'd have done was to marry your beautiful goddess. All this time alone and still not wed… the Ton are going to have a field day with this adventure.' Geoff sat down in one of the arm chairs as if he had all the time in the world.

'My first thought was to try and get us home before the break of day and prevent the scandal that will soon engulf us.'

Bella recognised the developing coolness in Rene's tone and was surprised after his warm welcome of his cousin; she slipped her free hand into the pocket of her overcoat to reach one of her pistols.

'Well I hope you've at least been enjoying your pretend marriage?' Geoff templed his fingers as the Earl sat down in the chair opposite him.

'Do I have to remind you that the Lady you're degrading is in fact my daughter?' Earl Stirling's tone was light but underneath was something harder than steel.

Rene agreed, 'Or that we should be focussing on how we're going to escape from the angry horde outside?' He drawled. 'Tell me cousin, are you here with a solution or are you part of the problem?'

Bella was actually surprised that Geoff smiled and was obviously not insulted by his cousin's deliberate accusation. He waved an airy hand.

'You don't think I'd stoop to anything as crass as burning down a beautiful building such as this?' Geoff executed a shudder that caused Bella to think vaguely of her own cousin. 'No, when I learnt that this was Nigel's ham-fisted effort to flush you out of your mouse hole, I knew I had to be at hand to help you get out of here with your heads still attached and not burnt to a crisp.'

'So,' Rene spoke slowly as if carefully weighing each word before it came out of his mouth. 'You're in contact with Nigel Sutherland…'

Raising his hand to interrupt that thought, Geoff forgot that his cousin couldn't see the gesture. 'Contact through Patrick, not collaborating with either of them… or that little toad Claude! Oh, that was something I've been longing to know… why have you been dallying in Paris? You could have been home two days ago?'

Bella's eyebrows rose sardonically. 'Surely if you've been in frequent communication with Patrick then you'd know that Aidan became ill and it is even now, still too dangerous to move him?' She was a little disconcerted as Geoff smiled up at her.

'No that is a piece of information that your cousin has chosen to keep to himself. Now then, I've arranged to have a carriage available at moment's notice but I'm afraid there'll only be room for us and not your French co-conspirators or any luggage.'

The cavalier way Geoff easily dismissed everyone else in the room forced Juliette Martin to speak at last. She had not turned a hair upon the use of the masqueraders real names but Geoff's intention to abandon their French friends to a brutal fate, if their role became known, was too much.

'They all leave together or no one leaves, Monsieur Delacourt!' Juliette said in English before switching back to French to address Bella. 'You understand that don't you, my Lady?'

Bella immediately nodded. 'Of course! I'd have it no other way Juliette,' she answered in French. As the image of a mutilated Marcelle flashed across her thoughts, she bit back a sob as she tightened her fingers around Rene's hand. 'Rene, I won't let what happened to Marcelle occur to Louise or Rosemary.'

'It won't.' His quiet reassurance in English made Geoff realise that whatever Bella had said to Rene in French meant that his plans would have to be revised.

'Well then,' Geoff sighed in resignation. 'If all that French jabber means we all go, then perhaps Madame Martin has another escape plan?'

Trying to not look smug, Juliette promptly answered, 'Actually yes I do! Before I brought you down here for safe keeping, I asked Bruno to arrange for Monsieur Guillaume's and Lord Stirling's carriages to be brought around to the service entrance at the rear of the hotel. By now, Bruno and the drivers should have loaded, on top of the carriages, your luggage that I asked you to leave in my office. If I'm not mistaken, indicated by Lord Delacourt reaching for his weapon, then this is probably Bruno at the door.'

Everyone turned to watch the door but Bruno, well attuned to Rene's habit of drawing his weapon on an intruder, announced his presence before he even laid his hand on the door knob.

'All organised Madame Martin,' Bruno nodded towards Juliette who permitted a small smile to twitch upon her lips.

'The fire?' Juliette asked, reverting to French.

'Well in hand, Madame,' answered Bruno, placing an arm around his sister's shoulders.

'The angry mob?' continued Juliette.

'Confined to the front of the hotel, along with the guests,' said Bruno.

'Good! Say good bye to your sister, Bruno as once we leave the hotel, we can't stand around outside where this child may catch a chill,' suggested Juliette Martin as Bella released Rene's hand so she could bend down to pick up Henri in his cocoon of blankets. Juliette removed a fur coat from the coat stand beside the door and threw it over her arm.

A Hasty Exit

Bruno drew Rosemary into a hug and kissed her cheeks. 'Monsieur Guillaume will bring you back to Paris when it is safe enough.'

Rosemary had been silent and wearing a worried frown ever since they had entered Juliette Martin's parlour. She had been carefully listening to the conversation going on around her and deciding suddenly to act upon a hunch, Rosemary reached up and placing her hand upon his neck, forced Bruno to lower his head as she whispered in French into his ear. When she released him to follow the others out of the parlour, Bruno looked down at her worried.

'Are you sure?'

'No, but...' Rosemary couldn't find the words to explain why that idea had popped into her head.

I know my sister so well that I don't need her to explain. 'It shall be done, Rosy.' A relieved sigh released some of the tension in the Maid's body and she silently followed the rest of their entourage out through the back of house of the hotel.

Following Juliette Martin through a maze of corridors and service areas, it was eerily silent of activity as most of the staff were attending to the fires, assisting guests out of the hotel or keeping out of the way. Bella kept pace with Juliette so that she could talk to her before it was too late.

'You didn't even react to the revelation of our true identities. How long have you known?' Bella spoke in French, mainly from habit but also just in case there were any other hotel staff lurking in the corridors and speaking in English would immediately betray their secret.

'Like Rosemary, I was on the lookout for you once it became common knowledge that you must be somewhere in Paris. Your story about your cousin was well constructed and I presume held a grain of truth. Your disguises are simple but also very effective. Even though you coloured your hair, you really do look like your mother.' As Juliette sighed wistfully, Bella looked at her in surprise.

'You knew my mother?'

'I'd already told you that my sister married an Englishman. Well, being French in England wasn't always easy. Lady Grace and Lady Isabella Delacourt were very kind and supportive to my sister. I met both of them the couple of times I went over to visit my sister.'

Juliette chuckled. 'Even without that connection, I don't think I could've betrayed you. I admire how you and your boys have tackled each obstacle with style, wit and elegance. Here, wrap your little man up in this coat. It will further insulate him from the cold.' Juliette threw the fur coat over the top of Henri as they reached the service doors.

Even as she tightly wrapped the fur coat around her son, Bella protested, 'We can't possibly accept such generosity.' She was silenced by a wave of Juliette's hand.

'Rosemary can bring it back when Monsieur Guillaume returns her to France.'

Oh! I haven't paid Doctor Girard for his services.' Bella lamented as the rest of the entourage caught up with them.

Andre said, from the back of the group, 'I settled your bill with the Doctor when I had your purse and sent the money and a set of signed books at the same time.'

'Thank you Andre. Oh! Your books! We didn't have to leave them behind did we?' Little things were starting to stress Bella as she drew the hood of the fur coat over the top of Henri's head.

'Calm down Bella! I distributed all copies earlier today and the set for Henri should already be on the carriage.' Andre glanced behind them as he heard footsteps making their way towards them down the corridor. 'Time we left! Thank you for everything Juliette,' he added.

Bella hugged Juliette and kissed her on both cheeks as the older woman opened the service door. She hustled the group out into the cool night air and breathed a sigh of relief that two carriages were waiting but no angry mob could be seen. Andre assisted Louise, Rosemary and François into his vehicle as Lord Stirling and Geoff helped Bella, Henri and Rene into his Lordship's carriage.

The laneway behind the hotel was extremely narrow and the carriage drivers manoeuvred their loads very carefully and slowly along its length. They were not going to draw attention to themselves by driving away in haste. Death for all of them lay a mere street away and no one aboard the carriages wanted to push their luck. So was brought to an end the temporary life of Captain Rene Du Bois, his wife Bella and their son, Henri.

As they watched the vehicles slowly disappear into the night, Bruno cleared his throat before he could trust his voice. 'I'm afraid I have to leave work for a little while Madame Martin.'

Juliette calmly nodded. 'Yes of course, Bruno. You need to let your parents know that Rosemary left the hotel safely. You could also inform Phillippe Du Bois that his cousin and uncle have also departed.'

There was a slight pause as Bruno's train of thought had been in a different direction. 'Yes, of course.' Wrapping her shawl around her shoulders, Juliette studied the young man as he struggled between his loyalty to his employer and his family.

'Something Rosemary told you has got you worried?' She surmised.

'Yes Madame.'

'Then you'd better go and do something about it like a good brother!'

Bruno let out a slow breath; the decision had been made for him. 'Yes Madame.' As he slipped easily into the darkness, Juliette turned and let herself back into the hotel to discover how much damage had been done by the fire.

Race To The Coast

It wasn't until she began to feel lightheaded, and not in a good way, that Tony realised she had been holding her breath. Letting it out slowly as the carriage began to pick up a little pace now that they were trundling down a real road rather than the lane way, Tony loosened her tight grip upon her brother and wished she could see Aidan's face to be certain he was all right. The Earl, sitting beside her on the back seat, laid his hand comfortingly over the top of his daughter's.

'One more hurdle baby girl and then it will all be over.'

'Yes Papa,' Tony's voice came out as barely a whisper that caused Caleb, sitting beside his cousin on the front seat to tighten his grip upon one of his pistols. Some of Tony's fear was being silently communicated to Caleb and in part it was about the doubt she had regarding the man sitting beside him.

Either I am so attuned to her thoughts or it is the fact that ever since we found Geoff in Juliette's parlour, I had also begun to doubt my cousin's loyalty. A small voice snapped Caleb out of his unproductive reflections and back to the present and the very real dangers that still surrounded them.

'Mama?'

'Yes Little Bear?' Tony stroked her hand along the five year old's fur covered back.

'We're finally going home now?'

Exhaling slowly Tony tried to release some of her pent up tension. 'Yes Little Bear, we're going home.'

'Good!' Closing his eyes, Aidan didn't protest as Tony drew the hood of the fur coat closer around his face and he presently went to sleep.

The fresh, young horses easily ate up the miles as they left Paris far behind them. Darkness completely surrounded the carriages now so that it was impossible to know if Andre's carriage was still on his Lordship's heels, even with the lanterns that hung from the corners of the carriages.

Half way to the French coast and the town of Dieppe, they had to draw up at an Inn to change horses in Beauvais and Tony was relieved when Andre's carriage pulled up behind them. As his horses were changed, Andre jumped down from his carriage and stuck his head inside the door of Lord Stirling's.

'Everything all right?' Andre's attempt at keeping his tone light and unconcerned made Tony smile.

'We should've asked Juliette for a basket of food and we could've stopped for a picnic.' She teased.

In response, Andre chuckled. 'We've already had our picnic, someone had the presence of mind to pick up the box of pastries from your room. I was all for finders' keepers but Rosemary said we had to share.' He pulled the box from behind his back and handed it to Geoff who was closest to him. Noticing the driver of Lord Stirling's carriage was ready to leave, Andre added, 'Oops! You're all ready to roll. We'll see you soon in Dieppe.' He just managed to draw his head and shoulders free and shut the door before the fresh horses were pulling the vehicle back onto the main road. Trotting back to his own companions, Andre had barely taken his seat when they too were once more on the move.

The countryside flashed past, silent and eerily lit only by the quarter moon. There were no traps, ambushes, angry pursuit vehicles or any other signs of influences from Nigel Sutherland, Patrick or Claude Henry. Without a single incident, the two carriages slowed as they entered the port of Dieppe and pulled up beside the dock where a large yacht was moored. When Lord Stirling had sent to London for money in case he needed it for a ransom demand, he had also arranged a special marriage licence from the Doctor's Commons and sought permission from an old friend to use his yacht to bring his family home.

As the Earl was about to leave his carriage, Tony, with a little difficulty as she tried to not wake Aidan, removed the two pistols from her overcoat and handed them to her father.

'Give these to Louise and Rosemary if they're unarmed.'

Nodding, the Earl took the weapons before addressing Geoff. 'Stand guard outside the carriage. I'm just going abroad the yacht to make sure that we can set sail immediately.'

'Of course, but shouldn't Tony keep one of those pistols?' Geoff followed his host out of the carriage.

Tony chuckled. 'No, we have Caleb to protect us!'

Glancing at Caleb's black glasses, Geoff was about to say something but he received an elbow in the ribs. Looking round, Geoff found that it was Andre and not the Earl beside him.

'Don't say it Monsieur Delacourt, your cousin is more than capable of protecting his family.' Andre shut the carriage door to keep the cool air, coming off the sea, from reaching Aidan.

Having handed the additional weapons to the other ladies, the Earl and François strode down the dock and boarded the yacht. Andre and Geoff stood guard on either side of the vehicles as the drivers of the carriages unloaded the luggage and carried it onto the waiting boat. Andre was more than a little anxious as he paced his side of the carriages. *We are so close to freedom that I can actually taste it on the air.*

Hearing a startled cry and a thump from the other side of the carriage, Andre started to circle the vehicles to check on Geoff. In the darkness he missed the huge mountain of flesh as Nigel Sutherland cracked the Author over the head. Stepping over Geoff's unconscious body Claude Henry ripped open the first carriage door and said, 'Get out!' but there was no one inside the vehicle.

Trouble In Dieppe

Having heard Geoff and then Andre knocked out cold, Caleb had opened the carriage door on the opposite side and he and Tony, carrying Aidan, had silently slid out of the vehicle. *There is no chance that we can make it to the yacht before we are seen but just maybe the poor visibility of the pale moonlight could be an advantage to us,* Caleb debated.

With Tony's hand tightly held in one of his, and his pistol in the other hand, Caleb inched his way along the side of the coach towards the horses of Andre's vehicle. *If I can place Aidan inside with Louise and Rosemary, then maybe Tony and I can get on top of the driver's box and drive away to hide and rethink our escape.* He had just grasped the handle of the door beneath his fingers when Caleb felt the muzzle of a pistol press against his temple.

'Just give me an excuse to blow y'r head off!' Nigel snarled. *For a big man, he can move very quietly.* Caleb tried to draw Tony and Aidan protectively behind him.

'No! Not yet!' They all heard Claude Henry wheezing for breath before he appeared around the side of the carriage. He led Rosemary and Louise with their hands bound. Pushing the women down to sit on the ground, Claude managed to drag in a deep breath. 'I want the child safe before you take care of the rest.' Claude reached out to wrestle Aidan out of Tony's arms but she was not about to let Claude anywhere near her brother without a fight.

'Get away from him you filthy mongrel! I'll never let you take my son!' Tony lashed out, kicking Claude hard on the shins. Colourful language exploded from Claude as Caleb tried to move between Tony and Claude. *Nigel's gun is still pressed against my head but I don't care, I have to protect Tony and Aidan at all costs.*

233

'He's not your son, bitch! Daughter of Satan! I've always hated you!' spat out Claude as well as copious amounts of spittle. His eyes watered in pain.

'And I have always thought you were an abomination of nature!' Tony stated calmly even though fear was beginning to seep through her body. *Not that I am going to let him know that.*

Roaring in anger, Claude lunged at Tony but surprisingly it was Nigel's hand on his shoulder that pulled the little man away. 'Don't let her rile ya, we've our orders to complete before we can leave this God forsaken country!' Nigel grasped hold of Caleb by the collar of his overcoat and threw him effortlessly to the ground. He pointed his pistol again at Caleb's head as he locked his eyes with Tony's. 'Give Claude the boy or I put a bullet through pretty boy's skull.'

'Don't listen to them, Tony, they're going to kill us all anyway!' Caleb shouted. *I know Tony's love for me will be in conflict with her love for her brother.*

'Shut y'r yap!' Nigel's pistol discharged.

Caleb slumped backwards and Tony screamed, 'No!' as she felt her heart shatter into tiny pieces.

Hoping to use her distraction against her, Claude made an attempt to grab Aidan out of Tony's arms but he had misjudged Tony's maternal instincts. Her closed fist smacked Claude hard in the face, breaking his nose for the second time in as many weeks. Even more explosive language erupted from Claude, slightly muffled as he clutched a handkerchief to his face to staunch the blood loss.

'You fucking bitch! I don't care what Patrick says, I will have you before we kill you all!'

'I'd rather join my husband in death than let a pathetic worm like you so much as lay one finger on me!' There was no hiding the contempt in Tony's voice as she shifted Aidan in her arms and reached into the cleavage of her dress for the stiletto blade Doctor Stevenson had given her before they had left England.

'Nice bluff,' said Nigel, 'Patrick said ya told him that ya weren't married.'

Tony didn't need for the two men to see her face clearly as her sneer at them was evident in her voice. 'That was then, this is now!'

A shot rang out from below the deck of the yacht, closely followed by a second shot. Startled Tony jumped and looked quickly at Nigel as he laughed.

'Well that should've been Patrick taking care of the Earl and the French toy boy!'

Drawing in a sharp breath, Tony felt her chest tighten remorselessly around her lungs as the thought of losing her lover and her father seemed too much to cope with.

'No! He couldn't...' Her eyes filled with tears as reality began to crash down upon Tony. *We're all going to die!*

Taking advantage of Tony's distress, Claude yanked Aidan out of her arms. In her despair, she was unable to stop him but striking swiftly in retaliation, she slashed her stiletto blade across Claude's forearm. Colourful expletives followed but Claude refused to release Aidan. He held the boy high over his head and laughed.

'I now have control over the new Earl of Stirling! Victory is mine!'

Shaking his head at the overly dramatic little man, Nigel took his handkerchief out of his pocket and tied it over Claude's bleeding arm.

'Calm down little man or ya'll be fainting from blood loss.' Nigel raised another pistol to point at Tony.

Claude laughed. 'At last everything has finally fallen into place for me! We knew that you'd see through the fire at the hotel and the angry mob outside so that you'd be ready to flee when Geoff offered you the chance to escape. Straight into our real trap! A pity you dragged these foreigners along with you Tony, now they'll have to be killed too.'

Raising her chin in defiance, she was not prepared to let death frighten her. 'There's no need to murder them as they're no threat to you.'

Laughing again Claude shook his head. He was having trouble retaining hold of Aidan as he threw himself about in his uncle's arms. 'We can't leave any witnesses. I'll take Aidan home to England and Nigel will dispose of the rest of you.' He tittered in glee. 'Even Patrick! It'll look like Patrick killed all of you but Delacourt managed to get off one fatal shot at Patrick before he died.'

Tony's eyebrows rose. 'Does Geoff receive the same betrayal or is it just for Patrick? Tell me Nigel, how do you know that this little weasel doesn't have the same fate lined up for you?' She was surprised when a grin formed on Nigel's face.

'I've an insurance policy. If anything happens to me a detailed account of everyone involved in this affair will be sent to the Bow Street Runners in London.'

'What do you actually get out of all this Claude? It's a little over the top just for revenge.' Tony wanted to extract as much information out of them in the remote case that someone managed to survive.

Claude was still struggling to subdue the wriggling Aidan. The boy may have been tightly bound in blankets but he was still able to thrash against his uncle.

'I have control over the new Earl! Unlimited money is coming my way!'

Tony chuckled, a response that surprised both men. 'I hope you're happy to wait then as Aidan won't come into his full inheritance until he is one and twenty! Until then the estate will be carefully managed by a board of trustees. They'll be even harder to get money out of than Papa.'

Nigel laughed as Claude swore violently. *I hadn't been aware that there would be anything else standing between me and a fortune!*

Bored with all this talking, Aidan thrashed harder in Claude's arms. 'I want to go back to Mama!'

Grunting in an effort to keep his grip around the boy, Claude was losing his patience. 'Shut up brat! You'll be back with Charlotte before morning.'

'No!' Aidan thrashed even more. 'I want my Mama... now!' He turned his head to look at Tony and seeing the pistol levelled at her head by Nigel, Aidan started to cry,

Aching to comfort and reassure her brother, Tony took a step towards Claude but Nigel cleared his throat, recalling her attention that his weapon was aimed at her.

'Shut up brat!' Claude shook Aidan but that only made the boy bawl harder.

'Claude, if you don't stop Aidan's tears, he will start coughing and then he won't be able to breathe. He needs to be somewhere warm now or you'll have a dead little Earl on your hands.' Tony tried to keep desperation or pleading out of her voice but she needed to use her last breath to continue to protect her brother.

There was a momentary hesitation but then Claude surprised even Nigel by handing Aidan back to Tony. 'Get on board the yacht Tony. I'm only keeping you alive so that I return a living Earl to Stirling Manor.' Using his own pistol, Claude gestured her towards the dock as she began to soothe her upset brother.

'I'll lock them in the cabin below the deck then come back to help you finish off everyone else.' Claude added to Nigel, who nodded but as the big man turned to make sure that he didn't fall over Caleb's dead body, Nigel swore. There was no body to fall over. Irritated Claude glanced back over his shoulder.

'What's wrong now?'

Nigel gestured to the empty ground beside Rosemary and Louise. 'He's gone! Delacourt! The bastard's not dead!'

Dead Man Walking

If this is what it's like to be dead, thought Caleb as he regained consciousness, *then why am I in so much pain?* Carefully he flexed his fingers before running a searching hand over his chest. When he encountered no bullet wound and no blood, he raised his hand to the throbbing pain in the side of his head. His fingers came away slick with blood and he bit down on his bottom lip to muffle his groan of pain. *Nigel's bullet has grazed my temple and although it has not entered my skull, I am bleeding quite freely from the wound.*

Lying very still Caleb concentrated upon what he could hear going on around him. When Claude attempted to grab Aidan and Tony had punched him, breaking his nose, Caleb had to stop himself from laughing especially as Claude burst into colourful language. *That's my tigress!*

Sliding his fingers over the hard ground Caleb heard a soft gasp of surprise as he came in contact with someone's foot. *Rosemary? Louise?* He wondered as he heard them shift closer to him.

'When I tell you, make your way round the carriages and wake Andre!' whispered Rosemary in French, trying to not move her lips too much so that she would be heard by anyone else.

When the first shot sounded from aboard the yacht, Rosemary whispered, 'Now my Lord! Keep true to your left hand and you'll reach the back of Andre's carriage.'

As they heard the second shot from the yacht, Caleb silently prayed, *I hope that regardless of how much blood I have lost I can rise noiselessly to my feet and disappear into the darkness before Nigel or Claude notice my movements.* His legs held him upright and taking a deep breath Caleb moved cautiously to his left, his hand extended ahead of him to try and prevent colliding into the carriages.

He was temporarily polarised when he heard Tony cry out in disbelief as Nigel explained that Patrick had just killed her father, but Caleb forced himself to keep moving. *If we survive this nightmare, then I can focus my energy upon comforting my beloved.*

When Caleb reached the rear of Andre's carriage, he was making his way round to the other side when he heard Claude snatch Aidan away from Tony and declare himself the winner. It took even more resolve for Caleb to not turn around and immediately attack. *I am outnumbered, out gunned and momentarily consumed with blood curdling rage that hampers clear thinking. That instinct to kill, to rip their heads from their bodies is quickly rising within me but before I can tackle them, I am determined to even the odds stacked against me.*

Gritting his teeth as Claude gloated about the brilliance of their trap, Caleb almost fell over Andre's unconscious body. Kneeling down, Caleb lightly slapped the Frenchman's face in an attempt to wake him while his other hand sought reassurance that Andre was still alive by trying to find a pulse.

'Come on Andre,' Caleb whispered, 'Rosemary needs you!' Placing a hand on either of Andre's shoulders, Caleb shook him and was rewarded by a brief groan of life. 'Wake up Andre!' He slapped Andre's face again and received a feeble protest.

Hoping that Andre would be able to recover without continuing to be roughly handled, Caleb crawled on his hands and knees until he located his cousin Geoff. He went through the same routine of trying to rouse Geoff, all the time trying to catch the conversation going on the other side of the carriages.

When he received no response at all, Caleb checked yet again that his cousin was actually still breathing, wondering if Geoff had been hit harder over the head than Andre, Caleb carefully ran his fingers over Geoff's skull. Although he located a bump, there wasn't any blood. Feeling a little dizzy, Caleb wiped away the blood running down the side of his own face before returning to Andre's side to give him another shake.

When Aidan cried out for Tony, Caleb was automatically jerked upright to his feet and immediately wished he hadn't moved so unwisely. The earth was spinning erratically around him but when Aidan began to sob Caleb tried to push aside his own disorientation as his family needed him. When arms suddenly circled Caleb's waist to steady him, he didn't fight against the support as the words whispered into his ear were in French and he recognised the voice.

'Steady mon cousin, reinforcements have arrived.'

'Phillippe? But how?' Caleb whispered.

Phillippe Du Bois chuckled as he eased Caleb down to sit on the ground. 'I'll explain while I tend to your head wound otherwise you'll be in no shape to help Tony and Aidan.' Tilting Caleb's face up so that he could utilise the meagre moonlight and the lanterns attached to the front of the carriage, Phillippe used his handkerchief to wipe away most of the blood oozing down the side of Caleb's head before tearing off his own cravat and binding the neck-kerchief tightly against the wound.

When Phillippe took out of his jacket pocket a flask of neat spirits and pressed it against Caleb's lips, he didn't resist as the alcohol was urged down his throat.

'I'm here with the Moreau brothers. Rosemary had told Bruno that she didn't like the vibe she had received from your cousin. She thought you could be walking into a trap.'

'I don't know about Geoff but she was right about it being a trap.' Caleb accepted the flask Phillippe placed in his hand and took another sip. Slowly the world began to stop spinning like a top. Caleb even accepted the hand under his elbow to assist him back to his feet. Aidan was crying and they had to act fast. Placing the hip flask into the breast pocket of his jacket, Caleb drew out both pistols from his holsters.

'Right then,' he sounded calmer than he felt. 'I need one person to keep trying to bring Andre and Geoff round. Is everyone armed? I want at least two men to surround them from behind the carriages. If possible I want two more with me as we complete the circle from the front of the horses of the first carriage. Any questions?' Caleb's voice was a little forced as he had heard the pause before Claude had handed Aidan back to his sister and ordered her to board the yacht. He received six 'Non mon Seigneur,' and nodded.

'Quickly now, they're about to discover that I'm not dead!' Accepting Phillippe's hand slipped through his arm, Caleb ran around the horses with Bruno and Isaac as Emile and Gilbert came from behind and Theodore knelt down beside Andre to wake him up. They all clearly heard the surprise and anger in Nigel's voice as he shouted, 'He's gone! Delacourt! The bastard's not dead!'

Caleb's Challenge

Spinning around on the spot, Tony's chest heaved as she struggled to drag a deep breath down into her tortured lungs. *Do I dare to hope that Caleb has actually survived?* Looking up to see first two Moreau brothers round the rear of the second carriage, Tony then turned to see Caleb, Phillippe and two more Moreau brothers appear to surround them.

With their weapons drawn as they circled the kidnappers, Nigel realised that he was not going to take on six gunmen and threw his weapons to the ground. Claude snarled and grabbing Tony by the throat, he drew her and Aidan in front of him and pressed his pistol against her temple.

Phillippe began to lower his weapon. 'The little weasel has Tony,' he explained in French to Caleb who continued to hold his pistols steady upon Claude.

'Release my wife and I will let you live!' Caleb spoke in English so Claude would not misunderstand him this time. Just able to see the glint of the moonlight off the black lens of Caleb's spectacles, Claude burst into laughter.

'You couldn't hit the side of a barn!'

One of Caleb's eyebrows rose. 'Do you really want to test that theory?' Bella, now?'

Tony stamped the heel of her boot into Claude's foot behind her as she sunk one elbow deep into his ribs. When Claude cursed her, she ripped herself out of his loosened grip and protecting Aidan, dropped to the ground.

'Now Rene!' She shouted and using the sound of Claude's cursing, Caleb fixed upon his target. Realising he had an opportunity to get rid of Caleb, once and for all Claude fired. The bullet pierced Caleb over the heart, causing him to slightly alter the direction of his arm so that as Caleb also fired, instead of striking Claude's body, the bullet went squarely through his forehead. Claude was dead before his body had hit the ground.

Struggling to her feet, Tony was unable to form any words as she watched Caleb stagger from the impact of Claude's bullet and then collapse back into Phillippe's supporting arms. Isaac Moreau had untied Rosemary and Louise and helped them to their feet. Tony thrust Aidan into Louise's arms, begging her to take the boy somewhere warm before she knelt down in front of Caleb. He struggled to breathe as Phillippe eased him to the ground.

'No! No! You can't leave me now! Please Caleb...' Tony reached out to lay her hand over his heart but instead of finding a pool of blood forming under her trembling fingers; it felt harder than flesh and was more fluidy and aromatic. In disbelief she raised her fingers to her nose.

'Brandy?'

Coughing, Caleb reached unsteady fingers into the inside pocket of his jacket and pulled out Phillippe's hip flask. 'Sorry

Phillippe, it looks like I owe you a new flask.' Caleb held up the metal object that had just saved his life. The bullet had pierced one side of the hip flask but only dented the other side. There would probably be a bruise over his heart. Tony uttered an unsteady laugh.

'Oh, I never thought I'd see the day that I was grateful for the presence of alcohol!' Tony buried her face into Caleb's shoulder and began to sob quietly as reaction set in.

A Pleasant Surprise

'Does that mean, I'll be allowed the rare glass without you looking worried?' The question came not from Caleb but the direction of the dock. Tony raised tear filled eyes as she recognised the voice.

'Papa?' She dashed away her tears to try and focus her eyes upon the three men who had disembarked from the yacht. 'But we heard two shots.'

Smiling as he approached those assembled, the Earl assisted Tony to her feet. 'That was done to make Claude disclose everything to you in the hope he'd reveal who masterminded this adventure.' He paused to cast a glance over the lifeless body of his brother-in-law Claude. 'Nice work my boy, right between the eyes. I wonder if you're even more deadly when you can actually see your opponent.'

Caleb sighed. 'I wasn't aiming for his head. I hoped to only wound him so that you could question him.' With Tony and Phillippe on either side of him, Caleb managed to rise to his feet.

'Never mind, my boy, if Claude hadn't shot at you, then you might not have killed him. Where are Andre and Geoff? Is Claude the only casualty or are there others?' Theodore appeared from the other side of the carriages, leading a very sheepish and head-sore Andre and similarly injured Geoff as Isaac tied Nigel's hands behind his back.

Tony was still looking at her father in puzzlement. 'But Papa, Patrick…'

The Earl waved a dismissive hand. 'He's been working for me this whole time. Patrick sent me regular updates on his progress as well as the others' plans.'

'Oh…' there was a lot of doubt in that one monosyllable. Smiling, Lord Stirling gently patted his daughter's cheek.

'Not all love will turn to hate even if it is unreciprocated. Patrick was hurt that you chose someone else but as you have never shown any indication that you would ever consider his suit, he doesn't feel any bitterness towards you.'

'Oh.' There was more acceptance in the monosyllable this time and Tony slowly felt a warming glow in their protection. 'Aidan!' She was suddenly filled with doubt again. *I should never have let him out of my sight!*

François answered, 'It's all right Angel, Louise took Aidan down to one of the cabins where we had already lit a fire in readiness for him.'

Watching as Rosemary warmly hugged each of her brothers, Tony used Aidan's question. 'Can we please go home now?'

Time To Leave

There was general laughter as Tony's statement seemed to sum it all up nicely.

'I want to thank you gentlemen,' the Earl said to the Moreau brothers. 'I'm grateful Rosemary felt the need to call on your services. With our departure and Nigel and Claude taken care of, there is no necessity for Rosemary to flee her homeland now. But we'd be more than happy to have her visit us for a short time. I think she mentioned something about a wedding to prepare for.'

Unexpectedly, Andre sighed. 'Will you people please let me conduct my own proposal in my own time?'

All eyes looked at Andre in surprise and Rosemary was glad that the moonlight didn't reveal her becoming blush. To break the awkward silence that had fallen, Tony laid a sympathetic hand on Andre's shoulder.

'I think Papa was referring to my wedding to Caleb. The sooner the better I think Papa but…' Just like Rosemary, Tony blushed. 'After Caleb has the bandages over his eyes removed. I want him to see me walk down the aisle in the most magical dress.'

Caleb found Tony's hand and raised it to his lips. 'And I will have shaved!' He drawled, knowing even without the use of his eyes that her blush would have spread all over her body in desire.

'Hang on!' protested Nigel, 'I thought you said you were married all ready.'

Reaching up to wipe her handkerchief down Caleb's cheek where blood had begun to seep from beneath his makeshift bandages. 'We are married,' Tony said as a matter of fact. 'This is the fifth night away from my father's house, without a chaperone and we've shared the same bed. We only need the piece of paper now to make it official.'

'I'm gunna be sick.' Nigel protested and received a push in the back from Andre.

'Well you can be sick over the side of the yacht as I'm not going to clean up after you.' Taking Rosemary's hand, Andre shoved Nigel towards the pier as he addressed the Moreaus. 'I'll take care of your sister gentlemen…' Andre uttered a rueful laugh. 'Or judging by the uncanny instincts of the lady, she'll be looking after me.' The brothers acknowledged the couple's wave before moving to speak with the Earl as Geoff joined his cousin who leaned more than a little upon Tony.

'You'd better take him below deck and clean him up,' Phillippe held up the remainder of the brandy in the hip flask to Caleb's lips. 'Here, you've done very well. I will be proud to call you cousin.' He forced Caleb to drink before handing the flask to Tony. 'A souvenir. Good luck Tony, you've got a good man there.' Reaching up to place her free hand behind Phillippe's neck she kissed both of his cheeks.

'Thank you, for everything.' Releasing her cousin, Tony directed Caleb's footsteps towards the yacht and Geoff fell in beside them, giving Caleb his support as well.

'So what did that little speech actually mean? Either you're married or you aren't, which is it?'

'What?' Caleb's voice was a little slurred, but not due to the small amount of alcohol he had consumed, but with his fight instinct dropping and the amount of blood lost from his head wound, he was close to collapse. Tony tightened her hold on Caleb as he occasionally missed his footing.

'Your cousin is asking if we consummated our union and therefore could I already be carrying your child.' Tony explained, carefully as she was still a little wary about whether or not they could trust Geoff. Caleb shook his head as if to clear the fog that was descending upon his brain.

'No, does that relieve you Geoff?' He had to concentrate for a minute as they helped him over the side of the yacht. Geoff didn't hesitate to answer.

'Nothing to do with me old bean! You still have doubts that I've secret yearnings for your title and estate? I was just wondering if you two managed to have any fun while you've been playing at being married.'

A multitude of images flooded their memories and their tell-tale blushes gave them away. Geoff chuckled as he opened a door so that they could descend below deck. He placed a hand on top of Caleb's head so that he didn't bump into the low beam.

'Brilliant! I don't suppose you're going to share any details?'

'No!' Both Tony and Caleb said in unison.

A door ahead of them opened and Andre poked his head out. 'It'll all be in the book! Come this way, Aidan is in here and Louise has the medical supplies ready for you Tony.'

Caleb had groaned at the first part of Andre's statement as Tony assisted him into the room. 'It will not be in the book Andre! You said if it's that pornographic no publisher would print it anyway.'

Tony eased Caleb down onto the edge of the double bed in the room. They were obviously in the owner's cabin. It was certainly more luxurious than the crew cabin they had shared going to France.

'Besides which, what would our children think if they were to read it?' she asked, undoing the temporary bandaging around Caleb's head and using a cloth and a bowl of water Louise had ready, mopped up the blood that plastered his face, hair and neck.

'Or our parents,' Caleb added, removing his dark glasses and the pads over his eyes. Tony's breath caught in an excited gasp.

'Or our grandchildren!'

A tired smile stretched across his face as he reached out to locate her standing in front of him and caressed his hand over her baby bump. 'I like the sound of that! I mean us growing old together and having grandchildren and not about them reading of our whole adventure.' For a moment Caleb submitted to Tony's medical attention and to Louise who was attempting to extract him from his blood soaked clothes.

Medical Care

It wasn't until Louise had stripped him of his jacket and waist coat and Tony had finished anointing his burns and bandaging the top half of his face that Caleb raised a feeble protest.

'There are too many people in this room if I'm to be completely re-dressed.'

Louise nodded and gestured with her head to the door. 'Go and help the Earl so that we can depart as soon as possible. I suppose we have to return the weasel's body to England?'

Andre spoke as he followed Rosemary, François and Geoff out of the cabin. 'I saw the two carriage drivers carry Claude on board from the window.'

'Port Hole,' corrected François.

'If port and starboard are nautical for left and right, does that mean that one side the windows are called port holes and the other side starboard holes?' asked Andre as he closed the door behind them.

Louise chuckled and they missed the answer as the group outside moved out of their hearing. 'They'll have fun trying to work that one out.' She continued to remove Caleb's clothes. 'Now then, my Lord, do we re-dress you or shall we place you into a night shirt?'

Softly Caleb sighed, it was becoming harder to remain conscious. 'Shirt and trousers, Louise. If I turn up at the Manor in a nightshirt, my mother will think I'm at death's door.'

Tony cleaned off any other regions of Caleb's body that had become covered with his blood before packing away the medical bag as Louise re-dressed Caleb. Tony bundled up the blood-soaked clothes and stowed them away in the bag with the rest of their dirty clothes. As Louise helped him off the bed so that Tony could turn down the covers, he lifted his head and reached out his hand until he found Tony's arm.

'Where's Aidan? Is he all right? Did he get cold?' There was an urgency in his voice.

'I'm all right Papa. I'm wrapped up so tight that I can't move.' Aidan continued to speak in French even though the adults had long since dropped their masquerade personae.

'Get into bed Caleb, I'll unwrap Aidan and he and I will join you.' Tony caressed her hand against her fiancé's ashen cheek.

Watching the tender look of love on Tony's face, Louise suggested, 'How about I take Aidan until we land in England?'

She received three, 'No!' almost in unison.

Bending down a little awkwardly as she still wore her baby bump, Tony picked up Aidan and placed him onto the bed to unravel him.

'Thank you Louise but Caleb and I have already discussed it and for a while Aidan will have to be constantly with us.' Removing all the blankets, Aidan's fur rug and the now cool hot water bottles, Tony re-dressed the boy in the fur rug before laying him down beside Caleb.

'That will make for an interesting honeymoon!' Louise stated, as she placed the medical bag on the floor and picked up the bloodied bowl of water to dispose its contents. Chuckling Tony removed her baby bump and her boots before slipping under the sheets with her boys.

'Who wants to be normal?' asked Tony.

Pausing with her hand on the door handle, Louse gazed deep in thought at the perfect family unit in the bed. Tony and Caleb lay facing each other, Aidan between them and one of their arms lay lightly over the boy with their fingers entwined. Smiling as she left the room Louise thought, *no, why settle for normal when you can have the extraordinary?*

It Won't Be Like This Every Day

With a sigh, Tony had begun to let her body relax until she suddenly thought of something she had forgotten.

'Damn!'

Caleb had been drifting through conscious states. 'If you say we're being attacked by pirates, aliens or an angry mob then I'll probably cry like a little girl.'

Laughing, she slipped her hand under his to caress her fingers against his chest. 'No my love, I didn't properly thank Phillippe and the Moreau brothers for their timely rescue. You were marvellous but it was nice that we didn't have too many wounded or... or dead.' She leant forward to kiss him and then again just because she could. *We are alive and finally leaving our French adventure!*

'You did thank Phillippe; and the Earl will make sure everyone else knows how grateful we all are for the last five days.' Caleb paused for a moment. 'I hope you know that the past ten days are not going to be typical once we're married. I just don't want you to be disappointed if you do crave the adventure and excitement.' He took her hand in his and raised it to his lips

'I think that something a little more normal will be a welcome relief. Except...' She became flushed at where her thoughts were leading her.

'Except what Bella?' Caleb said in French as he pressed another kiss against her wrist.

'I know we'll have Aidan with us for a while but I want... I don't want to have to control my desire to touch you, be touched by you. And not limited to the bedroom.' Tony stopped as she heard Caleb's breath hitch with an inward hiss as her words enflamed his imagination.

'I must ask the Housekeeper to ensure that all rooms have a key so that we can lock the door. We wouldn't want anyone to walk in on us.' Caleb's smile was very mischievous and naughty. Tony liked it, very much. It deserved a kiss but when she felt his hand trace up her arm and then down to curve around her breast, she reluctantly drew away.

'No sweetheart, you need to rest. We'll still be here when you wake and hopefully we'll be back home before dawn.'

Caleb accepted her gentle order and removed his hand from her desirable breasts to finally give into the darkness of sleep that had been calling him. *We've done it! Survived travelling incognito through France. Survived Aidan's illness. Defeated our abductors!* thought Tony and as the yacht left the dock. *We're finally going home.*

Trilogy Preview

Stirling Conspiracy

Finally making it home from their ordeal in France, Lady Antonia (Tony) Stirling, her brother Lord Aidan and Lord Caleb Delacourt still cannot relax their defences. Now, though, they have a wedding to look forward to as they contemplate their future life together. It is up to Abraham Bell, A Bow Street Runner to work out who, from his list of suspects, want to achieve their goals so badly that they are prepared to kill to get it. Can Bell solve the mystery before the killer or killers finally succeed?

ABOUT THE AUTHOR

Anne-Marie Price was born and raised in Perth, Western Australia. She lives with her parents Margaret and Laurence and has two cats, Mickey and Jackson.

She has been a member of the Society of Women Writers WA since 2009 and has been their secretary since 2011.

Anne-Marie has had articles and flash fiction stories published in the SWW In Print Magazine as well as The Readers World Magazine.

In 1997, she obtained a Degree– Library And Information Studies, in 1998 a Diploma of Comprehensive Writing and in 2009 a Cert IV Training and Assessment to assist her ability to teach others the craft of writing.

Writing is in the blood of the Price family with Anne-Marie being the fourth generation of writers. Anne-Marie has been writing fiction since the age of ten and still uses pen and paper as a preference for a first draft.

Also By This Author

Hostage Of Diplomacy
2015
Contemporary Romance

The Search For The King James Bible
2015
Supernatural Romance

Stirling Trilogy
2016
Historical Romance